EVERNIGHT PUBLISHING ®

www.evernightpublishing.com

THROUGH ROSCOE'S EYES

DEDICATION

To Mark who was the first to love me for who I am and who continues to love me and believe in me. For his unwavering support and inspiration, for his insight into the written, spiritual, emotional, and physical language of love, and for his gentle guidance during the honing of this novel, I am forever grateful.

To my friend, Christine Klocek-Lim, who has always been there to support my writing endeavors, I will always be in your dept.

To Karyn White, editor extraordinaire, for her gentle guidance and insightful suggestions. You've helped to make this story so much better.

To all members of the LGBTQ family who have experienced the love and support animals have brought into their lives when others have turned them away, this is for you.

THROUGH ROSCOE'S EYES

THROUGH ROSCOE'S EYES

Family Men, 2

Kory Steed

Copyright © 2019

Chapter One
Denim Legs

Early January, this year

Clad in a leather coat and denim jeans, Reggie sat quietly in his jet-black SUV, parked along the curb, while he drummed his fingers lightly on the steering wheel. From his vantage point, some thirty yards away, he peered through the windshield as he focused his binoculars on the huddled form on the sidewalk as it came in and out of view between the people hurrying by. He waited for a sign, a sign that would determine when his mission would end, but he grew impatient.

The smell of hot sandwiches and fries emanating from the last bag resting on the back seat seemed well out of place in his just under $100,000, top of the line, aniline leather-upholstered, Platinum Escalade, but it brought back fond memories from his childhood. Old Dudley, the family chauffeur, took pity on him to occasionally make a quick detour for the forbidden fast-food on their way home during his days at the private academy where he went to school. Dudley even took the blame for the smell that coated the interior of the limousine, claiming it was him who had succumbed to the lure of French fries and burger grease when his parents complained about the odor on those occasions when he didn't have time to air it out. Reggie wondered whether the recipient of the meal would relish its contents as much as he once did.

He'd already distributed twelve of the baker's-dozen, large paper bags that afternoon. With only the one left to go, he needed to make up his mind. Was the figure, sighted through other end of his binoculars, worth the risk? Regardless of his good intentions, charitable work had its hazards, particularly when on your own, and he'd already had run-ins with two anonymous recipients today. He didn't want a repeat of being accused of thievery, and this potential recipient looked to be closer to the risky end of the charitable acts' spectrum.

The work he'd begun years before had started with a promise, but as the years passed, he'd thought more and more of it as a mission. He set down the binoculars and sighed. *If she could see me now,* he thought. *Though I'm no missionary.*

Lost to his memories, Reggie had no idea how much time had passed when his eyes came back into focus. He recognized the sun would be setting soon, and he needed to be on his way. That's when he noticed movement coming from the direction of his target. Something shuddered in the breeze. He lifted his binoculars just in time to read the words, ***I ask not for me, but for them.***

Reggie put on his turn signal and pulled out into traffic, then pulled right back up to the curb after closing the distance to investigate the words that caught his attention.

Chapter Two
Cretin

Hurrying passersby glanced briefly at the words scribbled in rough, bolded-black letters, written with crayon in a child's hand on a crumpled, jagged-edged piece of cardboard. A dented, faded coffee can sat on the sidewalk in front of the propped-up sign. Drawn above the words were two artistic renditions of smiling figures with pointed ears, but the passersby kept passing by.

The sign was nearly as filthy as its author, also propped against a boarded-up door in the alcove of an abandoned deli, nestled between boarded up windows over blackened glass. There was evidence a fire had taken place there sometime in the past.

Cretin shrugged the once-colorful child's sleeping bag further up his neck as he repositioned himself against the door. He was the only one who knew a family of pink and purple unicorns still lived beneath the street-worn filth that now covered the quilted fabric. A cold north wind began to blow in, an omen that warned it was going to be another empty-stomach night for the three of them.

As the last rays of the early January sun began to slip behind the roof of the laundromat across the street, Cretin huddled against the advancing cold and tucked his head beneath the unicorns. "I'm sorry, babies, I did my best."

Reggie cleared his throat. "Who is them?"

Cretin continued to whisper into the sleeping bag. "Maybe tomorrow I'll find a better place to beg."

"Hey, buddy, I said, 'Who is them?'"

"Huh?" Cretin pulled his head out and blinked against the last rays of the setting sun until the shadow of a figure blocked them. Before him stood a pair of legs, covered by crisp, blue denim jeans, their rolled-up cuffs revealed a lining of blue and green, plaid-flannel. The jeans were propped up by a pair of expensive-looking brown, leather Boondockers.

"What'd you say? You talkin' t' me, Denim Legs?" Cretin followed the legs up to a wide, two-tone, brown leather belt with a matte, silver-metal buckle, just beneath a black and red, plaid-flannel shirt that was tucked into the jeans. Over the shirt was an expensive, brown, thigh-length, patchwork-suede, lambswool coat with the bottom two, large leather buttons undone, and there were gloves to match. The long end of a red and blue plaid-woolen scarf, wrapped around a neck, hung down the jacket's front.

"Yes, sorry, sir. I asked, 'Who is them?'"

Cretin followed the voice upward to a pair of broad, full lips, spread into a smile, and studded with white, shiny teeth that filled it from one side to the other. Above them, a noble, slightly crooked nose and a pair of blue-green eyes that crinkled at their corners finished the face. It was deeply tanned and surrounded by short brown hair with the ears cut out. There was a scattering of gray at the temples. Cretin couldn't tell whether the guy was rich, tanned-white or Hispanic, or some other combination thereof, but it didn't matter. He was talking out loud and to him, and he wanted to know who *them* was. Maybe there'd be food tonight after all.

"Sir? You callin' me sir?" Defying the greasy, matted, brown hair, tied in a ponytail, and the filth covering the bearded, Caucasian face, Cretin's amber-brown eyes with flecks of gold peered up at Denim Legs. "Sorry, but I ain't no sir, not no more, just Cretin. What you want?"

"I was inquiring as to who *them* is, or more properly, who *they* are. Your sign, with the beautifully drawn figures of a dog and cat, are they yours?"

"Yup, them's my family. Well really, only one is. Roscoe's mine, but Cinders is Roscoe's. Guess that kinda makes him family, too."

"Roscoe and Cinders? Who's who?"

Cretin flipped the sleeping bag open, and then looked back up at Denim Legs. "Them's Roscoe 'n Cinders."

Lifting its smooth, short-furred black and white head was what looked like a small terrier mix. Its ears pointed up while the tips drooped down, and its markings were like that of a killer whale, but in reverse—large, white regions with smaller, rounded and oval, black markings.

Denim Legs's face softened.

A two-toned, striped, ash-gray, juvenile cat, just out of kittenhood, was curled between the dog's front legs. The edges of its ears were scabbed, the ears themselves were red, and swollen, and oozing and there were crusts in the corners of its eyes. Crusted yellow wounds lay where bald spots covered its body, and both of its front and left rear paws were swollen, blistered, and hairless as well. Not taking its eyes off Denim Legs, the dog lowered its head and covered its ward with its paws.

Then the odor hit him. Denim Legs recoiled.

"Oh, for the love of God!" The stench that stirred into the air made him stagger backwards. "That smell!"

Cretin cowered and smiled weakly behind his several week-old beard, embarrassment evident on his face.

"Oh, I'm sorry," Denim Legs said. "I'm so sorry. You can't help it."

"No, I'm sorry, Mister. We been on the street off 'n on some past two years—but we been without means to bathe 'n shave fer only a couple weeks, ever since we got throwed outta that shelter. One animal's alls I's allowed, 'n they didn't even like that, but they had t' let us stay 'coz some rich folks done made a donation t' that effect. Once they found out Roscoe done adopted Cinders, they said to git. I begged and begged 'em, but they said no ways.

"I took one look at Roscoe, 'n her face done told me what I had t' do. After she pulled Cinders outta the rubble of that burnin' factory when he was a baby—well he been hers ever since. Can't break up her family so we packed right up 'n left."

"Roscoe is a girl?"

"Yup, I know. I know it's a boy's name, but I took one look at 'er when I found 'er nosin' by the tracks 'afore I knew 'n said, 'You looks like a Roscoe t' me.' She started waggin' 'er tail right off—been Roscoe ever since."

"And Cinders?"

"Baby boy, but he ain't gonna be a baby much longer. I'm savin' up some money so as t' git him fixed. I already tried once, but them animal shelter folks tol' me he was too young 'n weak at the time on account of his burns. I'm trying to build him up so as he can go through it. Only right with so many strays about. Maybe come spring I'll have enough saved up."

"I see," said Denim Legs.

"Not a lot of cans on the street right now seein' as folks don't drink as much soda pop since it got cold. I keep havin' to dip int' it t' pay fer their food. All used up three days ago, but I can start savin' again once the weather turns back. I been able t' scrounge up enough chow that be still half good right now out back o' them restaurants a couple blocks over, over on 47th, t' keep us going."

"Sir, it's going to be cold tonight. There's a big storm coming. A couple feet of snow is in the forecast for the city. You're going to have to find a place to take shelter."

"Ain't no place that'll take me 'n Roscoe 'n Cinders, 'n I ain't leavin' 'em. I can't. I promised 'em I'd always look after 'em."

"Hold on, maybe I have something that will help." Denim Legs turned around and walked to the curb. It was the first time Cretin noticed the big, black SUV with its motor running. Denim Legs returned a moment later carrying a heavy, quilted winter coat, a pair of knitted mittens, and a multi-colored, knitted scarf and hat—but most importantly, he carried a large, fast-food paper bag.

Roscoe lifted her head and sniffed the air. Her body began to tremble, and her tail started to wag, beating in time with the sound of the SUV's idling engine. Cinders lifted his head and sniffed, too, but he held fast beneath Roscoe's protective shield.

"Here you go," Denim Legs said, "These should keep you warm, and there should be enough in the bag to feed the three of you for at least a day."

A smile of stained teeth spread across Cretin's face. "Thanks, Mister. Sure 'preciate it. I'll put Cinders in the hat 'n then Roscoe 'n the hat inside this nice, new, warm coat. 'N zip it up real tight. That'll keep 'em both nice 'n warm tonight."

"Sir, the coat is for you."

"Ain't no sir, I told ya. I'm Cretin. I got this here sleepin' bag. It'll be enough fer me, but thanks again," he said as he reached into the bag of food and pulled out two foil-wrapped sandwiches, one a burger, the other fish. "Roscoe and Cinders sure do appreciate your generosity."

Denim Legs stood in silence as he watched Cretin carefully open the sandwiches and begin to pull the meat and fish apart, sucking the mayonnaise off the burger and the breading off the fish. After placing the breading among the remaining cheese, lettuce, tomato, pickle, and onion between the remaining buns, he broke up the meat and fish and fed the pieces to his little family. Once it was gone, he ate the contents of the buns in several bites.

"Sir ... sorry, Cretin," Denim Legs said with reverence. "There's plenty in there for all of you. You need protein just as much as Roscoe and Cinders do. Please have yourself a burger."

"Oh, I will, I will. It's just that I ain't that hungry right now, 'n they need it more 'n me, seein' as they only got fur, and there ain't much of that between the two of 'em. Again thanks, Mister. Guess I better get a move on afore that snow starts up."

"But where will you go? You said the shelters won't take you."

"Is right. There's a busted lock on a door 'round back of here. That's where we been holdin' up at night ever since we left the shelter. Too cold for kids and gangs to be botherin' us after the sun goes down. We hold up just fine in there.

"Good thing you stopped when you did, 'coz they done got our money out the can 'bout hour afore you come by. I was 'bout t' head out t' buy Roscoe 'n Cinders their supper. That's why I's still here—tryin' a little longer t' see if'n some good folks might find it in their hearts to toss us a few coins. Good thing I stayed, 'coz then I met you. So thanks again, Mister. Really, thanks."

"Here," Denim Legs said as he reached into his back pocket and pulled out his wallet. He took out a few bills. "Please use this and find yourself a room for the night. I'm sorry, but it's all I'm carrying right now."

"Sixty-five dollars! Sixty-five dollars! Mister, that'll feed us for a couple weeks!" Cretin exclaimed.

"Oh, thank you, thank you so much!"

"No, please get a room or you'll freeze tonight."

"Too late for tonight, but don't you worry none," Cretin promised. "Tomorrow'll be different. Now we gotta get a move on."

"But … but," Denim Legs stammered, but it was no use. Cretin shook his head. He'd made up his mind.

Denim Legs watched Cretin wrap the new scarf around his neck then fold up the sign and quickly pack up his meager belongings and the bag of food into a heavy, black-plastic garbage bag. Then he lifted a shivering Cinders and folded him into the hat under the watchful eye of Roscoe. After opening the new coat, he motioned for Roscoe to lie down in it, then placed Cinders, in the hat, beside her.

Once Roscoe curled up around the kitten, Cretin pulled the coat sleeves into the coat and zipped it up around them, leaving the top six inches open. He looked back over his shoulder at Denim Legs. "That's so as they can breathe." Then he pulled two pieces of twine from his pocket and tied the neck and bottom of the coat up tight. "So as they don't fall out 'til we get inside."

After opening the sleeping bag, Cretin laid the coat into its center and then drew up the four corners and tied them together to make a satchel. As he lifted the garbage bag over his left shoulder and scooped the satchel into his right arm, he nodded and smiled and then made his way down the sidewalk. Once he reached the end of the long row of connected buildings, he looked back and nodded his head again before disappearing around the corner.

Denim Legs waved and then turned and walked to his vehicle, shaking his head, wishing he could have done more. As he pulled out into traffic, he glanced in the rearview mirror at the pile of winter clothing behind the back seat and remembered why he was there.

Chapter Three
Charity

Ten summers ago

"After I'm gone, Reggie, you're going to have to take over giving away the clothing for me."

"Mom, you're going to get better, and besides, that's not my thing."

"I know 'it's not your thing', Reggie, but I need you to promise me that you will, at least until you've given away all of it, just in case."

"Mom, why couldn't I just donate it? There are plenty of charities that have better use for it and can get it to the people who really need it."

"That's what you'd think, but they throw away more than they keep, especially if they don't have room for it at the time you donate it."

Reggie averted his gaze and remained silent.

"Reggie, promise me now."

"Yes, Mom, I will."

"You'll what?"

"I'll see to it that all the clothing is given away."

"And that you're going to do it yourself, not someone else."

"Yes, I'll do it personally, Mom, I promise."

"You really don't want to do this, do you?"

"No, but I've given you my word."

"Then you better make yourself comfortable, because I'm going tell you a little story."

"Please, Mother, not that story again!"

"Mother is it now? Well…"

"Sorry, Mom."

"I know you've heard me tell the story before, but only in part. You don't know the half of it. It's time you heard it all and the truth this time. You're going to listen to it from beginning to end."

"Yes, Mom."

After Reggie took his seat, his mother began. "Had your grandfather, my father, not had a kind woman give him a coat and a hat and mittens one winter, you would not be here right now."

"What do you mean?"

"That's how he met your grandmother. She was the kind woman's daughter. It was snowing, and your great-grandmother noticed your grandfather on her way into the general store. He was wearing old, tattered clothes, and he had no coat, so she gave him some warm clothing that once belonged to your great-grandfather. She always carried several articles of his in her wagon's trunk and in this instance, the night before a blizzard blew into town. To thank her, your grandfather had gone in and walked through the general store with her, carrying her groceries while she shopped.

"As it turns out, you see, it was a good thing he did because as they talked, she learned he was new in town and had no place to live. By the time she came out with him loaded down with parcels and sacks, her wagon was stuck in the snow. A good two feet had already fallen by then. Fortunately, he got the wagon unstuck.

"He went back to the farm with her to be sure she got home safe, but by then, the snow had gotten so deep he couldn't leave, so your great-grandmother gave him a room with the intention he'd be on his way once the storm passed. But that winter, the blizzard never seemed to end, and a good month passed before the roads were open again.

"During that month, your grandfather became indispensable to the two of them. With her husband having passed on four years earlier, your great-grandmother and grandmother had barely been able to keep the farm going, but after that young man, your grandfather, arrived, things turned around.

"He pitched in to earn his keep and got the farm running right. He had a real knack for farm animals and machinery, so your great-grandmother decided to keep him on. Over time, your grandmother took a real shine to him, and before you know it, they were engaged."

"So that's why you've kept a stock of winter clothes in the trunk of the limo each winter, all these years," Reggie said.

"Yes, and every time I've noticed someone in need, I fit them with warm clothing."

"I never knew."

"Well now you know," she said, spreading her hands across her lap.

"I'm sorry, I never took the time to listen to the whole story before. Now I understand."

"You could continue the tradition, if you had a mind to do so, once I'm gone…"

"Mother, don't say that."

"I know, my boy, I know, but it will happen, Reggie, one day and whenever the time comes, I hope I can count on you."

"It's something to think about, Mom."

"I hope you think long and hard about it, Reggie. I know in my heart, you'll come to the right decision."

A month later, Reggie's mother's illness caught up with her, and she passed away.

Chapter Four
Negotiation

As Reggie approached the intersection, the light turned red. After he came to a stop, he switched on the radio. While he scanned the programmed stations, his mother's voice filled his head. *"Reginald Montgomery Scottsdale, you turn this vehicle right around and take that man to a motel!"*

Reggie jumped in his seat. "Holy shit!" He shook his head and looked in the rearview mirror, certain she was sitting right behind him. Then he was startled back to reality by several cars, blaring their horns behind him. The light had turned green, and he wasn't moving. Momentarily disoriented, he stomped on the gas, turned right, and headed down the street.

A moment later he regained his bearings and jerked the wheel to the right at the first place he found, a narrow alleyway. He headed for the far end, intending to make a right onto the next street, then another right to get back to the street he'd started on. After that he'd begin his search for Cretin.

In the distance, Reggie spied a group of male figures ripping apart a black plastic bag. An ominous feeling settled over him so he stepped on the gas as he leaned on the SUV's horn, startling them. The figures raced down the alley and scattered when they reached the street.

Halfway down the alleyway, he came upon the remnants of the garbage bag and spied an opened doorway and what looked like the satchel the homeless man, Cretin, had been carrying when he'd disappeared around the corner. There were also crumpled, foil-paper wrappers and French fry boxes scattered about.

As he slowed his vehicle, the satchel moved as he

came into view of the open doorway. When he lowered the passenger window, he heard mewing and whining, so he pulled the SUV to a stop and got out.

Rounding the front end of his vehicle, he called out, "Roscoe? Cinders?" As the whining and mewing became louder, he heard a muffled groan so he followed it until he saw a pair of legs just inside the opened door. When he rushed forward, he found Cretin lying in back of the abandoned deli with a gash on the top of his head. As he kneeled down, he pulled a handkerchief from his back pocket and placed it over the gash.

"Cretin, what's happened?"

Cretin moaned.

"Cretin, Cretin, what happened to you?"

Cretin opened his eyes. "Huh? What the hell?"

"Cretin, what happened?" Reggie asked again as he pressed down on the handkerchief.

"Sons-of-bitches! Those sons-of-bitches got my purse. Got my emergency money 'n stole my food."

"How much did they get?"

"Only five bucks. That's all I put in it, but they took it anyways. You learn to divide up what you got fer just such times. Didn't believe me when I said it was all I had, n' they was right, 'coz I lied. Didn't see me stash the rest of the money you gave me in my boots after I turned the corner between the buildings, but they was watchin'. Said they saw the rich man given me cash. Just didn't know how much."

Cretin started to giggle, but immediately stopped and grabbed his skull. "Cracked me upside the head with a brick when they opened it 'n didn't find what they wanted t' find. Sons-of-bitches!"

"Can you sit up?"

"Where's Roscoe? Where's Cinders? Where's my babies?"

"I think they're still inside the coat."

"They okay? Sons-of-bitches knocked 'em out o' my hands."

"Let's get you settled first."

"No, I gotta know they's okay. Take me to 'em."

"I don't think you should get up yet. You might be injured elsewhere."

"No, I gotta see my babies!"

"How about I bring them to you?"

"Fair 'nuf."

When Reggie returned with the coat, Cretin was sitting in the doorway with his back propped up against the doorjamb. He reached out and took the coat, ripping open the tied twine at the bottom. Out wiggled Roscoe, followed by a shaking Cinders. As Cretin lifted them to his face, and hugged them close, he began to cry. "Oh, my babies, my babies. Did they hurt you? Did those sons-of-bitches hurt you?"

Roscoe whimpered and cried as she covered Cretin's face with doggy kisses. Cinders mewed louder and louder while his near-skeletally-thin body shook. Once they'd all calmed down, Cretin began to stand up.

"Hold on there, Cretin, you're in no shape to stand."

"I gotta find a new place fer the night. Can't stay here now as they found us."

"Where will you go?"

"Don't know, Mister. Is almost dark now, but don't worry 'bout us. We'll be jus' fine."

"My name is Reggie. Please let me take you to a motel for the night."

"No! No, you done enough, Mister, 'n won't matter none anyhow. No place'll take us. Not me, 'n a dog, 'n a mangy kitten."

"You know what you have to do, Reggie." His

mother's voice filled his head. *"Now do it!"*

For a moment Reggie's face screwed up tight, but then he nodded his head and spoke. "Please, my name is Reggie. Let me help you. There's a place I know where I can take you."

"Thanks, Mister," Cretin said as he started to get up, "but like I said, no place'll take us."

"I know they will. I know the owner. It will be fine. Trust me."

Cretin stumbled and started to go down. "Son-of-a-bitch! Those damn sons-of-bitches!"

Reggie caught him and helped him back down to the ground. "You're in no shape to be out here on your own, Cretin. You're coming with me, you, and Roscoe, and Cinders. "It will be fine."

"I don't have no money to pay. I gotta keep the rest you gave fer food, 'n asides, we stink somethin' fierce, Mister. You know that! You don't want us in your fancy car."

"Please … call me Reggie, and I promise, you won't need any money where we're going. Now don't argue with me. I'll put a blanket down on the back seat if you like, and you can wrap all of you up in it. Will that work for you?"

Cretin looked long and hard into Reggie's eyes, wondering whether he could trust this stranger. "Give me a minute. I need to think about it."

"I see you're a tough negotiator. While you're thinking, I'm going to make a few phone calls to get the ball rolling. I'll be right back."

****

When Reggie returned, he found Cretin where he had left him. "It's all set. Ready to go?"

"Where we goin', Mister Reggie?"

"It's a nice place. I'm sure you'll like it, and

please, it's just Reggie. There's plenty of hot water with a tub and shower and a place where Roscoe and Cinders will be warm. There's also a bed for you, and there's plenty to eat. What do you say?"

"You're making this sound too good t' be true, Mister."

"It's Reggie," he said with a smile.

"Right … Reggie." Cretin lifted his hand to the wound on his head. When he pulled it away and saw the blood, he sighed.

Reggie kneeled down to him. "What do you say?"

"Okay, okay, you done twisted my arm, Reggie, 'n I'm too tired t' fight with you, but only fer the night."

"I believe you'll be allowed to stay as long as you want. I think there's someone there who can take a look at that cut on your head, and there's someone who can attend to little Cinders's sores."

"How's that, 'n how much? How much this all gonna cost?"

"I don't think they charge anything, but if you want, I'm sure you can work something out with the owner."

Cretin sighed again. He must have realized he didn't have much of a choice. It was getting dark, and he probably couldn't think clearly enough to try to figure out anything better. "Okay, Mister Reggie. Deal. I'm not one for such charity n' yeah, I beg on the street, but that's coz I don't got no choice, n' I earn money when I can.

"Stayin' someplace nice, like you sayin' it is, is another matter altogether." Cretin extended his hand. "But I'll take what you're offerin', but only fer the night."

Reggie took his hand, and they shook on it.

"Great! Now let's get you and your family in the

car. Then we'll be on our way." *Now, if I can only keep this from Aunt Virginia,* he thought to himself.

Once everyone was settled in, Reggie put the SUV in gear, just as the first snowflakes began to fall.

Chapter Five
Out of the Cold

The further they drove away from the city, the lighter the snow became. After forty-five minutes, Reggie turned the Escalade off the road through a fortified iron gate, between two immense stone pillars and along what appeared to be a paved, narrow lane that ran through a deeply wooded area. When nearly two minutes had passed and they hadn't reached their destination, Cretin started to squirm in his seat.

"Just how far we goin' down this road, Mister Reggie?"

"It's a driveway, and it's not far now," Reggie answered. "We're almost there. See." He pointed toward a building, off in the distance, as the vehicle entered a clearing.

A light snow was still falling, covering the shrubs, but here, the driveway was elevated from the grassy areas and was kept mostly clear by the blowing wind.

A moderate size, stone cottage, illuminated by lights mounted at the corners, just below the eaves, came into view. As they got closer, Cretin could see a two-car garage, made from the same gray and brown stone. Cretin's eyes grew wider and wider as they drew closer.

The two buildings were attached by way of a carport, through which the driveway ran. The carport was high and wide enough for the vehicle to pull under, and there was a side door that opened into the cottage. In front of the garage sat two, windowless vans.

As the SUV came to a stop, three women and three men, all dressed in hospital scrub suits and coats, came out through the cottage door.

Cretin grew more uncomfortable. He felt

completely out of place. He'd never seen such finery in his life. "What kind of place is this, Reggie?" he asked.

"It's a very nice place. I think you'll like it here."

Both rear doors of the SUV opened together, allowing the cold wind to blow through the vehicle as hands were extended inward. "Hello, Mister. Cretin, sir," a white woman with a kind face said from the left door. "I'm Jean. I'm a nurse. I'm going to assist Doctor Waters while he fixes up that nasty cut on your head. Let's get you inside where it's warm. Please, right this way."

"Here, Mister Cretin," a Hispanic woman with a broad smile said from the right door. "I'm Doctor Littleton. I'm a veterinarian. If you will allow me, I'd like to check over Roscoe and little Cinders. I understand they've had quite a fright this evening, and I've been told little Cinders has some sores that require some attention."

Cretin sat frozen in place. He grasped the quilted coat holding Roscoe and Cinders tightly to his chest, beneath the blanket wrapped around his shoulders. When the blanket was lowered by the two women, the coat was revealed, and it began to squirm. As he huddled his body around the coat, the odor, held in by the blanket, reached both Jean and Doctor Littleton, but they were professionals. Though their eyes began to water, the smiles on their faces remained unchanged.

"It's okay, Cretin," Reggie said as he turned around in the driver's seat. "They're here to help you." His eyes began to water as well.

"This ain't right, Mister. Somethin's awful fishy."

"Again, my name is Reggie. I promise you, everything is on the up and up. I told you. I know the owner. He's a nice guy, and he loves animals. When he learned about what happened to Roscoe and little Cinders, he wanted to help. Actually, he begged me to bring them here. He has a real soft spot for dogs and cats."

"There's a pot of beef stew simmering on the stove for you," Jean added, "and Miss Honey has just put a loaf of French bread into of the oven. It sure smells good in there."

Cretin shook his head. "Where is this man? I wants t' see 'im."

"He's tied up this evening," Reggie said, "but you'll meet him in the morning. I promise."

"Nah, this don't feel right. I don't know these people."

Jean pointed to two men standing behind her, one, with kind eyes, was tall, slender, and African-American. The other had a muscular build with brown hair and was white. "This is Doctor Waters, and next to him," she said pointing to the white man, "is Simon. He's a nurse, too." Then she pointed to the other side of the SUV, towards an African-American woman and an Asian man. "Over there, behind Doctor Littleton, are her vet techs, Veronica and Trevor. We're all here to see to it that you and your family are taken care of."

"Would you feel better if I went with you, at least to get started?" Reggie asked.

Cretin sat thinking. He pulled the coat even tighter to his chest.

"I'll be happy to accompany you, Cretin," Reggie said. "Look, I'm sure Roscoe and little Cinders could use a good meal with real dog and cat food and nice, warm beds to sleep in tonight, and little Cinders will feel so much better once the doctor fixes up his sores. Now what do you say?"

"Dog n' cat food? Where the hell'd that come from? What's goin' on here, Reggie? How can there be dog n' cat food?"

"I brought it, Mister Cretin," Doctor Littleton said

as she rested her hand on his forearm. "Just a few cans. When I heard about Roscoe and little Cinders, I thought they might be hungry. Truly, there's nothing more to it."

Cretin finally relented. "Okay, but only if you come along, Reggie. You been real nice t' me. I guess I can trust ya."

"Thank you, Cretin." Reggie exhaled deeply. "I'll be happy to go with you." He unbuckled his seatbelt and stepped out to wait behind Jean.

Cretin kissed the coat and then began to hand it to Doctor Littleton, but then stopped. "Them's my babies, Doc. They's all I got in the world. You promise me you won't hurt 'em or put 'em down or nothin'."

"Mr. Cretin, sir, I would never do such a thing. I only want to help them."

"You give me your word on that?"

"Of course."

"Then say it, out loud. I want t' hear ya say it."

"I give you my word, Mister Cretin. I'm here to care for them, and I won't hurt them or put them down."

"Good." Cretin handed the coat to Doctor Littleton and then turned towards Jean. As she took his hand, he pulled against it and slid himself from the back seat. While Simon held the cottage door open, everyone walked in, with Reggie bringing up the rear to close the door against the cold behind them.

The first room Cretin entered was a large mudroom with a long, waist high, stainless steel counter along the right wall. A large, deep, stainless-steel sink, with a spray hose anchored to the base of the faucet, was cut into the counter at its far end. Beyond the counter sat a full-size washer and dryer, next to a closed door that led into the cottage.

Along the opposite wall and closest to him was a five-foot long, stainless steel table that stood out, lengthwise, from the wall and beyond that, an examination table like those found in a doctor's office. Across both the counter and table were spread various supplies, equipment, ointments, creams, and bottles of medications.

In the far-left corner, by the door, was a large six by six-foot shower with a floor to ceiling wrap-around curtain pulled to one wall.

Doctor Littleton placed the coat atop the counter and untied the twine, revealing a shaking Roscoe and Cinders. Cretin stopped and watched.

Veronica picked up little Cinders in her gloved hands and murmured to him as she wrapped him in a towel, then held him close to her chest while she gently stroked the top of his head.

When Trevor reached for Roscoe with a towel, Cretin said, anxiously, "I wouldn't do that, Mister. You might git bit. She's real picky 'bout people." But it was too late. Trevor already had Roscoe in his arms and was petting her and whispering kind words into her ear. Roscoe's tail began to wag. She was eating up the attention.

"I wouldn't of believed it if I didn't see it fer myself!" Cretin exclaimed. Then he thought, *If'n she trusts 'em, maybe I can trust 'em, too.*

"I think the best thing to do for little Cinders is to start by giving him a bath so I can get a good look at his sores and clean them in the process," Doctor Littleton said. "Do you agree, Mister Cretin?"

"Yeah, Doc. Sure, sounds good to me."

"While we're at it," Doctor Littleton went on, "I think Roscoe would enjoy a nice warm bath as well. It will help to warm them both up much quicker, too. Is that all right with you?"

"Sure, sure, whatever you think is best, Doctor."

"They're both a bit thin. We'll give them both some medications and supplements to help them along. Would it be okay with you if we run a few tests to check on their health?"

"Sure, Doc, sure," Cretin said.

"As soon as we have the results," Doctor Littleton continued, "I'll review them with you."

"Thanks, Doc."

"Have they been treated recently for rabies, distemper, heartworm, Feline leukemia, those kinds of things?

"No, Doc, I can't afford 'em."

"Not to worry, we'll take care of that, but we'll hold off on most of the inoculations for little Cinders until we have his blood work back. He might be a little young for some of them, and I'll want to know his health status before I decide what he should receive and when."

"Thank ye, Doc."

"Now it's your turn, Mister Cretin," Doctor Waters said. The man radiated kindness. "How about you let me have a look at that head wound of yours?"

"Yes, sir, Doctor, sir. You want me up on this here table?"

"Yes please."

"Mind if we run some blood tests on you as well?"

"Might as well, Doc, seein' as we're all getting tune-ups."

****

While Cretin's head was being cleaned and sutured, Reggie stood by and watched. After his blood was drawn, and he received a tetanus booster, Simon helped Cretin down from the exam table. "Would you enjoy a nice, hot shower yourself, Mister Cretin, to warm yourself up as well? Why should Roscoe and Cinders get pampered a little and not you, too?"

Cretin looked over at his little family. As Doctor Littleton and Trevor finished up with treating and dressing Cinders's wounds, Roscoe was in the middle of having her coat brushed by Veronica under a stationary blower. The look on her face was one of pure bliss.

"Yeah, I think I probably should, afore I sleep in somebody else's bed."

"You can use the shower right here in the corner. I have it all set up for you. There's shampoo, soap and a washcloth and loofah."

"Thanks, young man. I appreciate it."

"I'm just going to go check on your dinner," Reggie said as he excused himself and opened the door to the cottage. "I'll be right back."

"Now that Doctor Littleton has finished with Cinders," Jean said, "and Doctor Waters has finished with you, we can all just step out and give you some privacy. There are beds for both of them inside. Veronica can move them there just as soon as she's finished with Roscoe."

"I appreciate it, Miss, but Roscoe won't leave my side, and Cinders won't go nowheres without Roscoe."

"Then I'll bring the beds out here for them while they wait for you to finish."

"Mighty nice of you, Miss, but they only need one 'coz Cinders only ever sleeps with Roscoe."

"I'll stay back to wash your hair, Mister Cretin," Simon said. "You can't see those nine sutures Doctor Waters just put in, and you certainly don't want to pull them open. There's a chair here for you to sit in while I do that."

"Okay." Cretin smiled meekly as he lowered his eyes. "If you think that's best."

Doctor Waters smiled. "It is."

"I'm jus' sorry I'm such a sight."

"There's nothing to be shy about," Doctor Waters continued. "You'll need to be careful with your sutures for the next ten days, and don't forget to apply the ointment to the wound at least daily. Once I take them out, you'll be good as new."

While Doctor Waters was speaking, Reggie returned.

"While you're in the shower," Jean added, "I'll just run your clothes through the washer and dryer."

"I think there might be a few outfits that will fit you in one of the bedroom closets," Reggie added. "We'll pick out some things for you to try on once you're finished. Then Miss Honey has that pot of stew and the bread she just took from the oven waiting for you. How does that sound?"

"Sounds great. Thanks."

Chapter Six
A Name

After everyone but Simon and Veronica left the room, Cretin began to undress. While he did, Simon began to pull off his own shoes and socks.

"What you up to there, young fella?"

"I have to get in the shower with you to wash your hair."

"Yeah, but I don't want no naked young man in there with me. Been a while." Cretin sighed and then thought to himself, *'N you're a looker. I can't account fer what that just might do t' me.*

"Sir?"

"Oh, never mind. I appreciate the offer." Cretin closed his eyes then sighed and thought, *You're bein' naked's likely to make me feel things I aint' felt in a while.*

Simon chuckled. "It's okay, Mister Cretin. I won't be naked."

As Simon removed his scrub top, he revealed a tank top underneath. He then rolled up his pants to above his thighs and slipped on a pair of shower shoes.

"That'll work," Cretin said. "That'll be safe."

Simon laughed, not realizing that Cretin meant safe from him. "Thanks, Mister Cretin."

When Cretin pulled off his boots, the sixty dollars he'd stashed in them fell out. He picked the bills up and handed them to Simon. "Here, it's all I gots, but take it fer me, 'n Roscoe, 'n Cinders."

"Oh, Mister Cretin, there's no charge."

"No. No," Cretin insisted, "You all done so much fer us, now please take it."

"Mister Cretin…"

"How about I put it with your belongings,"

Veronica said, "and we can sort this all out later."

Cretin nodded. "Fair 'nuff."

Once Cretin was behind the shower curtain and had finished undressing, Simon went to the door and called to Jean. "We're getting started, so you can take his clothes."

Jean returned to the mudroom from the cottage and placed the pet bed on the floor. "I have their bed ready, Mister Cretin, and just in time. Veronica has just finished up with Roscoe."

Cretin stuck his head around the curtain. "Go lie down, babies," he said as he waved his arm at Roscoe and Cinders.

Veronica handed Cretin's cash to Jean as she finished. "Mister Cretin has offered this for taking care of him and his family."

Jean nodded. "Oh, I see."

"Yes, I offered to place it with his belongings until we sort everything out."

"Good idea," Jean answered.

As Veronica passed the shower on her way into the cottage, Cretin lifted his hand for her to stop. "Thanks, Miss. I'm sure my babies appreciate all you done fer 'em."

"Of course, Mister Cretin. Any time."

A moment later Roscoe and Cinders curled up together. After they were settled, Cretin pulled the shower curtain closed.

While Jean began to empty his pants pockets, she began to hum softly to herself. "Your wallet is a bit soiled, inside and out, Mister Cretin," she called into the shower. "Do you mind if I give it a once over with some saddle soap?"

"Sure thing, Missy. That sure is nice of ya."

"It would be my pleasure, Mister Cretin. Once

your clothes are finished, I'll give your sleeping bag a good cleaning, too."

"Again, mighty nice of ya, Missy," he called out.

Jean jotted the information she gathered from the wallet onto a small notepad. Then she loaded the clothes into the washing machine and began to pack up the remainder of supplies they had used that were left out on the counter and table.

After Simon turned on the shower and adjusted the temperature of the water, he noticed a chain around Cretin's neck. "Oh, you're wearing dog tags." Simon said. "What branch did you serve in?" So encrusted were they with the same grime that covered every nook and cranny of Cretin's body, he apparently hadn't noticed them at first.

Cretin began to wash his face. "Army—First Gulf War. They been a part of me fer so long, I forget about 'em, most times."

"They're awfully tarnished. Would you allow me to give them a bit of a scrub?"

"I've never had 'em off, not since I got out, but I guess it'd be okay."

After Cretin handed them over, Simon read the tags out loud, "Chadwick, CA—O pos—P. It's Mister Chadwick then."

On the other side of the curtain, Jean pulled out the notepad and added what she'd heard.

"Ain't nobody called me Chadwick in longer 'en I can remember."

"Why Cretin then?" Simon asked.

"'Coz that's what folks on the street kept callin' me. After a while, it stuck, 'n I forgot all about Chadwick."

"Oh, you poor man," Jean whispered.

Simon continued. "What's the P stand for?"

"That's fer Protestant."

"How long have you been out of the Army, Mister Chadwick?"

"Since '01."

"I'm sorry, Mister Chadwick," Simon said after a minute, "but I can't get the tarnish off these tags with just soap."

"No matter," Cretin said, "but I appreciate you tryin'."

Jean stopped humming and called into the shower. "Mister Chadwick, would you do me the honor of allowing me to polish your dog tags for you? It would be a privilege to do that for an American military veteran."

"That's might…" Cretin's voice caught. He cleared his voice several times as he blinked tears from his eyes. "That's mighty kind of you, Miss. Ain't nobody … nobody ever wanted to do somethin' like that fer me 'afore."

"It would truly be my honor, Mister Chadwick."

"Thank you, Miss." Cretin's voice caught again. "You can hand 'em out to her, young fella."

"I'll have them finished before you're out of the shower," Jean called in. "By the way, there's two little souls out here who can't take their eyes off the shower curtain."

"Don't worry, Miss. They won't move, not 'til I tell 'em they can."

"I'll be right back with your dog tags, Mister Chadwick," Jean called out. "There should be some polish in the kitchen."

"Ready to get your hair washed now?" Simon asked. Cretin nodded. "Then your throne awaits you." Simon waved his hand toward the chair.

As Simon helped Cretin wash his hair and then

the parts of his body he couldn't reach, years of dirt and grime fell away and disappeared down the drain. By the time they'd finished, Cretin was unrecognizable from his former self.

"How about you let me give you a quick shave and a trim?" Simon asked. "You'll feel so much better, and it'll help to keep your hair out of your eyes."

Skeptical, Cretin asked, "You sure you know how?"

"I sure do! I'm not a pro, but I do a decent job at shaving, and I can give a respectable haircut. It'll only take a few minutes."

"Then let's go fer it, young man. Might as well get the full treatment, but no full shave. I'll let ya give my beard a trim though, if'n you like, but not too short on account of the weather."

****

While Cretin rinsed himself off of the last of the hair trimmings, Simon called through the ajar door to kitchen. "We're all finished." He carried the used towels that caught Cretin's hair to the trash can, shook them out, and tossed them in the washer. Meanwhile Jean came in and laid out a set of underwear, a gray sweatsuit with slippers, and also an outfit consisting of a pair of khaki slacks, a blue oxford dress shirt, a pair of socks, and shiny, brown leather shoes with a matching belt.

Simon returned to the shower and helped Cretin put on a robe. Then he opened the shower curtain, and Cretin stepped out.

"I thought I'd save you some time, so I've picked out some clothes for you to choose from, Mister Chadwick," Jean said as she turned around to face him. Suddenly she sucked in her breath. "Oh my!" she exclaimed. "Mister Chadwick, you look amazing, and what a looker you are. I barely recognize you!"

"Well thanks, Missy. I sure do feel good."

For a moment, Jean just stood there taking in the man who stood before her. "I just can't believe…"

Cretin smiled. "'S okay, Missy. I have that effect on people." Then he laughed out loud. "I must've sure been a sight t' behold."

"Yes. I mean … I'm sorry. Um. Darn…" Jean waved a hand in front of her face. Then she turned back to the counter as she waved her hands in front of her eyes to dry her tears. "Here," she said a moment later as she turned back to face him and offered the two sets of clothes. "I'm pretty good at guessing sizes, but please let me know if something doesn't fit."

"Them's new shoes!" Cretin exclaimed as he stepped forward.

"Your old boots were worn all the way through their soles. You need another pair, and these are available."

"I'll have to be sure to thank that man, once I meet 'im. How come he's got all these extra clothes lyin' around?"

Jean smiled. "I don't know, Mister Chadwick."

"Maybe that Mister Reggie knows his story."

"Maybe," Jean answered. "Are you ready to eat?"

"Sure thing. I done smelled that stew when you opened the door. My mouth's a waterin'."

"There's a place set for you at the dining room table. Oh, and these are ready for you," she said as she pulled his dog tags from the breast pocket of her scrub top and handed them back."

Cretin looked down at the shiny metal. "Just like new," he said. "Thank ya, Miss."

"It was my pleasure, Mister Chadwick."

"Ya know," Cretin said, "I'd sure like it if'n you'd call me by my proper name, Calvin."

Jean inhaled sharply and drew the back of her hand to her mouth. The tears that had nearly abated began to form in the corners of her eyes again. "It would be my honor, Calvin," she choked out.

"Wow!" Simon said, as he turned away and pressed his palms to his eyes, wiping them in the process. "So Calvin is the C in CA?" he asked.

"Yup," he said.

"Would you mind telling us what the A stands for?" Simon asked.

"Oh, that's fer Austin, like the city."

"Thank you, Mister Chadwick," Simon said, clearing his throat.

"Oh, you can call me Calvin, too."

"Thank you, Calvin." Simon cleared his throat again, and then leaned forward to whisper into Jean's ear. "You've broken through the first barrier. Mister Scottsdale will be so pleased."

****

As Calvin walked through the door, dressed in the slacks, shirt, and new shoes, everyone who was seated around the kitchen table, including Reggie and a plump, middle-aged, auburn-with gray-hair worn in a tight bun, white woman, were seated at the kitchen table, talking.

"Well," Reggie exclaimed as he looked up from a small notepad, "look who's all spit and polished."

Bringing up the rear was Roscoe, half-carrying, half-dragging a complaining, paw-bandaged, Cinders in her mouth, followed by Jean, carrying in their bed and then Simon with the extra sweatsuit.

The plump woman rose from the table and walked around the group as she approached him. The top of her head barely reached Calvin's shoulders. "Hello there, Mister Chadwick," she said with a faint, British accent, extending her hands and taking his into hers. "I'm

Miss Honey, the caretaker of this cottage. It's a pleasure and honor to meet you."

Calvin squeezed her hands back.

"Please have a seat at the dining room table," she pointed through an archway, "and I'll bring you your dinner."

"What about Roscoe and Cinders? I never eat before them."

"They've already been fed, Mister Chadwick," Trevor said, "just a half hour ago, in the mudroom, while you were in the shower. Their bellies are quite full."

"Thanks, but they won't let me out of their sight."

Miss Honey didn't miss a beat. "That's fine, Mister Chadwick. I'll just set a place for each of them as well." She excused herself from the kitchen.

"That's good, 'coz they'd be out of sorts if I didn't share with 'em."

"Right this way, Mister Chadwick," Reggie said as he stood up. "If you'd follow me."

"Mister Reggie, 'bout time you started callin' me by my proper name, Calvin. Chadwick's too formal."

"Certainly, Calvin."

"Have you 'et yet? Come sit with me a while, all y'all. It'd be nice t' have some company."

The group declined in murmurs, and then Reggie spoke up. "Thank you, Calvin. Everyone else has already eaten, but I'd be happy to join you." Then he placed a hand in the small of Calvin's back and directed him from the kitchen.

"Good," Calvin said.

After they walked through the archway together, Reggie pulled out the chair at the head of the table and seated Calvin. Then he took the seat to Calvin's left. Calvin rested his hands on the table and looked over the tall, lit candles rising from a sterling silver candelabra, a low floral arrangement, and each piece of silverware, china, crystal, and linen. Then he looked up at the ceiling and took in the crystal chandelier.

"I ain't never had such finery, Mister Reggie. Never in my life have I seen such…"

"Please, Calvin, no more mister. Just Reggie will do."

Miss Honey approached the table carrying two large, china soup bowls nestled into matching platters, both filled with her hearty beef stew. She set them down in front of the two men and then moved a butter plate with a silver knife and the bread platter to within arms' reach. Several pieces of bread had already been cut from the loaf. After pouring a glass of water for each of them, she stepped away from the table.

Behind her came Veronica carrying two small, shallow bowls with matching plates. They held small amounts of gravy and mashed meat and vegetables. She set them down on the table between two, less formal place settings, to Calvin's right and across from Reggie.

Trevor followed carrying Roscoe and Cinders in his arms, each wearing a small bib. The moment he set them down at the table in front of the bowls, they began to lap away. "I usually have 'em wait 'til after grace, but this is a special occasion." As Calvin's family crouched down at their places, Miss Honey, Veronica, and Trevor disappeared into the kitchen.

After lowering his head and folding his hands in front of him, Calvin began to murmur a quiet prayer. Reggie followed suit and waited for him to finish. After saying grace, Calvin turned to Reggie. "Thank you for bringing me here Mister … um … Reggie. I don't know how I'll ever repay ya fer lookin' out fer me and my family."

"It's been my pleasure, Calvin. I'm so happy you

came." Reggie poured a hearty burgundy from a bottle that had been opened to breathe into the wine goblets in front of each of them. "Now why don't you get started before your stew gets cold, and don't forget, there's plenty of bread and butter and a whole pot of stew to finish, so dig in."

While Calvin ate, Roscoe and Cinders moved to his lap once they'd finished the stew in their bowls. Calvin consumed several pieces of bread slathered with butter while he worked his way through the bowl. No sooner had he taken the last spoonful than Miss Honey appeared with a second bowl on a matching platter. After removing his empty bowl and replacing it with the new one, she cut several more pieces of bread and then placed the animals' bowls into Calvin's and returned to the kitchen.

So focused on his meal, Calvin spoke nary a word.

****

When he finally pushed himself away from the table, Calvin exhaled slowly and patted his belly. As he moved, Roscoe and Cinders lifted their heads from his lap. Roscoe sat up and looked between Calvin and his empty bowl. Cinders remained lying down. He lifted Roscoe to the table and watched while she cleaned the remaining scraps of stew from his bowl, then he lowered her back to his lap and began to speak. "I can't remember when I ever et so good, Reggie. That Miss Honey's one fine cook."

Reggie smiled. "That she is. It was wonderful."

Calvin stretched his neck and let his head fall back. "This day is 'bout all I can take," he said as he straightened up. "I'm sorry, but I'm pooped. I know I owe you some conversation, but I'm no good at it no more. With just Roscoe and Cinders to talk t' fer so long,

I'm plumb out of practice. I think it best if I just hit the sack afore I fall asleep here at this fine table."

"Perhaps we'll find time to talk sometime in the future."

"I'd like that, Mister Reggie, I really would."

"Please, it's just Reggie. I'll show you to your room then."

"'N Roscoe 'n Cinders? Where they gonna sleep?"

"With you, of course."

"Thanks … Reggie. Thanks a heap."

****

No sooner had Calvin buried his head into the plush, feather pillow than he was fast asleep. With Roscoe and Cinders under the blanket and down comforter and lying along his flanks, they all slept soundly for the first time in a very long while. There were no horns blaring, no voices shouting, and no one to watch out for who could do them harm. It was just like home.

Chapter Seven
Fess up

With no city noise coming from outside, Calvin came to consciousness slowly. He stretched and yawned and then rolled over as he opened his eyes and reached down to say good morning to his family. They weren't there.

"Roscoe, Cinders?" he called. *They're gone!* his mind shouted.

Calvin sat bolt upright. It was dark. He was in a strange bed, and the room he was in was foreign. Glints of sunbeams glistened from the edges of wide, heavy drapes pulled across an enormous window. There was just enough light for him to make out a bedside table with a small lamp. His body began to tremble.

He turned on the lamp and threw off the covers as he searched the bed for Roscoe and Cinders, but they were nowhere to be found. Looking down at himself as the lamp cast its dim light over him, he saw that he was wearing pajamas. *Pajamas!*

As he continued to look around, he spied more light coming from under a door. Just below his feet, he saw a pair of slippers on the floor. He slid them on and made his way towards the door, calling out Roscoe and Cinders's names in a hushed but urgent voice.

From a distance, Calvin heard the pitter-patter of nails approaching as they danced across a wood floor, and then there was scratching, whimpering, and mewing at the bottom of the door from the other side. "Roscoe, girl, Cinders," he whispered, "is that you?"

As gentle knocking began from the other side of the door, Calvin jumped back. "Mister Chadwick," a woman's voice spoke softly. "Mister Chadwick? Are you awake?"

Calvin remembered the previous night—and a kindly woman: Miss Honey. "Yes," he answered. "Yes, I'm awake?"

"I'm sorry," Miss Honey called, "but the little ones were whimpering at the door. I took them outside for their morning constitutionals several hours ago. They've been keeping me company. Are you decent?"

Calvin opened the door. Roscoe began to dance around his feet while Cinders rubbed his head up against his calves and mewed.

"Oh, there you are," Miss Honey said, "You'll find the change of clothes I laid out for you last night over the back of the chair. There's a fresh washcloth, soap, and towels and a toothbrush and toothpaste in the bathroom to the right of the bed," she said as she leaned into the room and pointed.

"There's also a razor and shaving cream if you like." She walked in and headed to the window. When she pulled the drapes open, brilliant sunlight, reflected off the surrounding snow, entered the room. Calvin shielded his eyes against the glare.

"Ain't got no use fer no razor, Miss, I needs my beard 'coz of the cold."

Miss Honey nodded and smiled. "As you wish."

Roscoe and Cinders were insistent for his attention. When he leaned down and picked them up, Roscoe covered his face with wet kisses while Cinders rubbed his head beneath Calvin's chin.

"Would you like breakfast, or shall I serve you lunch once you're dressed?"

Calvin lowered Roscoe and Cinders to the floor. "Huh? Breakfast? Lunch? What time is it?"

"It's 11:25, Mister Chadwick," Miss Honey said, "What would you like to eat?

"11:25? In the mornin'?"

"Yes, sir. Perhaps a cup of coffee to start? Or do you prefer tea?"

"I don't know. I'm only here fer the night. I gotta fig're out how I'm gonna git back."

"Oh, I don't think that's going to happen any time soon. I understand Mister Scottsdale will be paying you a visit."

"Is that the feller who owns this place?"

Miss Honey smiled. "Yes, sir."

"You know how to git in touch with Reggie? He's the one done drove me here. I gotta catch a ride back t' the city."

Miss Honey took his right hand and gently patted it between hers. "All in good time, Mister Chadwick. Now first things first, what would you like to eat?"

"Don't go t' no trouble, Miss Honey. If there's any of that fine stew left, me 'n Roscoe 'n Cinders'll be more 'n happy with that."

"Nonsense!" she said with a fluster. "And besides, they've already eaten. Now what would you like? Eggs? Pancakes? Waffles? Do you like BLT sandwiches? We have plenty of bacon, and there's sausage. I could make you red-eye gravy to go with a nice ham steak, or perhaps biscuits and gravy if you like, or maybe … grits? I do make a passable pot of grits. Egg salad? Ham salad? How about tuna-fish? I even have a nice slab of that old-time, Philadelphia scrapple in the icebox."

"Too many choices," Calvin said as he pressed his palms to his temples. "There's too many choices. I eat what's put in front of me."

Miss Honey lowered her voice. "My apologies, Mister Chadwick, I didn't mean to overwhelm you. I'll prepare a few things while you're washing up. How does that sound? Then you can choose whatever you like."

"Thank you, Miss Honey, but still, don't go to no trouble on my account."

"Very good, Mister Chadwick. You'll find me in the kitchen whenever you're ready."

****

Roscoe and Cinders followed Calvin into the kitchen where he found Miss Honey busy at work. She was placing several platters in the oven to warm. Set out on the counter was a bowl of batter next to a bowl of fresh eggs, and a variety of breakfast meats in various stages of preparation. Atop the gas stove was a cast-iron griddle set over two burners, warming over low flames.

"I asked you not to make no fuss over me," Calvin said as he entered the room. "Now look at all you gone n' done."

"I'm sorry, Mister Chadwick, but my orders are for you to not want for anything."

Calvin scratched his head. "Huh?"

"And besides, we need to put some meat back on your bones."

"What're you sayin', Miss?"

"Just that those are my orders."

"From who?"

"From Mister Scottsdale, of course."

"Speak of the devil!" a voice boomed from the doorway to the mudroom.

Miss Honey and Calvin turned towards the voice. Standing in the doorway was Mister Scottsdale himself. "And I meant what I said."

"Reggie?"

"Hello, Calvin. How did you sleep?"

"Huh? I don't get it?"

Reggie stood there, his face beaming.

"What's goin' on, Reggie? Fess up."

"I'm sorry for the deception, Calvin. Please have

49

a seat and let me try to explain." As Reggie pulled out the chair at the end of the kitchen table, Calvin backed away a step.

"Please, Calvin, I had my reasons," Reggie said softly as he extended his hand toward the chair beside him.

Calvin hesitated a moment as he looked into Reggie's eyes, searching. Reggie nodded his head. His smile softened as he rested a hand on the chair. "Please, Calvin."

After Calvin sat down, Reggie joined him.

"You, Reggie? You're Mister Scottsdale?"

"Guilty as charged."

"But you said you knew the owner."

"Well, that's true … in way. I am the owner."

"Then how come you didn't tell me that up front? Why all the secrets?"

"Because I didn't think you would come with me if I told you I was going to bring you to my home. It's a long story. A very long story."

"This is your home? Then where'd you sleep last night?"

"This cottage is part of my home, my estate. There are several cottages on the grounds."

"Estate? Grounds?"

"Yes, my estate. It might make more sense if you saw it for yourself. Why don't you come outside and let me show you?"

Reggie pushed his chair out and stood up. "Please, come with me. You can see most of it from just beyond the garage. We'll keep to the driveway so you won't need boots, but you'll need your coat. It's still quite brisk out there."

With a bewildered look on his face, Calvin got up from the table.

"It's okay, Calvin, really it is. Just come with me. Please," Reggie said as he opened the mudroom door.

"I don't know where my coat is."

"Oh, sorry, it's hanging right in here." Reggie lifted a different, new coat from a hook just beyond the door and held it out for Calvin as he slipped it on.

As Reggie led him out along the driveway, Calvin noticed the two vans that had been parked in front of the garage the night before were gone. Reggie made a grand, sweeping gesture with his arm towards the surrounding snow-covered grounds. "That roof you see, beyond the hill," he said, pointing in the distance, "that's my home. This cottage is one of four my family has maintained for years for staff and most recently, visitors—friends who are writers, like me, or artists, who have all needed a quiet place to work."

"You rich or somethin'?"

"My family is or was. I'm all that's left. It's mine now."

"So why'd you do it, Reggie? Why me?"

"Do you want the truth?"

"Heck yeah."

"Because my mother told me to."

"But you just said it's just you now."

"It is. I'm sorry for the confusion. After I left you in the city, she came to me. I heard her voice in my head, telling me to take you to a motel. Then I found you, injured. I knew you needed more help, so I brought you here."

"Then who was all them people last night, those doctors and nurses and such?"

"They're from organizations I support, or rather my foundation supports. I called in a few favors."

"'N they just dropped what they was doin' and come a runnin'?"

"Sort of, but it's not quite like that. They're also my friends, and I work right alongside them when they hold their free clinics."

"Somethin's not addin' up here, Reggie. You on the up 'n up?"

"Why don't we go back inside, and I'll tell you the whole story about my mother and her philanthropic work and about my foundation and why your plight touched me so deeply. Have you eaten yet?"

"No."

"Then we'll talk, or I'll talk and you can listen while you eat. How does that sound?"

"I don't know, Reggie. This is all too much fer me t' handle. It's like I'm in a fairytale or somethin'."

"I realize how strange this all must seem to you, Calvin, but will you give me a chance to explain? If you don't like what you hear, I'll drive you back to the city myself or wherever you want to go."

Calvin took a step back and looked Reggie up and down. Then he focused on his face, and his eyes. There was a kindness there he hadn't seen very often. Reggie smiled.

"I got your word on that?" Calvin asked.

"Yes, I give you my word."

****

Over the next hour, as they sat in the dining room while Calvin ate from the bounty of platters on the table Miss Honey had piled high with her sweet and savory delectables, Reggie told him the story his mother had told him about his grandparents, years before. He talked about the foundation he had established in the years that followed her death, and about his monthly visits to the city where he gave out food and clothing and sometimes even paid for a motel room for a few days, for people who needed one.

Chapter Eight
An Offer

Reggie leaned forward in his chair. "When I saw your sign, I knew I had to go to you. Then, you told me the story about how you and Roscoe and Cinders became a family. It touched me deeply. There is so much humanity in how Roscoe adopted little Cinders and how you've sacrificed for both of them. I remembered the friendships that animals had brought to my life when I was younger, much younger, Calvin. I've been deeply moved by your sacrifices, and I'd like to help you."

"Ain't humanity ... is motherly instinct. When I found Roscoe, she was still wet with milk. She was stumblin', try'n t' carry a little'un in her mouth, but there weren't no life left in that wee little girl. I think she 'n her babies got dumped in the river. She had a collar on, and there was water-weeds stuck in it. I looked and looked fer a sack of pups along the bank, but I couldn't find nothin'. She carried that wee one fer pert near a day 'til she finally let me take 'er 'n bury 'er in the tall grass by the side of the tracks.

"Ever since, she's mothered any little critter she come across, 'cept of course for rats. She hates rats. Snaps their necks. We et 'em sometimes when I couldn't rustle up no food. Skin 'em 'n gut 'em 'n roast 'em. Not too bad really, 'n there's a decent amount to 'em, when they's big 'nuff."

Reggie cringed at the image of a human being eating rats, but then his face softened. "I can't imagine the life you've had to live, Calvin. Will you allow me to help you?"

"I ain't no charity case, Reggie."

"I'm not talking about charity, Calvin." Reggie leaned back in his chair for a moment and tented his fingers together against his mouth as he considered another possibility. After a few moments, he folded his hands on top of the table. "Tell me, what did you do in the Army?"

"I don't like t' talk about the Army—too many bad memories there. I ain't been able t' cut it ever since."

"Cut it? Do you mean make a go of it? Make a life for yourself?"

"Yeah. Exactly."

"Is that why you lived on the street?"

"Mostly. After I got out, I worked my way through a couple jobs, but never held on t' one fer more 'n a few months, 'n 'coz of that, I couldn't hold on t' my life. I was alone back then. That was afore Roscoe—way afore. I went from livin' in an apartment, then t' a motel fer a couple nights at a time, then t' my car, 'n then the street. Been on the streets since '04."

"Is there anything you'd feel comfortable telling me about what you did in the Army? Anything at all? I'm here to listen."

"How come?"

"Because I think you might be able to help me fulfill my mission."

"What's your mission?"

"To help people in need. What I need help with is managing logistics. Someone who knows how to get help to people who need it, getting them the right kind of help they need and the tangible things they'll require to improve their lives. I've been outsourcing most of it, but I've been thinking lately that the foundation should be managing it, rather than just paying for it. That way we'd have more control over how things are done."

"Like a quartermaster?"

Reggie straightened up in his chair. "Yes, exactly! A quartermaster is exactly what I need. You could be my foundation's quartermaster!"

"Quartermaster's the work I did. I was a sergeant, but why me?"

"Because you've lived it," Reggie said as he leaned forward. "And because you have a good and kind heart."

Calvin lowered his head. A moment later, his shoulders began to heave. Roscoe was instantly by his side. She jumped up into his lap and began to whimper as she nuzzled his face. When Calvin raised his head there were tears in his eyes. "Ain't nobody willin' to give me a chance no more."

"I'm sorry, Calvin." Reggie felt a stirring in his chest. His heart went out to the man and instinctively, he placed his hand over Calvin's. At his touch, Calvin froze for a moment, and then he abruptly pulled away.

"Don't be touchin' me like that, Reggie. I can't go back t' that. It hurts too much—cost me way too much. Don't Ask, Don't Tell didn't work fer me, 'coz somebody done told. I appreciate all you done, but I can't go down that road again—can't risk that no more … a man's touch … not like that again. My heart's been broke too many times."

"Calvin, I didn't mean…"

"Can't let nobody in, just can't."

"Calvin, I'm sorry. I didn't mean it any way other than one human being making a connection with another human being, in empathy."

"Empathy means you had the same thing happen. You mean sympathy. Don't get 'em mixed up."

"No, I meant empathy."

"You mean … you…"

Reggie frowned. "This conversation is not going at all the way I thought it would, not in the least, but yes, Calvin, I've been hurt, too. I've had my heart broken, and I've lost relationships and friendships. As a result, I've also been afraid to let people in. I've known how much the touch of another ... *person* ... can mean and how vulnerable it can make you."

"You mean you're a..."

Reggie looked beyond the top of Calvin's head. His eyes were focused far, far away.

Calvin's voice was soft. "You said a person. You mean a man," he swallowed, "like me, or a woman?"

Reggie didn't answer. Memories came flooding back—of all the people, mostly women he had been intimate with, and especially, one of the men who had been a friend since his school years. Then it all came into focus as he realized every damn one of them had tried to use him for their own personal gain. The women he had dated, whether they had known from the start or learned somewhere along the way, were only interested in his family's wealth.

Thank God I'd found out before any of it ever became serious, he thought to himself.

And then there was Darren. I could never forgive Darren. No, I never will. Damn it, we'd grown up together, and I believed it was safe to take him into my confidence, but he betrayed me, too. Darren betrayed me the most.

Chapter Nine
Flashback

Fifteen years earlier, Reggie's suite at the family estate

Reggie sobbed on Darren's shoulder over his most recent failed relationship, but as it turned out, Darren had his own agenda, and as they say, money is a terrible temptation.

"Come on, Reggie," Darren said with a kind smile, as he rubbed his hand across Reggie's shoulder. "We'll go out, have a nice meal, and if you're up to it, maybe even party a little later on. Get your mind off it. What do you say?"

"I don't know, Darren. I don't feel like partying, not now, maybe not ever again."

"Okay, okay. How about we just go out for dinner at my family's place? You know it. You love it there. You know you love our prime rib. We'll have a few drinks and then ... who knows? Now wipe the snot off your face and put on your jacket."

Reggie sniffled then sighed. "You promise?"

Darren stood up from the sofa and picked up Reggie's suit jacket. "Yeah, of course," he said as he shook it, enticing Reggie to put it on.

****

When Reggie woke, he had little memory of the prior night, but as he slowly came to, he remembered more and more.

After a big, satisfying meal, in the private dining room of the hotel restaurant Darren's family owned, he introduced Reggie to the marvels of adding pot and diazepam to liquor. Then, in his own way, in his own time, he took advantage of what Reggie believed to be a deep, lifelong friendship.

****

"Here's to you Reggie," Darren said, clinking his tumbler of whiskey against Reggie's glass, "My best bud."

"Thanks, Darren," Reggie slurred. "You're the bes'."

"You know, Reggie, I just can't understand why you keep striking out with the ladies. You're a handsome guy, and you've got a body most men would kill for. Maybe you're just not using your assets to your advantage."

Reggie slurred his words again. "Oh, you're just saying that, Darren. You're gonna make me blush, but I 'preciate the compliment."

Darren assessed his friend's state of inebriation, as he looked for cracks in his resolve. "I'm not just saying it," he said sincerely as he scooted to Reggie's side along the padded leather bench-seat that wrapped around the back half of the table. Once their thighs touched, he threw his arm over Reggie's shoulder. "You're my friend, and I care about you ... a lot."

When Darren leaned in and brushed his fingers through Reggie's bangs, moving them to the side, Reggie closed his eyes and sighed. Darren leaned in and whispered into Reggie's ear. "You really are a handsome man."

Reggie smiled. "Thanks, buddy," he said as he eased his body against Darren's. When Darren brushed his lips against his earlobe, Reggie sucked in his breath as goosebumps ran over his shoulders and down his back and arms. When Darren began to nibble on the lobe, Reggie felt his groin begin to stir. He groaned and then slurred again. "What are you doin', Darren? You puddin' the make on me?"

"Something like that, buddy," Darren said

huskily. "Like I said, you're a stud, and your body ... my God, your body." Darren drew his lips along Reggie's cheek.

"Oh," Reggie moaned. "Darren."

Darren nuzzled his neck. "Let me show you how to use that body of yours to your advantage."

Before he knew what was happening, Darren had taken Reggie's face into his hands and plastered his mouth against his lips. Reggie's mind began to reel, but his body betrayed him. As he tried to pull away, Darren slid his tongue into his mouth and his hand down the inside of Reggie's pants and grasped his partially engorged shaft.

He began rub his thumb around the head of Reggie's cock, spreading the slick liquid that began to ooze from the tip across its surface.

Reggie groaned loudly, throwing his arms around Darren and pulling him into a hug as he melted into his embrace. When Darren slicked his hand with his saliva and returned it to Reggie's cock, Reggie's hips began to thrust upward, forcing his growing erection into Darren's tightening fist.

"That's it, buddy," Darren said, as a torrid smile spread across his face. "You know you want this, and I'm the one to give it to you."

Reggie surrendered. The next thing he knew he was in the elevator and then they were in a suite. He did things that night he'd never imagined. He felt things he'd never felt before, and he liked it—God how he liked it. He fell head over heels in lust with Darren, and he wanted more, so much more.

****

As Reggie came to, he realized how much his ass was burning. "Oh, fuck ... my ass is on fire," he moaned.

"Well, you earned that fire, buddy, and then

some."

Lying on his belly, barely covered by a sheet, Reggie lifted his head and looked around for the voice. There, on the bed to his left, naked and smiling, and watching him, Darren sat with his legs crossed beneath him.

"Good morning, lover, how'd you sleep?"

"Huh? What? Darren? Where the hell are we? What are you doing here?"

"Oh, come on, lover, you're not saying you don't remember last night, that you don't remember me making a man out of you, are you?"

"Oh, fuck!" Reggie cried out. "That wasn't a dream?"

"No, lover, it wasn't, and your ass is proof of that."

Flashes of images came flooding into Reggie's mind.

****

Reggie thrust his cock into Darren's hole with the intensity of a jackhammer. He couldn't remember ever being this hard, this thick, this aroused. "There, right there," Darren moaned as he was driven on his back towards the headboard. "Oh, baby, pound my orb with your knob," he cried out. "Pound me! Pound me now!"

"You're so tight," Reggie moaned. "Oh, God, you're so tight! I never knew it could be this good."

"Oh, you're gonna make me come, Reggie." Darren's head twisted back and forth as he licked his lips. "Oh, baby, just like that. Just like that!"

Reggie began to pant. "I'm gonna blow my load. Oh, fuck, I'm gonna blow!"

"Give it to me, Reggie. Fill me with your hot jizz! Flood my ass. Flood me now!"

Reggie grabbed Darren's thighs and leaned

forward, plastering them up tight against his chest as his shoved his cock into Darren's hole even deeper. "Hold on, baby," he cried out as Darren locked his ankles behind his back. "Here it comes!"

He reached down between Darren legs and began to jerk his cock, slicking it with the stream of pre-cum that flowed freely from the slit. As he did, Darren began to buck his ass against Reggie's thrusts, driving his cock even deeper inside himself.

Rabid with drug-induced cravings, electricity began to flow from deep within Reggie's core. As connections zapped from nerve to nerve, he felt like he was ablaze, consumed by an uncontrollable fire. His shaft swelled even more against Darren's hole, stretching it to the point of tearing.

"Rip me open, baby," Darren squealed. "Tear me apart!" Darren's eyes grew wide as the pressure in his prostate began to build. His balls drew up tight as his sack contracted. Like a flash fire, musk and sweat steamed from every inch of his body.

The muscles in Reggie's legs began to buckle, and his abs contracted, pulling him down against Darren's hot and heaving chest. He closed his eyes, clamped his hand against Darren's shaft and jackrabbited it for all he was worth, as they came together.

When Reggie's muscles locked, he was driven forward, pressing his balls tightly against Darren's spasming hole, as he began to gush his load into Darren's guts. The first was one long continuous stream of milky, thick cum that scorched past Darren's tetanic prostate as Reggie's cock contracted with every fiber of its muscle, trying to empty itself completely into the depths of Darren's core.

And while that moment of explosive ecstasy

seemed to last forever, as if Reggie would pass out, his body began convulsing as he uncontrollably pumped out another seven streams, each slightly less than the one before, his cock spasmed again and again, until it was empty, but still wanting release, as if it had a mind of its own.

When Reggie's body locked, Darren pulled his chest tight against him, and then bounced his ass in rhythm with his own ejections, intensifying the pounding that Reggie's cockhead produced against his prostate. Like a shot across the bow of a ship, his first load traveled the length of Reggie's chest, coating the tips of the hair there as it spewed upward, only to be stopped as it splashed against Reggie's chin.

Darren tilted his head forward, wedging it against Reggie's chest so he could catch his next several bursts in his mouth. He swallowed greedily as each stream passed his lips, savoring the musky sweetness of his own milky essence.

When it was over, Darren wiped Reggie's chin and fed the remnants of his cum to his new lover. Reggie relished the taste, sucking every last bit from his fingers.

"I love you, Reggie," Darren whispered. "I'll always love you for what you've done for me."

Reggie saw the entire night repeat over and over again in his mind. They'd made love three times, each taking a turn on top, but what he remembered most clearly, what he'd enjoyed the most was swallowing Darren's cum while Darren swallowed his during the first 69 session he'd ever experienced. Coming while savoring his best friend's cum at the same time was something he knew he'd remember for the rest of his life. He knew he wasn't gay-gay, but he wondered what he was, what it all meant now. Then he didn't care. It was the most exquisite sexual act he'd ever experienced, and he knew it was something he could not live without ever again.

A new chapter was about to open in Reggie's world, and he embraced the possibilities of what a new, secret life with Darren, his best friend, could mean for them.

****

"It was a dream," Reggie said over and over. "It had to be a dream."

"Fuck no, buddy!" Darren's voice pulled Reggie back to the present. "And I've got pictures to prove it."

Reggie shook his head and blinked. "You have what? Why? No! We made love, Darren. We made love!"

"Yeah, and it was great, buddy."

"But you told me you love me!"

"Heat of the moment, Reggie. Heat of the moment."

"What? What do you mean?"

"Just what I said, buddy. Passion's a funny thing. Once those juices start flowing, they can make you do things you'd never consider doing otherwise."

"What are you saying, Darren? What are you thinking? Darren, you've got to get rid of them!"

"What these?" Darren said as he held up his phone and clicked through more than twenty images of Reggie, naked—Darren, naked—and what Darren had done to him—and what he had done to Darren.

Reggie staggered up and immediately winced at the burning coming from his anus. "Darren! You're not thinking straight! You've got to get rid of them!"

"Me? What do you mean me? They were your idea!"

"No! Never!" Reggie shouted.

Darren fixed Reggie with a cold stare.

"Darren, you son of a bitch!" Reggie screamed.

"I would have never wanted that! My family! My mother!"

"Well, that's the way I remember it. That'll be my story."

"Your story? What the hell are you talking about?"

"When it comes out about us."

"Darren, you wouldn't!"

"You're right, Reggie, I won't. Not if you're willing to help me out of a jam. You'd help a friend out of a jam, wouldn't you?"

Reggie saw red. He lunged at Darren and grabbed for the phone while simultaneously striking him in the jaw with his fist. As his fist connected, Darren flew backward.

Reggie wrestled the phone out of his hand and ran for the bathroom, locking the door behind him. He deleted image after image until he heard Darren knock on the door.

"I really am sorry, buddy," Darren said from the other side, "but it won't matter what you do to my phone. I've already emailed all of them to myself at home."

Reggie staggered against the vanity, dropping the phone, as his body slid to the floor. Darren's betrayal was complete. "Why?" Reggie cried from the bathroom. "Why, would you do such a thing to me, Darren?"

"I'm sorry, buddy. Really, I am, but I'm in a jam, a terrible jam. If you help me out, I'll delete them all. I swear it. They'll be gone forever, and no one will ever know."

Reggie pulled himself together as he stood up and walked to the door. "What jam?" he asked, his face red with tears as he opened it. "What jam could ever be worth blackmail?"

"I need ten grand, to clear my debts with my

bookie and my dealer," Darren said meekly.

Reggie staggered backward. "Your what? Who?"

Darren pulled himself together and straightened up. He had to do this. His voice was clear and direct. "I'm sorry, Reggie, really I am, but I can't go to my parents. It would kill them. They can never know."

Reggie seethed. "You bastard! What about my mother? You're a bastard, Darren. A real bastard," he said through gritted teeth as he grabbed Darren by the throat.

"I've had to do things I never dreamed I would," Darren said as his shoulders slumped, "but I have to draw the line somewhere."

"And you drew it at me? Me?"

"Sorry."

"After last night, I thought we meant something to each another."

"We do, Reggie. We're friends, and I need my friend's help."

"But you said you loved me!"

"Yeah, I did, and I meant it at the time."

Tears began to slide down Reggie's cheeks. "But now?"

"Sorry, Reggie, I need the money."

"By blackmailing me? You could have just asked. I would have given it to you. You should have just asked me."

"I didn't know that, and I'm not going to prostitute myself to pay off my debts. That's what I'd have to face, and I almost did it, but I ran out of the room before it really got started."

"What do you mean, 'the room'?"

"My dealer set me up with a high-end escort service. Until he's paid off, I have to 'entertain,'" Darren made air quotes, "paying male clients, but now

he's after me, because I bailed. I'm not gonna do it. I just won't go there."

"You've already gone there, Darren. You already have. You just did!"

A day later, Reggie handed Darren a personal check. Not true to his word, Darren threatened Reggie with revealing the photos three more times. Until his funeral, two years later, they were the only times Reggie set eyes on his childhood friend. Darren was found in the city with a needle in his arm, dead from an overdose in an abandoned building, frequented by addicts.

Reggie never forgave himself for his lapse of judgment, and the guilt he felt following Darren's death haunted him for years. He knew it wasn't his fault, yet he alternated between blaming himself for not being strong enough to help Darren beat his addiction and hating his guts.

Though the impact of the financial payouts were significant, they were nothing compared to the embarrassment it brought to his mother, once he had admitted his part in Darren's death. Since that time, though he'd found release in the arms of others, he never allowed himself to develop feelings for anyone—not even once.

Chapter Ten
An Offer

A tear formed in the corner of Reggie's left eye. When it began to run down his cheek, he shuddered, then quickly wiped it away as he lowered his eyes and then looked up, into Calvin's. "I'm sorry, Calvin. What was I saying?"

"You was sayin' a lot o' stuff, 'bout yer broken heart."

"Oh … yes."

"You a homo, too … a queer, Reggie? Is 'at why you brought me…"

Reggie felt a sinking in the pit of his stomach.

When Calvin recognized the pain on Reggie's face, he stopped what he was saying and spoke softly. "I'm sorry, Reggie. Don't worry. Makes no never-mind to me."

A faraway look settled across Reggie's face. Before today, he hadn't thought of Calvin that way. He hadn't even considered it. Suddenly he saw evidence of a younger, once muscular Calvin, in the much thinner version sitting before him. Then he envisioned him decked out in his military uniform.

Calvin had mentioned Don't Ask, Don't Tell. Without him saying it outright, those words told Reggie that Calvin was gay, and now he'd just confirmed it. Images of him began to flash through Reggie's mind. Try as he might, he couldn't shake the idea of the young, buff Calvin, locked in an embrace with another man, go away, and that made him immediately feel guilty.

He realized his empathy for Calvin could quickly turn into an attraction, and from past experience, he knew how quickly attraction could turn into lust. A tremor ran through his body as he steeled himself against those images, and he swore to himself he would never allow those kinds of feelings to begin to develop.

After a few moments, Calvin said, "You okay there, Reggie?"

Reggie startled, then focused intently on Calvin. "It's called gay now, but no, that's not why I invited you here." He cleared his throat. "I had gay friends in my youth, good friends. I still do to this day, and many support my foundation, but that's not the issue. I had no idea about that part of you yesterday. I never would have suspected it."

"Ain't you ever heard of Maslow 'n his Hi-R-Key?"

"You mean Maslow's hierarchy of needs? Yes, of course."

"Livin' on the street, you huggin' the bottom, Reggie—food, cover, clothes … gotta always find cover, gotta survive. Sometimes ya move up, like me, after findin' Roscoe 'n Cinders, but ya move down a lot more 'n up."

"Yes, I know about those needs, and there's more than just those few."

"Yeah? No kiddin'. 'Course I know that. I ain't stupid, Reggie, but you only git what you can find. Spendin' all y'ur time just survivin'… ain't no time fer nothin' else, 'n 'sides who'd ever want somebody like that … like me? Nobody! 'N on top of that, I know what I look like, 'coz it's how I have t' live. No reason fer nobody t'ever look further 'n what they see."

Reggie's eyes softened. "Calvin, the only thing I saw in you was a kind man with two small animals who was down on his luck, and who needed some help. I tried to do that. Then when you were injured and had no place to go, I realized I had a place, and I offered it to you. It's as simple as that."

"I believe you, Reggie. I do, but I don't think I can help you. I'm too far gone. I'm too, and I'm sorry for the word, but I'm too *fucked up* to be of any use to nobody no more."

"I don't believe that, Calvin. You don't give yourself enough credit. Look at how you've kept Roscoe and Cinders alive, and you've done it with almost nothing. Imagine what you could do for the world with some support."

"I been on the street fer too long, Reggie. I don't know how t' talk t' people no more. I only had Roscoe and Cinders, 'n they ain't choosy."

"You're doing pretty darn well with me right now."

"Nah, I'm too out o' practice. I didn't used t' talk like this. I got me a college education, Reggie … a college education! I used to write proposals. I used to paint and draw. Heck, I even dreamed of becomin' a writer one day, but it's too late now."

Reggie smiled. He pushed away his bitter memories of Darren and the images he'd had of Calvin and focused on the man sitting in front of him. "All of those things are like muscles, Calvin, that haven't been used in a while. They just need to start stretching and exercising again. They need to be challenged with real work. That's the only way they can remain in shape, by being put to work. I'm challenging you right now to do that. Put those muscles back to work, Calvin.

"I'm offering you a real job with a real paycheck and real benefits, a job where you can make a life for yourself and Roscoe and little Cinders, a job where you can make a difference for you and your family and so many other people. What do you say?"

"I'm afraid I'd let you down, Reggie. I'm afraid I'll fail."

"Then we'll train you to do all the things you need help with. Remember, you would bring something to the job that no one else could."

"What's that?"

"Heart, your heart, and your experiences, all you've lived through and survived. You're the right man for the job, I just know it."

"You'd be willin', I mean willing t' do, um … to do all that fer … there I go again. I mean *for* me? Sorry, talkin' right's hard fer me … *for me*."

"Yes, I am, and you're doing just fine."

Calvin looked down into his lap. He hadn't noticed that Cinders, now curled up against his belly, had crawled up there, and Roscoe was curled around Cinders. Two little heads lifted and looked up at him. Two sets of eyes blinked with complete trust. A tail thumped against his thigh—a soft mew rose up from a little mouth that yawned.

Calvin looked into Reggie's eyes. When Reggie smiled back, he knew what he had to do. "You've got a good heart, Reggie, and you got you a deal."

Calvin lifted Roscoe and Cinders and lowered them to the floor. "Shake," he said as he stood up and stuck out his hand. Reggie rose from his chair, and took Calvin's offered hand.

"Thank you, Calvin."

"No, thank you, Reggie, just thank you—fer me 'n Roscoe 'n Cinders. Thank you."

"You're the one doing me the favor, Calvin. Now, I need a moment with Miss Honey. Then how about I give you a real tour of the place?"

****

Back from their car ride, Roscoe and Cinders raced ahead through the mudroom and into the kitchen the moment Reggie opened the cottage's door from the carport. When he and Calvin came in, Miss Honey was preparing two cans of food. Roscoe sat patiently at her feet while Cinders mewed and wove himself around and between her legs.

"All right, all right—patience, my precious boy. Patience," she said as she lifted the cat food can from the electric opener and then inserted the other one. "It will be ready in just a moment, just a moment." She looked over her shoulder. "Did you ask him?"

"No, not yet," Reggie said.

"Ask me what?" Calvin asked.

Reggie sat down at the end of the kitchen table and waved Calvin to a chair next to him. "Calvin, Miss Honey is my cook, but she's more than that. She keeps my house running and keeps the staff in line. I guess you could say she's my Chief of Staff."

"Could!" Miss Honey said with a fanciful scowl. "Could indeed!" which she then followed with a smile.

"You mean mansion, don't you," Calvin said as he soft-punched Reggie's arm. "That's the biggest *house* I ever seen."

"I'll give you two some privacy," Miss Honey said as she lowered the two food bowls to the floor. Roscoe and Cinders wasted no time and dug in heartily. Then Miss Honey excused herself from the room.

"Thank you, Miss Honey," Reggie said. He turned his attention to Calvin.

"Calvin, Miss Honey lives in my home. She stayed here last night so she would be available if you needed anything and to make you breakfast this morning the moment you woke up."

"Yeah, and I sure do appreciate it."

"The thing is, she really needs to come back to the main house. I need her there."

"Sure, I understand. I can git by on my own."

"I'd like you to come with us. Really, I need you at the main house. Everything runs from an office out of my home, the foundation … everything.

"Logistically, having you here in the cottage would make it more difficult to coordinate everything. I need you there, in the office. Actually, you'll have your own office with your own staff. It's a big house, and some of the wings are devoid of occupants. You'll have your own suite of rooms to live in."

"I don't know, Reggie, I ain't used t' such finery 'n besides, I like my solitude. It's all movin' kinda fast. I have t' think of Roscoe 'n Cinders, too."

"You'll get used to it. They'll get used to it. Actually, my hope is you'd grow to love it!"

"'N Roscoe, 'n Cinders? How's it gonna work fer them, goin' from the street to a mansion? They ain't gonna know how t' act. I ain't gonna!"

"All that's required is a little patience."

"Yeah, but this here ain't no mansion. It's small 'n cozy. Mansion's a lot t' take in—I mean yesterday I was hunkered down in front of a burned-out deli 'n today you're askin' me—all of us—t' move into a mansion. A job's one thing, but all this? All that?" he said, pointing in the direction of the mansion, "Yer makin' my head spin like I been possessed by the devil."

"Give yourself a little credit, Calvin. Give them a little credit. All three of you adjusted to this cottage after coming from the street. There weren't any problems, were there? You slept well, didn't you?"

"Yes, but a mansion is a whole different ball of wax."

"I'm sorry if I wasn't clear about this at the start, but the more I think about it, the more it makes sense. Don't look back, Calvin. Keep your eyes forward."

"But it's too much … too much to think about."

"Do you really need to think about it? Do you?"

Calvin's face began to flush. Then his hands balled into fists. "Don't pressure me, Reggie! Please!"

Calvin noticed movement from the corner of his eye. When he turned, he saw Roscoe sit up in her bed. Her ears were up. Then Cinders sat up. His hackles rose as he crouched back down while a low rumble came from his throat, and his tail began to flit back and forth. Calvin realized they must have moved to the bed after they'd finished their lunch.

Roscoe barked softly, once, and there was a slight growl beneath it.

"I'm sorry, Calvin. I'm not trying to pressure you," Reggie said, seeming completely unaware of Roscoe and Cinders's agitation. "It's just that I believe in this so much. I believe in you."

Calvin noticed Roscoe look at Reggie, and then she came running to Calvin's side, barking something fierce. "It's okay, girl. Ever'thin's okay," he said as he reached over and patted Reggie's arm to show Roscoe there was no danger. "Don't take this the wrong way, Reggie," he said to him. "I'm just calmin' her down."

Calvin looked back at Cinders. "It's okay, boy. We're all good here."

Roscoe sat down at Calvin's feet. Her little tail began to wag a mile a minute. After a moment, Cinders eased down into the bed, but his tail continued to flit back and forth.

"Go lay down, girl," he said to Roscoe. "We're fine."

"I'll tell you what," Reggie began.

"Hold up, Reggie," Calvin said softly. "Give 'em a moment."

Reggie began to rub his chin, as he looked back and forth between the cat and the dog and Calvin.

"Fascinating," he said. "They can read you."

After Roscoe returned to the bed, she wrapped herself around Cinders as she lay back down. Once she was settled, Calvin removed his hand from Reggie's arm, then continued. "Course they can. Now, you was sayin'?"

"Yes. How about a trial period, let's say one month? If after a month you're not happy there, we'll find you another place, one of the cottages even, this cottage, if you like. Though it wouldn't be ideal, we'd make it work."

"Could I go there to work and then come back here? After?"

"You won't even consider it?"

Calvin looked over at Roscoe. "Girl?" he said softly. Roscoe lifted her head to look up at him. Then she seemed to smile before setting it back down.

Calvin realized he should take the chance. If he wanted a better life for Roscoe and Cinders then he'd need to be agreeable, within limits.

"Okay, Reggie. I'll do it, but can we start with a week? Would that be okay?"

Reggie relaxed back into is chair. "I can do that, but I really believe you're going to love it there. You'll see. Once you're all moved in, it's my hope you won't want to leave."

Calvin smiled cautiously. "Good, 'coz we got nothin t' move," he said. *We'll see,* he thought. "So when do we leave?"

****

While Calvin collected his meager belongings, Reggie spoke briefly with Miss Honey, then they all left together and drove to the mansion. While Reggie gave Calvin a tour, Miss Honey put the ball in motion in preparation for Calvin and his family's stay.

Chapter Eleven
A New Life

Later that afternoon, Calvin's suite

At the end of the tour of the mansion, while Calvin carried Cinders in his arms and Roscoe walked by his side, he followed Reggie down the second-floor hallway of the residential wing. They came to a stop in front of a set of large, ornately-carved, heavy, double-doors.

"This will be your suite, Calvin," he said as he opened them and walked in.

Calvin followed him. Immediately, he began to turn around and around, faster and faster as he took in the ceiling with its crown molding, the leather and expensively upholstered furniture, the oriental rugs, and the doorways that opened into adjoining rooms. When he began to stumble, Reggie caught him by the elbow.

"Sorry, got dizzy there fer a minute," Calvin said as he grabbed hold of Reggie's arm.

"Here, sit down." Reggie waved as he directed Calvin to an overstuffed chair.

"All this? Fer me?"

"All this is for you, Calvin."

"I ain't never…"

"I know it's a lot to take in, but yes, this is all for you. This is where you're going to live."

"I'm a get lost in all o' this."

"You'll do fine, just fine. Now, dinner is at six. I usually wear a coat and tie, but we can forgo that for the evening if it will make you more comfortable."

"No matter, I ain't got nothin' t' wear 'cept what I got on."

"Oh, sorry … there's clothing, I believe it's your size, in the wardrobe, in your bedroom. May I show you?"

****

Calvin plopped down on the edge of a small sofa. "I don't know what to say, Reggie. I ain't never had so many clothes, not like this. 'N closets that are furniture that hold clothes, 'n set inside a closet that's a room, big enough t' sleep a dozen people? Even in the Army, I only had five uniforms. Where'd they all come from?"

"Well, you're not in the Army any more. Those are called wardrobes," he said pointing. "They're in *your* dressing room." Reggie extended an arm and rotated around slowly, taking in the room. "And these are your clothes now. Miss Honey picked them out from what was in the cottage and from my dressing room. Except for the inseams, we're the same size, and everything is brand new. Until we get you properly fitted, they'll suffice.

"This is how I lived growing up. Why don't you take some time and get acquainted with your suite? I'll come and find you just before dinner."

"Where can I get washed up afore supper? I ain't even got a comb t' run through my hair. That nice young feller, Simon, combed it fer me last night, 'coz of the stitches I got. I just used my fingers this mornin'."

"Let me show you your master bath."

****

After seeing the bathroom, Calvin became overcome with emotion. The words he had said to Reggie earlier about being touched by him were momentarily forgotten. He turned around and embraced Reggie, pulling him tight against his chest as he wept with unbridled joy. Over and over again, he repeated, "Thank you."

Reggie embraced him back as he stood there, allowing Calvin to cry. Then Calvin let go and stepped back. "I ain't never seen no tub so big afore. So much water t' fill it, 'n all these bottles and powders and creams and lotions and oils, what're they fer?"

"Hair, face, body, there's a product for everything."

"Is too much, Reggie. Is too much fer me t' take in. There's a carved hairbrush. I ain't never had me a hairbrush afore, let alone one of such fine stone."

"It's jade," Reggie said, smiling. "Oh, my barber is coming tomorrow. I've kept Mother's salon. It's across the hall in what used to be my parents' suite. Would you like to have him give you a professional trim and maybe a shave while he's here? I know Simon gave you a basic cut last night, but my barber is top notch."

"Ya know, Reggie, I held on t' this beard fer years 'n I just let it grow in the winter. Keeps my face warm."

"Maybe it's time to lose it. Think about it. You're not out in the cold anymore."

"I won't know my face in the mirror."

"It's completely up to you, but you'll never know unless you at least have it trimmed down a bit more. It's still quite full. Perhaps if he does it in stages?"

"Okay," Calvin hesitated. "I'll think on it."

****

The following afternoon, Calvin's sitting room

There was a knock at the door. "Come in," Calvin called from the sofa.

Miss Honey opened the door and approached him. "Mister Chadwick, Doctors Waters and Littleton have arrived. They're waiting for you in Mister Scottsdale's office."

"Thanks, Miss Honey. T' be sure, can you tell me again where it's at? I still can't find my way around this place."

"Certainly, Mister Chadwick. From your suite's

main door, turn left down the hallway, then make your way down the grand staircase. Turn right down the hallway off the front of the grand foyer. It will be the first door on the right."

"Thank you. I'll be right down."

Miss Honey folded her hands in front of her. "I'll take you there, if you like."

"Thank you. I think I'll do just that."

Calvin stood up and called out with an upward lilt in his voice, "Roscoe, Cinders, we're going fer a little trip."

Immediately, there was the pitter patter of Roscoe's feet as she hurried from her bed, just inside the doorway of the bedroom. Following close behind was Cinders as he limped along on his bandaged, sore paws.

Calvin leaned over and picked up his brown and gray tweed jacket with the leather elbow patches and put it on. With Cinders in his arms and Roscoe at his heels, he followed Miss Honey down the long hallway of the residential wing to the top of the left staircase.

"Reggie told me that's the guest wing," he said pointing along the banister that led to the other side of the mansion. "Is it ever used?"

"Yes, the north wing or guest wing is used occasionally," she said, "when we have guests, usually over the holidays and when extended family comes to visit. You're in the residential wing, the south wing."

"Two wraparound staircases and all that room, n' half of it ain't hardly never used. It boggles the mind."

Miss Honey smiled as she patted his arm. "Quite." Then she began to lead him down the twenty stairs to the center landing at the rear of the mansion.

"It's just down there." She pointed towards the hallway off the foyer to the right. "I can take you there directly."

"Thanks, Miss Honey, but I can manage from here."

"Very good." She patted his shoulder then accompanied him down the remaining stairs and turned to the left toward the dining room and kitchen, humming as she went. As Calvin approached, Bernard Ainsworth, the family butler, stopped busying himself with adjusting the position of ornamental figures on a table and stood at attention. The tall, portly, gray-haired man nodded, then *harrumphed* after Calvin had passed.

"Mongrels, all," he said to himself. "What has this family come to?"

****

"Here he is!" Reggie stood from his chair at the end of a glass coffee table and smiled. "All spit and polished."

Reggie took in the man walking toward him. Already he had more color in his face, and the tweed jacket fit him well and provided a really dapper appearance.

Doctors Waters and Littleton got up from their overstuffed chairs along the table's length and waited as Calvin approached.

"Don't you look handsome," Doctor Littleton said.

"I wouldn't have recognized you, Mister Chadwick ... with just a hint of beard," Doctor Waters added.

"Didn't reco'nize maself, Doc," Calvin answered, "but I think I like it."

After shaking their hands, Calvin took the chair to Reggie's right, placing Cinders in his lap. Roscoe jumped up and snuggled in by his side.

"So you got some tests t' tell me 'bout?"

"Yes, Mister Chadwick..." Doctor Waters began.

"Please, call me Calvin. You too, Missy." He nodded to Doctor Littleton.

"Certainly, Calvin," Doctor Waters continued, "I have the results of your blood work."

"I want t' hear 'bout Roscoe 'n Cinders first."

"I have those results, Calvin," Doctor Littleton said. She cleared her throat. "To begin with, they're both malnourished, Cinders more so than Roscoe, and they both have intestinal parasites and worms. That's why they're both so thin. They've affected Cinders the most because it's likely he contracted them very young, and they've continued to sap his strength, which has been a tremendous strain on his immune system.

"We gave them both a preliminary treatment for worms the night before last, but we'll need to continue to monitor them and treat for the other parasites a while longer. We gave Roscoe all her vaccinations; but until he's healthier, we should hold off on most of them for Cinders.

"We believe most of Cinders's sores began as burns that haven't healed properly because of his poor nutritional status. I was told he was found in an abandoned factory after a fire. Is that correct?"

"Yes, Doctor, Roscoe found 'im."

"I see. On top of that, his sores have bacterial infections, and he's developed mange. That's a skin disease caused by mites. It's still at an early stage, which is good. Mites are parasites that burrow under the skin. He's a perfect candidate to host them because his immune system has been so compromised from malnourishment, and on top of that, he's young."

"I tried t' keep 'im warm, Doc, 'n I fed 'im all I could get."

"Of course you did, and that is what likely kept him alive. We began treatment for all these things, but the treatment will need to be continued for a while longer. Once we see a turnaround in him, we'll know how long we'll need to continue the treatment.

"His coat will begin to grow back where it has thinned out once the infections have cleared up and the mites have been killed. From what I can see of him right now, I believe his stamina has already improved, likely because the food he's been receiving is more nutritionally appropriate for a growing, young cat, and from what I understand, he's getting plenty of it."

"Yeah, I watched him eat this mornin'. He was chowin' down somethin' fierce."

"Wonderful! I'd advise withholding any table food from him for the time being. Let him eat just the canned cat food. It contains all the vitamins, minerals, and trace elements that cats need. I've left several cases of it with Miss Honey, and I've also brought some supplemental vitamin and mineral drops with me to add to his and Roscoe's food. Table food doesn't contain those things, and anyway, it should be given only as a special treat."

A look of fear and guilt spread across Calvin's face. "I'm sorry about that, Doctor. I couldn't afford special food fer 'im. I fed 'im what I could find."

"It's okay, Calvin." Reggie reached out and rested his hand on Calvin's arm. A warm feeling spread through him when Calvin smiled back at him.

"No one's blaming you, Calvin," Doctor Littleton continued, "not at all. I know you did your best for him. The truth is, you saved his life. You're to be commended for how well you've cared for him, considering what you've had to face. I've seen how devoted both you and Roscoe are to him. I'm simply advising you of what would be best for him in the future. I think we'll see tremendous improvement in both of them very soon."

"Thank you, Doctor."

"One last thing, Cinders hasn't been neutered, and I couldn't find a scar on Roscoe to indicate she's been spayed. We can take care of those things, if you'd like, once they're returned to proper health."

"I didn't have the money fer it, Doc, but I would like Cinders done. We're livin' in a nice place now, and I don't want him spryin' the furniture. I know that can be a problem in a tom. As far as Roscoe's concerned, I always felt bad on account of her losin' her litter of pups, and I always wanted her to have the chance t' have one more, if'n I was ever able to find steady work."

"Very good, we can discuss that at a later date. Now, if you'll permit me, I've brought my mobile clinic with me. I can treat them both for their other intestinal parasites, and we'll clean Cinders's sores again while you're speaking with Doctor Waters.

"We'll come back every day until they're both in tip-top shape. Trevor's waiting out there right now. What do you say?"

"Sure, Doc, sure." Then he looked down at Roscoe. "Wha'd'ya think girl?" Roscoe stood up in the chair and sneezed, then wagged her tail.

"I think that's a yes, Doc," Calvin announced as Roscoe jumped to the floor, and then he handed Cinders over.

After Doctor Littleton carried Cinders from the room, with Roscoe walking at her side, Doctor Waters leaned forward in his chair. "Now it's my turn."

Reggie reached over and squeezed Calvin's forearm. "I'll just step out to give you some privacy with the good doctor here."

"How come?" Calvin asked. "You gone an' paid fer it all, an' asides, I ain't got no secrets."

"Are you sure, Calvin?" Reggie asked softly.

"Some of those test results could be rather personal."

"Nonsense, Reggie! You sit tight. I spect they ain't gonna tell me nothin' I don't already know." Calvin turned to Doctor Waters. "G'on, Doc—spill."

Doctor Waters cleared his throat. "First, I'd like to take a look at those sutures I put in the other night."

"Sure thing, Doc, poke away."

"Yes, very good," Doctor Waters said as he stood over Calvin and separated his hair to inspect his work. "Very good indeed. They look just fine, and the wound isn't infected."

"Great, Doc."

"I see you've been applying the ointment as I directed."

"Sure thing. What's next?"

After he returned to his chair. "Your blood work reveals that you are also malnourished, Calvin, but I think we can turn that around pretty quickly. With the right diet and some vitamin, mineral, and iron supplements, you'll be in peak condition in less than a month."

Doctor Waters pointed to several small boxes on the table. "Those are the supplements I want you to take for the next several weeks. You'll be as good as new in no time."

Reggie patted Calvin's arm. "Oh, we'll see to that, Doctor. Don't you worry."

"Right." Doctor Waters nodded. "You're also free of any infections of any kind, no STDs that we tested for, and there's no evidence that your body is fighting an occult infections processes..."

"Occult? You mean like Voodoo? I ain't never had no Voodoo done on me, Doc, least not as I knows of."

"Oh, no. Sorry, Calvin, in medicine that means

hidden. An occult infection is one that hasn't revealed itself yet, like Hepatitis C or tuberculosis, however, there are other routine tests that should be done to establish a baseline of normalcy."

"Like what, Doc?"

"Like a chest X-ray, and an EKG, and what I already mentioned, a tuberculosis check—things like that."

"Whatever you think best, Doc."

"Ah…" Doctor Waters paused.

"What's up, Doc?"

"It's a sensitive matter, one I should really discuss with you in private."

"Already said, Doc, I ain't got nothin' t' hide. Ask away."

"It's another infection test I think is important to consider, particularly if you've never been tested for it before."

"What test?"

Doctor Waters slid a form across the coffee table. Reggie looked down at it and recognized immediately why the good doctor had hesitated.

Reggie straightened up. "What's this, Doctor?" he asked, surprise registering on his face. "I wasn't aware…"

Calvin picked it up and read the heading aloud. "Consent for HIV/AIDS testing."

Doctor Waters cleared his throat. "Yes."

"Sure, Doc, sure thing," Calvin interrupted, "but ain't no chance of that. I been celibate fer years, 'n Reggie needs t' know fer sure if'n he's gonna give me a job. Last time I got tested was right after I left the Army."

"Actually, no, Calvin," Doctor Waters answered. "Employers can't require, let alone request this testing. It would be illegal."

"No matter. Go ahead and do it."

"Don't do it for me, Calvin," Reggie said.

"'S only right, Reggie. Don't you never mind 'bout it. What's next, Doc?"

"Very good. I'll set that up for you. Now, when I examined you the other evening, I also noticed you have some problems with your teeth. I have a dentist colleague who can take care of that for you."

"I think that would be a good idea, Calvin," Reggie said with a warm smile. "You only get one set of teeth, and you need to take care of them."

Calvin shoulders slumped, then he covered his mouth with his hand. "I did the best I could with 'em, Doc. I still brush after every meal, but I don't always got toothpaste. It's true, I ain't seen a dentist since I been on the street, not really since I got out the Army."

"I'm not an expert on teeth, and I didn't see anything major, but you do have several small cavities that should be taken care of before they get any worse."

Calvin looked sheepishly at Reggie. "I'm sorry, Reggie. I'm so ashamed."

"Don't you worry about it," Reggie said, as he patted Calvin's arm. "We'll get them taken care of right away. You'll have a dental plan as part of your health insurance. I've already signed you up."

"But, Reggie, I haven't even started any work yet."

"I know, but officially, you begin today. As soon as we're finished here, I'm going to walk you to your office and introduce you to your staff."

****

As the afternoon progressed, Calvin became more and more uncomfortable with his new staff, but it wasn't them, it was him. He hadn't overseen the work of other people for many years, and these were normal civilians, educated folks, not military, and not like him at all. Though they spoke with *"highfalutin'"* words, they were kind, considerate, and deferred to everything he did and said. Calvin could tell they knew better than he did; they just didn't say it.

Chapter Twelve
Adjustments, Corrections, and Fantasies

The dining room

The following morning, Calvin met Reggie for breakfast.

"How was your night, Calvin? I hope you slept well."

Calvin pulled out his chair and sat down, then motioned Roscoe to his lap. "Course. I didn't fidget or fit, not once, 'til I woke up."

"Well, that's certainly a plus."

Distracted, Calvin lifted Cinders to his chin while he pet him repeatedly. "I guess."

Reggie poured a cup of coffee for each of them. "Is something wrong?"

Calvin shrugged and lowered Cinders to his lap. As he did, Roscoe moved to the chair beside him. "Nah, just not used to ever'thin' yet."

"I know it's an adjustment, but I want you to know how proud I am of you for trying. Just continue to give it a chance."

"I will. I promised, one week. Though seems like somethin' so simple, all this grandeur 'n all, shouldn't take fig'rin' out a'tall. Take this dinin' room fer example, when it's opened up without these here partitions." Calvin pointed to the privacy screens that separated the smaller area in which they sat off from the rest of the immense room. "How many it seat? Couple hundred?"

"Yes, but not in many years. My parents and grandparents entertained quite regularly, once upon a time."

"Seems a waste, fer sure. Least with me it's doubled its occupancy from afore I come."

"True, but it's always been that way. Miss Honey

would join me for meals on occasion, as well as the other staff."

"Well, that's good. You got tables enough fer that many? Plates 'n cups 'n such?"

"Yes, but I'm more interested in hearing how you're settling in. I hope you'll like it here, Calvin." Reggie began to serve eggs, ham, bacon, and sausage to Calvin's plate. "I'd be lying if I said otherwise. I really do hope we can make this work."

"Don't you worry none. I gave my word, 'n I'm gonna keep it." As Cinders extended his bandaged paw toward the plate, Calvin picked up a piece of egg and fed it to him, and then he offered a piece of bacon to Roscoe.

"I'm glad to hear it." Reggie nodded toward Cinders. "And remember what Doctor Littleton said about table food."

"Darn, yer right. It's a habit. Thanks fer remindin' me. I plumb forgot." Calvin put down his fork with a piece of sausage he was about to offer to Cinders.

When Cinders protested, Reggie reached for the bell on the table and rang it.

"Sure thing. So, how do you find your office? Is it comfortable? Do you like your staff? Is there anything you need?" Though his words were upbeat, Calvin noticed Reggie's eyes said otherwise. There seemed to be a hint of worry behind them.

"It's gonna take some gettin' used t' … sorry … to … getting used to. Dang, I gotta start workin' on ma talkin'! I sounded like a fool yesterday, talkin' to folks who're supposed to be workin' fer me 'n who talk so good—so much better 'n me, 'n know better 'n me."

"Everything in its time, Calvin."

The kitchen doors opened to reveal Miss Honey. "Yes, Reggie," she said as she reached the table. "What do you need?

"I think Roscoe and Cinders could do with some breakfast."

"Of course," she said as she lifted Cinders from Calvin's lap. "You too, Miss Roscoe. Come with me. Your breakfast is waiting for you by the stove." At the sound of the word *breakfast*, Roscoe jumped down and hurried by Miss Honey's side as she made her way back to the kitchen.

Calvin smiled as he watched them disappear through the doors. Then he turned back to Reggie. "Can you do me a favor?"

"Sure, anything."

"From now on, 'n I mean ... and I mean this. Ever' ... every time I talk ... speak, every time I speak like a yokel, please correct me. I got better in me ... ah ... I know I have it in me to do better. I'm just out of practice."

"I think you're doing quite well on your own, Calvin. As you said, you just need a little practice, but consider this—immediately you know the words you meant to speak—they're just not part of your patterned consciousness, they're not habit. May I make a suggestion?"

"Shoot ... I mean, yes, please do."

"Pause for a moment before you speak. Think about the words you want to say and then say them. If you do, I think that will be more helpful to you in the long run than having someone interrupt to correct you."

"... Agreed ... Let's try that. Thank you, Reggie."

"Anytime."

****

As the days passed, Calvin grew more and more comfortable with his surroundings. At the end of the first week he agreed to stay in the mansion another week and then a third. His new job, however, was another matter.

No sooner had he mastered one task, than he was faced with something new that threw him for a loop, but eventually, each new task, each new challenge helped to make the next one easier. What tested him the most was keeping everything in motion. At times, he felt like a juggler with too many balls in the air, and sometimes, he dropped them. If he hadn't had Roscoe and Cinders close by it would have been a real struggle for him.

Though he recognized it was going to take time for him to grow into his new position, he knew he had made the right decision every time he felt Cinders purr in his lap or recognized an acceptance of their new life in Roscoe's eyes. What he hadn't expected was how easy it had become to be around Reggie, how much he enjoyed his company, and how much he craved his attention.

He was like a sponge, sucking up every scrap of knowledge Reggie shared with him, and when Reggie looked at him with approval in his eyes, it made his heart leap. What he wasn't prepared to accept, what shook him to his core, was the resurfacing of memories from his past, memories of friendship, and family … and intimacy.

On an afternoon in Calvin's office during the fourth week, after he'd completed a particularly delicate negotiation with a supplier, concerning how their brand name would be removed from a large lot of sneaker seconds that hadn't passed inspection for sale, Reggie squeezed Calvin's shoulder in a display of sentimental good will. He told Calvin how proud he was of the progress he'd made and the ease with which he was transitioning into his new position. When Calvin hugged him in return, he held the hug just a little too long. Reggie's touch had sparked something in him, something he hadn't felt in a very long time.

When Reggie abruptly broke the embrace and excused himself from Calvin's office, Calvin became confused. He wondered whether Reggie felt he'd stepped over some invisible line of propriety. He wondered whether he'd done something wrong.

****

When Reggie returned to his office, he could still feel Calvin's embrace. It had sparked something in him he hadn't felt in many years, something he was ill prepared for. Yes, there was the first hint in his loins of a physical stirring, but it was more than that. It was an attraction for Calvin, the attraction he'd sworn over a month before that he would never let happen.

****

That evening, Calvin's suite

With his ears under the water, the silence was a wonderful respite for Calvin while he soaked in the tub after his first month of working with Reggie. As he stared at the ceiling, the scented oil he'd added to the water began to lull him into a state of serenity, and his mind began to drift. It reminded him of how Reggie smelled.

He remembered the first time he'd looked into Reggie's eyes the day they'd met, how they crinkled at the corners, how they shone as brightly as his smile, and he thought about his mouth—his full lips, and how genuine and unassuming his smile really was. His voice was soothing, inviting, and kind, and his touch … his touch the first morning was … so gentle, and his embrace, just that afternoon … it was electric. He hadn't felt that in years—he couldn't, he dared not, but Reggie had been so open as he complimented and joked and laughed and spoke encouragingly while they ate dinner.

As he closed his eyes, Calvin brought his left arm up and rested the back of his head in the crook of his elbow, leaving his other arm free to roam.

****

Suddenly, Reggie was there, smiling down at him. His voice was soft, and comforting and the words he spoke were words Calvin hadn't heard in more years than he cared to remember.

When his loins began to tingle, Calvin's right hand crept down and grasped his stirring manhood. *He opened his mouth to receive Reggie's kiss—his manhood grew. Reggie's hand wrapped around his shaft. He began to squeeze it, gently, and stroke it, slowly.*

As Reggie cupped Calvin's balls, he drove his tongue deep into Calvin's mouth, and Calvin opened himself completely to receive him. His scrotum pulled up tight. His shaft strained against Reggie's advances. His body began to quake as Reggie ran his palm over the slick swollen head.

"No, Reggie," he murmured. "This is wrong. You don't want someone like me. I'm no good for you."

"You're exactly who I want, Calvin. You're exactly who I need."

"Oh, Reggie ... Reggie..."

"I love you, Calvin."

"Then love me, Reggie ... love me."

Reggie stepped between his legs as he slid down into the water with him. His cock was enormous, and he knew exactly what to do with it. As Reggie advanced his hips forward, his cockhead pressed against Calvin's pulsing hole while he teased and tested Calvin's ability to receive him.

Calvin moaned. His grip tightened against his shaft as his dream state allowed him to feel Reggie press inward.

When Reggie leaned down and drew Calvin's cock into his mouth, a warmth he only faintly remembered began to form in the pit of his loins. Reggie's grasp on his manhood tightened even more, as he began to stroke along its length. His pace quickened.

The warmth grew in intensity as Reggie pushed forward, entering him in one, firm, continuous thrust.

Tingling sensations rose in Calvin's groin. The warmth and tingling spread outward into his abdomen and down his inner thighs, and continued to spread until they enveloped his entire being.

When Reggie began to thrust in and out, he slurped Calvin's cock against the back of his throat.

Calvin's hips began to buck, and his scrotum tightened around the globes that urgently needed to release his manly essence.

As his back arched, Calvin's hips thrust out of the water, and his head was driven backwards. *Calvin clenched his eyes tightly shut as he felt Reggie fuck and suck him to a fevered pitch.* When his mouth opened, a feral moan filled the room as he lost control and gave into the impending release.

As searing streams of semen spewed from his cock, Calvin emptied himself of years of pent-up sexual energy as his body bucked and twisted in love's embrace. Thick ribbons of hot, musky spunk ejected like a geyser erupting from his core, landing in his hair, across his face, and down his chest and abdomen.

Time stood still.

****

When Calvin opened his eyes, his right hand was still clamped tightly around his shaft and his left was massaging his loosening sack. He looked around the room for Reggie, but he was alone. He had imagined it all.

Reggie had never been there.

Chapter Thirteen
Revelations

Reggie's office, late the following morning
    Miss Honey entered, carrying a silver serving tray, as Reggie finished up a phone call.
    "Thank you, Mister Tasker. Thank you very much. I look forward to receiving those documents." He returned the phone to its cradle.
    "I brought you a fresh pot of tea and scones with jam and clotted cream, Reggie," Miss Honey said as she set the serving tray down on the coffee table. "Presently, Calvin is at his last appointment with Doctor Lin. He's due back at three."
    "Yes, he told me before he left. Have you noticed how proud he is of his new smile?"
    "Yes," Miss Honey said, beaming, as she poured a cup of tea and set it down at the coffee table's end. "And a beautiful smile it is." She waved him from his desk to the high-backed chair.
    While Reggie got up and moved around his desk to sit down, she continued. "I'm so pleased with how the good doctor has been able to put him at ease. Even though he was excited about having his teeth repaired, he absolutely dreaded seeing a dentist. He told me how ashamed he was of his mouth."
    "Well, that's all in the past now," Reggie said as he slathered clotted cream on one of the scones. "His smile is now as white as the snow outside."
    "Yes, it is. Um, not to change the subject..." Miss Honey cleared her throat and nodded toward the phone on the desk, "but good news I hope?"
    "Yes. Oh, yes! Good news indeed." Reggie motioned for Miss Honey to join him at the table. "He's located a sister, and his mother is still alive, but the sister

was sketchy about her condition. Apparently, her health is poor."

"A sister, *and* his mother!" Miss Honey clapped her hands together. "How wonderful! Calvin will be so pleased."

"I'm not so sure about that. He's never mentioned his family, and he's faced so many new things these last few weeks, I don't know how much more he'll be able to handle. With all of that and now this ... I'd hate to see him pushed too far. Too much, too soon, you know."

"It's true, he has been a bit overwhelmed by it all, but a sister and mother! That has to be good news!"

"One would think, but..." Reggie sipped his tea.

With a serious expression, Miss Honey interrupted. "But nothing, he's managing, quite well— really he is, with Roscoe's help."

"Roscoe? What do you mean?"

With a sparkle in her eye, Miss Honey leaned forward. "Haven't you noticed how often he looks to Roscoe whenever he faces a new challenge?

"No, no, I haven't. I've noticed how she and Cinders are tuned into him, but nothing more."

"It's the most precious thing. If Roscoe doesn't seem to be disturbed by it, then Calvin accepts it and moves on. It's as if he looks at life through Roscoe's eyes. She's become his barometer for new experiences ... his life barometer."

"Really?"

"Yes, really." Miss Honey poured herself a cup of tea.

Reggie crossed his legs and leaned against the left armrest. "Tell me about it."

"The first week after he began, he had asked me to sit with him a few times for moral support while he made phone calls for the foundation. I could see in his face he was feeling stressed. Roscoe sensed it, too, and she immediately jumped up into his lap. He looked into her eyes—she has such calming eyes, don't you think— and then she nuzzled his face. She put him right at ease."

"Maybe I am giving him too much, too soon. I had thought it was the other way around, that Roscoe and Cinders drew strength from him. I'll try to be more mindful in the future of how the staff and I introduce new responsibilities to him."

"I don't think you've done anything wrong, Reggie, and you may be right to a point. Perhaps they draw strength from each other. Regardless, I don't think you need to worry anymore. Just yesterday I was bringing him a fresh pot of coffee when I noticed he had picked up the phone. He took a deep breath and looked down at Roscoe, curled up around Cinders. She lifted her head and looked back at him, and I swear she seemed to smile as she slowly blinked her eyes. He whispered, 'Thanks, girl.' She sighed gently, then put her head back down and snuggled back around Cinders. It's how he's learned to cope with change. I think he's doing marvelously, all things considered."

"You're right, he is, but he's taken on quite a bit and everything is new to him. At least new compared to the past … however many years it's been. I've seen him draw from his experience in the Army, so he has what it takes, even if all of this is presenting a challenge. But now there's his family on top of it."

"Oh, but family's different—a sister will be different. And a mother! He'll be over the moon. He must have thought about them both, at least from time to time. He must have missed them terribly."

"Mister Tasker told me, she—the sister I mean— didn't even know whether he was still alive."

"No! I don't believe it."

"It's true, Miss Honey."

"You mean there's been no contact between them … any of them?"

"Not since he enlisted in the Army. Apparently, the father was the problem."

"Oh, poor Calvin. That sounds terrible."

"The sister didn't say it outright, but she did suggest their father was very rough on Calvin. He didn't approve of his lifestyle."

"Oh, you mean…"

"Yes, I believe so."

"I never even considered that."

"So you knew?"

"I've suspected, but even if I didn't, it wouldn't matter one iota. You of all people should know that. I always say, 'Love is love and gay is gay. It's just another way.'" *And I've seen how he looks at you, my boy,* she thought to herself. *And I've seen how you've started to look at him, too.*

"It isn't news to me, either. He told me as much, when we spoke at the cottage. Has he mentioned family to you at all—any family?"

"No, Reggie, not a word, but remember, you've transplanted him into, as he calls it, 'a fairytale land.' He's still adjusting. He will be for quite some time, I suspect. Family may help to ground him."

Reggie clasped his fingers behind his neck and leaned back into his chair. "I wonder if I should hold off telling him about the sister, let alone the mother. I don't want to push him too hard, too fast … not if she's in ill health."

"That might not be a bad idea, considering, but you mustn't wait too long. I'm sure that now that the sister knows he's alive, she'll want to make contact with him, and soon. Is she going to tell their mother?"

"I don't know."

"Well, if you wait too long to tell him, they may wonder why he waited so long to contact them, once they all finally do meet?"

"That's what Mister Tasker said. I'll have to think about this."

She patted Reggie's knee. "Well, think fast, and don't forget, if his mother is in poor health, who knows how much time she may have left? What if she suddenly takes a turn for the worse? What if she suddenly passes? Time may be a very precious commodity."

Reggie smiled meekly and nodded.

Miss Honey frowned.

Reggie sat up in his chair. "What is it?"

"I don't mean to add fuel to the fire, Reggie, but that other matter shouldn't wait much longer."

"What other matter?"

"That other matter you've been putting off.

"Oh, you mean..."

"Quite."

Reggie leaned forward and pressed his fingers against his temples. "Aunt Virginia! How do I broach the subject of Aunt Virginia?"

"Gently—very, very gently, but also, directly. No hemming and hawing about it."

"She could ruin everything and just when he's beginning to settle in."

"You don't have much time, Reggie. *Forewarned*, as they say, *is forearmed*."

"She could send him running for the hills."

Miss Honey chuffed. "He deserves a little more credit than that."

Reggie's forehead furrowed. "He's still fragile, emotionally, I mean."

"He is that, but he's faced worse, I'm sure. He's

KORY STEED

also a very kind and gentle soul. If anyone can win her over, Calvin can. After the dust settles, that is."

"Dust! Ha! You know," he raised his voice, adding a conspiratorial tone with a smirk on his face, "whenever she arrives, she comes in riding a hurricane … on her broomstick."

Miss Honey scoffed as she waved her hand towards him dismissively.

"She could eat him for lunch, Miss Honey, and spit out the bones."

"Reggie! She would not, and you know it!"

Reggie giggled. "Seriously, what's today?"

"The twenty-fourth."

"Then I only have three or four more days."

"Yes, if she keeps to schedule. So you need to get to it."

"Then it's settled. I'll mention her at dinner this evening."

"You better do more than mention her to him, Reggie. Prepare him is what you must do, but don't exaggerate. Just be forthright."

"Good Lord! How do you prepare someone for the Wicked Witch of the West? She'll *get him and his little dog, too!*"

"Reggie!" Miss Honey snickered. "Yes, your Aunt Virginia can be difficult, but she doesn't mean to be, not really. At her age she's become accustomed to … to a certain lifestyle … a certain level of social status and manner of behavior. Now Peabody on the other hand … if he had a finger, she'd be wrapped around it."

"You're too generous, Miss Honey. She can be a stuck-up, stuffy, old bit—"

"Reggie!"

"Okay, okay. Old witch then … most of the time. You know as well as I that she can turn into the devil incarnate at the drop of a hat! I wouldn't put it past her to use that Pomeranian to stir up trouble. She'll use Peabody as an excuse to force Roscoe and Cinders out, and Calvin will be right behind them."

"Your aunt is only one hurdle. There's more than the foundation riding on her being difficult, and you know it. There's more riding on this, period."

Reggie's eyes narrowed. "What do you mean?"

"I think you know exactly what I mean, Reggie." *He just might turn out to be the one for you,* she thought, *so don't do anything to jeopardize that. It's been too long since I've seen you smile at another man, or woman for that matter, without a glint of pain in your eyes. You need someone.* She continued. "I've seen a change in you since Calvin arrived. You walk straighter, you smile easier, and there's laughter in this house again, genuine laughter. Everyone has noticed it. This is a happier place now, for you … for all of us, and also for Calvin. He's come so far in such a short amount of time. It would be a shame if…"

"Miss Honey, I…" Reggie's lips trembled. He looked at her, then lowered his head and sighed. Miss Honey had seen it in his eyes. He knew she knew. What she had implied was the truth. Because he'd been denying his growing feelings for Calvin, how could he possibly begin to admit them to her?

She leaned forward and took his hands between hers. "There's an opportunity here, Reggie. An opportunity that may not come to you again. I'd hate to see you not embrace it."

Reggie lifted his eyes to meet hers. As she smiled back at him, she patted his knee, just like she did when he was a boy. "Just consider it … please."

Chapter Fourteen
Confessions

While at the dentist, Calvin had reimagined his fantasy about Reggie. When he returned to the mansion, he stopped by Reggie's office, claiming the need to lie down after the hours-long procedure. Just before dinner, he called Reggie asking to be excused, stating his teeth were aching too much to eat. He then asked whether Miss Honey might be able to bring him some broth or light soup.

So, seeming concerned for his welfare, thirty minutes later, Reggie himself appeared at Calvin's door with a cart and tray and stayed with Calvin while he ate. Though he mustered through it, Reggie's presence in his bedroom, just one room away from where he'd fantasized so vividly about him, made Calvin so fearful that something might happen between them, he feigned fatigue and asked Reggie to excuse him so that he could sleep.

The following day, Calvin was revisited by the images from his fantasy about Reggie once again. Though he'd pressed on, Reggie noticed his distraction and asked several times whether he was all right. Each time Calvin made an excuse, saying he'd become temporarily confused or overwhelmed by the task he was working on. When the images became all-consuming, he'd excused himself, claiming a headache, and said he needed to go to his suite to lie down, but it didn't help. In the quiet of his bedroom, the visions became even more intense.

****

Reggie's suite
As he dressed for dinner, Reggie's mind drifted. Since his earlier talk with Miss Honey he'd finally come

to admit how fond he'd grown of Calvin. He almost couldn't remember what his life had been like before Calvin had arrived. The warmth and good humor he'd brought into the house were palpable.

Everyone felt it, and yes, there were more smiles each time the staff, himself included, encountered Roscoe and young Cinders. They all enjoyed the pitter-patter of Roscoe's happy, little feet and the nearly healed Cinders, with hardly a hint of kitten left, who now raced past his adoptive mother whenever Miss Honey called them to dinner, was endearing. Even old curmudgeon Bernard had begun to warm to them and was even seen cracking a smile and chuckling at Cinders's antics when he crashed into Roscoe as he jumped over her while playing.

Reggie had come to realize how much more he looked forward to each new day, beginning from the first moment he awoke and remembered he would be working with Calvin. As much as he tried to deny it, he recognized that his feelings toward Calvin were growing in that other way, and that scared the hell out of him. How could he jeopardize what he'd hoped to accomplish with the foundation if he complicated their working relationship by even considering a more personal one? He'd failed in personal relationships so many times before, and always because he wouldn't allow himself to trust.

Then earlier that day he became concerned when Calvin said needed to excuse himself because of a headache. He believed Calvin when he said he'd become overwhelmed by the work he was doing. He believed he was pushing Calvin too hard, and it had to stop.

Right then he decided he couldn't take a chance. He just couldn't. Calvin was too fragile. There was too much at stake. Come hell or high water, he was going to save Calvin, not destroy him for his own benefit.

****

Dinner, that evening

As he walked into the dining room with Cinders in his arms and Roscoe at his side, Calvin averted his gaze to above Reggie's head. He barely saw the table, so strong were his visions of Reggie on top of him. Again, he felt the sensations course through his body as he remembered Reggie's thrusts, pounding his prostate, and those images made him shiver as he reached his chair.

When Reggie saw him tremble, he stood up and moved to his side. "Is it too chilly in here for you?"

"No, it's okay, I guess. Still not used to such finery."

He pulled out Calvin's chair. "How are you feeling?"

"Still troubled," Calvin answered, distracted.

"Well, please know, I'm very impressed with how you've managed the distribution of foodstuffs, clothing, and toiletries to the new organizations the foundation has begun to support." Reggie moved to his place at the head of the dining room table. "I know how complicated it all can be, but you handled it marvelously.

"Not only that, the schedule you created to handle everything will really streamline deliveries. We'll be able to make a positive impact in so many more lives. Though after what happened today, your headache, I'm concerned that you might be pushing yourself too hard. Perhaps we should back off a little to give you more time to adjust."

"Thank you, Reggie, and no, I'm doin' okay now. I think it was 'coz I wasn't completely over bein' at the dentist yesterday. It was a lot, but I'm fine now."

Reggie exhaled audibly. "I'm so relieved."

"You know, I remembered something you said

that first morning I was here."

"That first morning? What was that?"

"You said you wanted me because I lived it."

"I hope you don't believe that's the only reason, Calvin."

Then Reggie became quiet. Calvin noticed his eyes glaze over. He gave him a few moments, then called his name when he still seemed lost in thought.

"Reggie! Reggie where'd you go just now? Looked like you was far away."

"Oh, sorry, I'm sorry. Something just popped into my head. What were you saying?"

"It was you who was sayin', but t' answer, no, I know there were others reasons…"

"Other what?" Reggie seemed lost to the conversation.

"Other reasons. You was … were sayin' you hoped I knew the reason you wanted me wasn't only 'cause I lived it … ya know, for the foundation, t' help you run it."

"Right. Right! Sorry," Reggie said, his voice tinged with embarrassment.

Calvin continued. "But I want you t' know, it helped me to remembered my childhood and how we wouldn't have gotten by if it hadn't been for the generosity of others."

"Can you tell me about it?"

"Me 'n my sister 'n my brother … oops, there I go again. I mean, my sister and brother and I couldn't wait until our mother returned from the donation center with food and new hand-me-downs. Them's used clothes that people donated."

"Yes, I know what hand-me-downs are."

"My brother was the oldest. He usually got the new hand-me-downs, and then I would get his grow'd out o' stuff, but sometimes my mother would find something new that would fit just me, like shoes."

"So you have an older brother ... and your sister is..."

"Eloise, she's younger by three years."

"And your brother?"

"Caleb, he's older by the same."

"You haven't talked about your family before. It means a lot to me that you feel comfortable enough to do that now."

"Yeah, I can't believe it either. So much has changed these past few weeks. They suddenly came into my head today when I was working on assigning different lots of shoe seconds to several of our organizations. I realized how grateful I'd've been to get a new pair of shoes, even if they was seconds."

A smile spread across Reggie's face. "You just said *our*, Calvin ... our organizations. Thank you."

"Course. That's how I'm startin' to feel about 'em ... um ... *them*."

"Have you been in touch with any of your family recently?"

"No, not in years. I wouldn't even know where to begin. I wrote to my mama dozens of times when I was overseas, but I never heard a word back, not even a peep.

"When I started living out of my car, I was desperate. I drove home to see if I might be able t' stay for a while, but I didn't know whether my daddy would even let me in. He was the reason I joined the Army."

Reggie leaned forward in his chair. "What do you mean?"

"He was a drunk, and one day we had a real row. It came down to blows. For the first time in my life, I knocked him on his ass. I realized then 'n there that if I stayed, one of us could wind up in the hospital ... or even dead, so I left. I wasn't about to go to jail for killin' my own daddy, so I went right to the recruiters and signed up."

"I'm sorry, Calvin."

"It's not your fault, Reggie. My daddy didn't accept my," Calvin made air quotes, "*lifestyle*. Gawd, I can't believe I'm telling you all this."

"It means a lot that you trust me enough to talk about it. I can't imagine how difficult it must have been for you."

"No different than it was for all us queers, I suppose."

"So you were saying, you drove home and…"

"And they was gone—all of 'em. I knocked on a neighbor's door. Miss Sarah told me my daddy died two years earlier from drinkin'. He bled out 'coz of the damage it done … I mean, did to him … to his liver, I mean. She told me he was dead in less than a minute—said it was horrible. My mama and sister had to move away 'coz they couldn't afford the rent without his pension, but the neighbor didn't know where they went."

"And your brother?"

"She told me Caleb left a year before my daddy died. Mama woke up one mornin', and he was plumb gone. No one knew where he went, not even my mama and sister, least not that they was sayin'. I didn't know where to even start to look for him."

"I'm so sorry, Calvin."

"I visited my daddy's grave before I left so as to make peace with him. Then I just started to drive. I was on the road for perty near two years by myself, stopping for a week here, a few weeks there–earnin' money where I could. When my car finally gave out in the city, that's when I really became homeless. I was there ever since, 'til you found me."

"You still have family, Calvin. I don't mean to pry, but would you want to try to make contact with them again?"

"I wouldn't know where to start, but I think I'd like t'—at least try to, but I don't know about them ... where they stand, I mean. None of 'em ever spoke up against my daddy when he went into one of his tirades about my life—my life ... style I mean. I don't know how they feel about me ... really feel about me. I wouldn't want to open up any old wounds ... for them or for me. Like my mama always said, 'Ya don't never go pickin' at scabs.'"

"Would you want to see any of them if they were open to it?"

"Yeah ... I mean yes, I think I would, at least to see how they are ... maybe someday. But look at me. I'm nobody now. I'd be embarrassed fer 'em to see what I've become, Reggie."

"Calvin, what are you talking about? That was before. Look at you now, where you are and what you're doing. Have you taken into consideration what you're doing—really doing ... now?"

"Nothin' personal, Reggie, but this all just got started. Who's to say? You might get tired of me, decide I can't hack it and just cut me loose. You don't owe me nothin'."

Reggie's true feelings suddenly burst to the surface. "That's not true! I owe you a lot. You've done so much for me, for the foundation, and for all of us here. You've brought light into this home, my home..."

As Reggie heard his words, he regained control of himself and began to put on the brakes. What followed was measured, restrained, and calculated. "I mean you and Roscoe and Cinders. I've got a real good feeling about you ... about your future. I see something in you, even if you don't see it yourself … at least not yet."

"That's real nice of you to say so, Reggie, but nobody can predict the future."

****

The double-hinged, double doors that led to the kitchen opened as Miss Honey backed in carrying a tureen and bowls on a serving tray. "I know how much you enjoyed my stew that first night, Calvin," she said as she reached the table and set down the tray. "I thought tonight, being so cold, would be a good time to make it again."

"It smells wonderful, Miss Honey," Calvin said as she lifted the lid. "Thank you so much."

"My pleasure." She ladled out the stew and placed bowls in front of both men. "I'll just leave the tureen here, in case you want more."

"Thank you, Miss Honey." Reggie nodded.

"Will there be anything else?" she asked as she moved the bread and butter trays closer to them.

"We'll be fine," Reggie answered.

"Very good," she said as she backed away. "Enjoy."

Chapter Fifteen
With the Best of Intentions

Once Miss Honey had returned to the kitchen, Reggie placed his hand over Calvin's. "Calvin, there's something you should know."

A chill ran up Calvin's arm. Reggie was touching him again, and the chills began to run down his spine and spread between his thighs. Calvin swallowed. "What's that? What do I need t' know?" Images of Reggie and the bathtub filled his mind.

Please say it, he thought. *Please! Please say we can be more.*

"I hope you won't be angry, but we use a private investigator, Wallace Tasker, to do a background check on all our new hires. And while his report didn't show anything other than what you told me about being discharged from the Army, it did identify several people from your past. I wanted to know whether those people might be your family."

The only words Calvin heard were, *background check.* His mind shifted gears so abruptly, he was nearly knocked to the ground. His head flew back, as if he'd been struck in the jaw, causing his shoulders to crash into the back of the chair. His heart began to pound in his chest, and his ears and neck flushed red with blood.

"You what?" he shouted, once he'd regained control of his faculties. Calvin stood up so quickly, his chair toppled to the floor behind him. "Why?" he yelled. "Why would you do that? Why would you look into my past?"

Reggie began to stammer. "Calvin ... I ... I only..."

****

High-pitched, angry barking began to echo from

deep within the kitchen and travel along the hall to the dining room doors. The doors began to bulge outward. When they finally squeezed open enough to allow Roscoe passage, she shot through. As she raced toward the table, her bark echoed through the room. Reggie had never heard such shrill sounds come from her.

"Don't you trust me, Reggie?" Calvin shouted. "Why would ya go behind my back like that?"

"Calvin, I know how much family can mean. My parents are gone, and while I still have my Aunt Virginia, I didn't have any brothers or sisters. I always missed that. I thought you might, too."

Roscoe took up position next to Calvin's chair. Her barking, directed at Reggie, continued as her body bounced up and down from the floor.

"That's your life, Reggie, not mine! You can't never understand what my life's been like!"

"I'm sorry … I'm so sorry, Calvin. I didn't mean to upset you. I was trying to help."

Suddenly the kitchen doors blew open. "What in the world has happened?" Miss Honey scolded. "Little Cinders is cowering under the stove."

"Upset me? Upset me?" Calvin continued to shout, completely unaware of Miss Honey's approach. "You done more than upset me, Reggie! Just when I finally admit t' myself that I got feelings fer … fer … fer ya! Just when I thought …"

Reggie sucked in his breath. "You have feelings for me?"

Calvin recognized the stunned look on Reggie's face—and on Miss Honey's face as he caught her out of the corner of his eye. He hadn't revealed his deepest, innermost feelings in years. Not to anyone, not even to himself. *What the hell did I just say?* He tried to pull himself together and began to backpedal.

"Yeah, God-dang-it! I got feelin's fer ya, fer all y'all, okay! Feelin's, Reggie! Fer you 'n Miss Honey, 'n all these folks that's been helpin' me. Jesus Christ, Reggie!"

"Calvin, please … let me explain."

****

All Reggie heard was Calvin's tempered wrath, but Miss Honey recognized the haunting, wanting look in his eyes. "Oh," she whispered as she drew her hand to her mouth. A smile spread across her face as she turned and hurried back to the kitchen. Neither Reggie nor Calvin noticed the little jump her feet made when she pumped her fist into the air. *Yes!* she said to herself as she pressed through the doors, then "Yes!" she shouted, once she reached the confines of the kitchen. "Yes! Yes! Yes!"

****

Calvin took a deep breath. He leaned down and righted his chair, and then he turned to Reggie. His voice was low and slow as he tried to control its intensity.

"I need time t' think, Reggie. Don't talk, 'n don't ya dare come after me." Then to Roscoe, "Roscoe, come!"

"Calvin, I…"

Calvin raised the flat of his hand, silencing him. Abruptly, he turned and walked from the dining room.

Reggie struggled to decide whether to blurt out that Calvin's family had been found or let him leave. In the end, he believed no matter what he said, Calvin wouldn't hear him, so he remained silent and watched him go.

****

Several minutes later, Miss Honey went to check on the progress of the meal. Being a short woman, she used a stool to peer through the kitchen door windows.

Reggie sat alone at the table, slumped to one side of his chair. Calvin and Roscoe were gone.

Miss Honey went to Reggie and rested her hand on his shoulder. "Where did he go, Reggie? What happened?"

"I don't know, Miss Honey. He wouldn't let me explain."

"What started it all?"

"I told him I had Wallace do a background check and then to see if he could find his family."

"Is that what you opened with, checking into his past?"

"I guess. I don't remember."

"I think I understand now."

"You do? What?"

"Reggie, you've dropped Calvin into a world he could never have imagined. In the midst of all this grandeur." She waved her hand around the room." "You gave him shelter, a job, creature comforts … all your attention. But he was forced to leave his life because of his father, and then the life he had created for himself was ripped away by the Army. He's been alone on the street for years, with Roscoe and now Cinders as his only family.

"Then you stroll in, rescue him, and hand him a fairytale life on a silver platter … you encourage him, compliment him, build him up, give him tremendous responsibility and as a result, overwhelm him, leaving him struggling to keep up, to please you, to pay you back."

"Miss Honey, you make it sound like I'm some kind of sinister entity, moving him like a pawn around a chessboard."

"That's not what I meant, Reggie, and I think you know that. All I'm trying to say is that it was too much, too soon for him."

"Do you think that's all it was? He was overwhelmed?"

"That was a big part of it, but the straw that broke the camel's back was his believing you didn't trust him. He felt betrayed."

"Of course, I trust him. Why else would I have brought him into my home and given him all that responsibility? I thought I was being careful not to push him or give him too much at a time. When he proved to himself, he could do something, I offered him more, and he took it."

"Sort of like the Army? Sort of like him rising to the rank of sergeant, taking on all that responsibility, then having it ripped away, and not because he couldn't do the job but because of being who he was? Like that?"

"Oh, my God! What have I done to him?"

"You didn't do it to him, Reggie, but I think it was inevitable. At each step of the way it could have gone one of two ways, he stayed, or he left. Unfortunately, at this juncture, he didn't stay. Did he say anything when he left?"

"Yeah, he said he needed to think and for me to not follow."

"Oh, well that's different."

"What do you mean?"

"Didn't you notice the look in his eyes, the haunted, craving that was there? Didn't you hear his words? He said he has feelings for you."

"I heard him say that, but then he just went off on a tirade."

"Unless I completely misread him, I think Calvin realized in that moment just how much he cares for you, but it happened in the same split second that he felt betrayed. It was too much for him to sort through."

"Do you really think so?"

"Yes, I do, and it shows a level of maturity for him to remove himself from the moment so he didn't say something he didn't mean. Remember, he said he needed to think."

"I hope you're right."

"I think I am."

"He did say he became confused and overwhelmed while performing a task this morning."

"See … it's as I said. It was inevitable. Give him time. Give him a day or two or even a week—however long it takes."

"Okay, I will. Thank you, Miss Honey. You've always been there for me."

"That's because I love you, Reggie. Now, what am I to do with all this stew?"

"I'm sorry. I'm not hungry."

"It will keep. I'll wrap it up."

Chapter Sixteen
Mediation

Reggie's office, the next day, late morning

Miss Honey entered pushing a tea cart. "Good morning, Reggie, no sign of Calvin yet?"

Reggie looked dejected. "No."

"What about Roscoe and Cinders?"

"Not them either."

When neither Reggie or Calvin showed up in the dining room, Miss Honey decided to take matters into her own hands. She began to set out Reggie's breakfast at the conference table.

"I suspected as much. He tried to sneak into the kitchen early this morning, but I saw him when he took several cans of food for the little ones. I didn't mention anything about last night, but I think he suspected I knew something. He wouldn't make eye contact with me, so I just told him good morning."

"What did he say back to you?"

"He looked hurt, emotionally hurt, but then he righted himself and calmly told me he 'wasn't up to snuff' and that he 'won't be taking breakfast in the dining room so I 'shouldn't go to *no* trouble.' Then he left."

From behind his desk, Reggie lowered his head and slowly rubbed his hands down his face, then he raised his eyes and looked at her. "I haven't tried to talk to him or contact him in any way. I don't want to push."

"That's probably wise. Now, come eat your breakfast."

Reggie stood up and walked around his desk. "I'm not that hungry."

"You will be, soon enough, once you get started. At least try to eat a little."

"What am I going to do, Miss Honey?"

"You're going to let time take its course. He'll come around, I'm certain of it."

****

By early afternoon, Calvin had yet to make an appearance. With Reggie so down in the dumps and Calvin AWOL and not eating, Miss Honey decided enough was enough. Ignoring her own advice to Reggie, she put a tray together of finger sandwiches and cream of chicken soup and went to Calvin's room with the intention of giving him a little poke.

After knocking on the door, she entered and found him looking dejected, sitting in his pajamas in a chair in his bedroom, petting Cinders and Roscoe in his lap.

Silently, she pushed the cart to the table beside the chair and then set down the tray. Roscoe and Cinders immediately took notice, once she uncovered the food. She leaned back and placed her fists on her hips. "Well, at least someone is happy to see me."

Calvin looked up as if noticing her for the first time.

Miss Honey pointed to the tray. "Eat, Calvin. You need to keep up your strength."

Calvin averted his gaze. "I guess you heard by now."

"Heard what?"

"Heard about me 'n Reggie's row last night."

"I couldn't help but overhear the beginning of a misunderstanding; but a row, no, that was no row, at least not where I come from."

"He investigated me, Miss Honey, like some criminal."

"Are you sure that is why he did it?"

"That's what he said."

"Is that all he said?"

"Yeah, he made some excuse, sayin' he was lookin' fer my family."

"All I can say to you, Calvin, is it wasn't an excuse."

"Why, did he find somethin'?"

"That's not for me to say. If you want to know more, you're going to have to talk to him."

"Wha-da-ya-mean?"

"Exactly what I said, Calvin. Reggie is a good man, a kind man. Give him a chance to explain."

With that, she lowered her arms and began to walk from his room. When she reached the suite's outer door, she called over her shoulder. "I'm going to serve your favorite stew for dinner tonight, Calvin. The stew you never touched. I hope you will come because I'd hate to have to keep another night."

The past twenty hours had been eating away at Calvin like a buzzard on a carcass. He needed to know. He had to know for sure just what was behind Reggie's actions before … before he said any more—before he acted.

****

The dining room, dinner time

Reggie's heart leapt when Calvin entered and approached the table carrying Cinders with Roscoe following right behind. Calvin stopped and stood by his chair. "You've got sixty seconds, Reggie. Then I'm walkin' out the front door if'n I don't like what I hears."

Roscoe hopped up onto the chair.

"Calvin, I wanted you to have your family, if they could be found and if you wanted them. You've had such a difficult life. I wanted you to be complete, with a family who loved you. I didn't mention it to you at first because I didn't know whether they existed, and then I didn't talk to you about it because I didn't want you to get your hopes up. I had to know if they were still alive, before I told you anything."

Calvin recognized the look in Reggie's eyes. It told him there was more Reggie had yet to reveal. As Calvin pulled out his chair and sat down, Roscoe moved aside. He lowered Cinders to his lap. "Yer face says you know somethin', Reggie. How long you known? How long ya known about my family?"

"Just yesterday … I only learned yesterday afternoon, while you were at Doctor Lin's. I give you my word."

"And?"

"And what?

"What did ya learn?"

"We found your sister. She wants to see you."

Calvin's body thrust forward in his chair. "You found my sister … my sister, Eloise?" he shouted!

"Yes."

"No one else?"

Reggie hesitated a moment as his expression turned to concern. Calvin read his face.

"Who, Reggie? Who?"

"Your mother—your mother is still alive, but that's all I know. Your sister was reluctant to offer any information about her."

"And my brother? Any word on Caleb?"

"Not so far, but I think this is a start, a damn good start."

"And they want to see me!" It was a statement, an exclamation, not a question.

"Your sister, yes."

"Not Mama?"

"I don't know. It's as I told you. All we know is, she's alive."

Calvin's mind reeled. Images of his family filled his vision. Not only did they not reject him, they wanted to see him, or at least his sister did.

****

As Calvin jumped up from his chair, Cinders became airborne and landed on the table, hissing and crouching with his hackles raised. Roscoe yelped as she jumped to the floor, out of the way. Reggie stood up at the same time. With his arms braced in front of himself, he winced, unsure of what Calvin would do. Would he strike out for not telling him yesterday, even though he was the one who walked away? Would he hug him? Would he... He just didn't know.

As Calvin rushed around the table's corner, Reggie recoiled, but instead of receiving a fist to the jaw, he was encircled in an embrace, so firm and so sudden, the air was forced from his lungs in a strained whoosh. Stunned, he returned Calvin's embrace and held on tight.

"Oh, Reggie, I don't know how to thank you. You found my sister and my mama! I'm sorry! I'm so, so sorry I yelled at ya. I'm so sorry I thought badly of ya. Oh, you beautiful man. Can ya ever forgive me fer all the hurtful things I said t' ya—'bout ya? I was so wrong t' say those things. I was so wrong 'bout ya. Ya done so much fer me 'n fer Roscoe 'n Cinders. I'm so, so sorry, Reggie."

Two lips pressed against Reggie's cheek. "Thank ya, Reggie. Thank ya!" Calvin cried.

"You're welcome, Calvin."

"Thank ya! Thank ya! Thank ya!" Overcome with joy, Calvin forgot himself. He leaned in and began to plant kisses all over Reggie's face until finally the only place left untouched was his lips.

Barking began to fill the room once again, but this time it was joyful. Roscoe bounced up and down on her hind legs, reaching her front paws up to their thighs as she jumped. Cinders, confused by the commotion, ran for the kitchen.

"You really have feelings for me?" Reggie asked softly.

****

Hearing the shouting once again, and dreading the worst, Miss Honey hurried to the dining room. As she opened the kitchen door, Cinders flew past her and raced for the stove. Witnessing the embrace, Miss Honey backed through the doors and using her stool to peer through the window, she was just in time to witness Reggie pull Calvin tight to his chest.

****

"Yes." Calvin leaned in. Feelings he hadn't felt, hadn't dared to feel, for so long began to bubble up inside him. Tenderly, he planted his lips against Reggie's and held them there until their faces slid cheek to cheek against each other, as if neither would ever let the other go.

****

Thinking about how lonely Reggie had been for so long, tears began to spill from Miss Honey's eyes as she watched the scene unfold. She pulled out a hanky and blew her nose loudly, nearly toppling herself from the stool.

****

Reggie's mind began to fill with possibilities, possibilities he hadn't dared to dream of in years. *A life— I could have a real life with him. Someone to wake up to in the morning. Someone to hold me late at night, night after night. Someone to love. Someone to love me.* His body began to sway from side to side. Calvin's body followed, and they began to slow dance in place. It lasted for only for a few moments, but it felt like hours.

Reggie leaned back and searched Calvin's face. Calvin's eyes met his, and he smiled.

"Say it again," Reggie whispered. "Tell me you really have feelings for me."

"Yes, Reggie, I do. I really have feelings for you."

"I never imagined, Calvin—I wouldn't have believed it possible, not after all you've told me about what you went through with the Army and about your heart being broken so many times."

"Me neither, but I can't help it. You done all this fer me—ever'thin'—and without askin' fer nothin' in return. But it ain't just me. You done the same fer so many folks through the foundation, folks you don't even know. Folks you have no cause to care about. You're a beautiful, incredible man, Reggie. How could I not have feelin's fer ya?

Reggie stepped back, but kept his hands on Calvin's shoulders as he looked deeply into his eyes. "Oh, Calvin, of course I forgive you, but really, there's nothing to forgive. It was all my fault. I should have been more sensitive to your feelings. I should have been more mindful of everything you've experienced before I acted. If I had been through what you've been through, I would have reacted the same."

"Thank you, Reggie. Thank you fer forgivin' me, but no—'tain't your fault. You gots a good heart, 'n I knows it. I knows you'd never do nothin' t' hurt me, so please don't say no more. This is all on me."

Reggie drew in a breath and began to speak, but Calvin moved in and pressed a finger against his lips as he shook his head. "Not a word," he whispered.

After a moment, Reggie nodded, then smiled. "So where do we go from here?" he asked softly.

****

THROUGH ROSCOE'S EYES

Miss Honey dabbed at her eyes with her hanky. *Honey*, she thought, *remember today, because you're witnessing the rebirth of two men.*

Chapter Seventeen
Passion Rising

The bubbling inside Calvin turned to rumbling. "Where d' ya want t' go?" He felt a tingling in his loins. Then he felt his shaft begin to stir, and then before he knew it, his balls began to undulate in their sack.

"I think you should call your sister and arrange to meet her ... and soon. We can fly..."

Calvin's pupils dilated. "That's not what I meant." As he peered deeply into Reggie's eyes, the intensity of their shine matched his own rising passion. The rumbling inside him turned to quaking. It grew stronger and stronger, and his loins responded in kind.

Before he realized what was happening, Calvin felt his cock come to life. As blood began to surge, filling its shaft, he wrapped his arms tightly around Reggie's back. He leaned in and kissed him again, passionately. His tongue darted against Reggie's lips, seeking entrance until they began to part on their own. Sensing an opening, Calvin became consumed with a sense of urgency as he drove his tongue into the depths of Reggie's mouth.

As he began to grind his pelvis against Reggie's, Reggie opened his mouth and pressed his tongue forward, forcing Calvin's tongue aside, wrapping itself around Calvin's, tasting every inch of it, exploring every crevice in his mouth. Then Calvin felt a firmness began to form in Reggie's groin as the outline of his shaft pressed forward in his pants. When Reggie suddenly broke away, Calvin began to gasp for air.

"What is it, Reggie? What's wrong?" he asked between breaths.

Reggie's body began to stiffen, and his cock began to soften. "No, this ... this is wrong."

Calvin took a deep breath and exhaled slowly. "Ain't nothin' wrong with it."

As Reggie's body became more rigid, he began to press his hands against Calvin's chest. "Yes, there is. You're my ward ... my responsibility."

Calvin released his arms from Reggie's back and gently took Reggie's hands in his. "I ain't yer ward, Reggie," he said as he gently squeezed them. "I ain't no child. I'm a grown man."

"No ... sorry. You're right. You're not. You're my partner. We're partners for the foundation, but now I've taken advantage of you."

Calvin began to chuckle. "You? Advantage? I'm the one done started this."

"Maybe, but I let it happen. I should know better. You're still so vulnerable."

"I ain't vulnerable nothin'!" Calvin couldn't decide whether he was incensed or amused.

With his breathing now returned to normal, Calvin smiled sheepishly. As the smile began to spread across his face, he grasped Reggie's shoulders and began to grind his groin into him.

****

Miss Honey averted her eyes. "Honey," she whispered, "you should be ashamed of yourself." She stepped down from the stool and placed it against the wall.

Cinders mewed as he peeked his head out from beneath the stove. "Everything's all right, my little man," she said. "Everything's going to be all right ... from now on. Now, let's find you a saucer of cream to celebrate."

****

Calvin sensed the rigidity in Reggie's body begin to drain away, only to be replaced by something else he felt begin to grow rigid between his legs once again. Calvin's stare burned into his eyes. "I don't know what came over me," he whispered, "but I ain't feelin' vulnerable. I'm feeling excited and very, very…"

Reggie's eyes twinkled as he smiled. "Horny?" he whispered back.

Calvin's brow rose, then furrowed. "Yeah, and a tad bit … afraid."

"I can see that, at least the horny part."

Calvin swallowed. "Then let's not go ruinin' the feelin', not now. Not when we got this momentum goin'. If'n not, I'm afraid I might not be able t' start it up again."

"Okay. This will be okay," Reggie said as he nodded. "It will be okay."

"Damn straight, Reggie." Calvin pressed on. "You asked me where I wanted to go. You said I should call my sister, but I was thinkin' more along the lines of…" Calvin rubbed the bulge in his paints against Reggie's growing erection, suggestively.

Reggie's eyes cautiously lifted to meet his. "Sex?"

"Not at first. I didn't know what was happenin', but dang. Now? Yeah!"

"I'm thinking the same thing, but…"

"Come on kinda sudden, huh?"

"Yes, but maybe we should wait, like you said."

"Wait? Hell! I didn't say so. I said I ain't had the courage to go there in … can't remember when." *'cept, that is, when I was fantasizin' 'bout ya*, Calvin thought to himself. Aloud he said, "It's now or never, Reggie."

"It's all good, Calvin. These feelings are good, for both of us, I think … right?"

"Hell's bells, yeah. We's both adults."

"Yes, we are."

"Just one thing, Reggie. I ain't … sorry, I haven't been with no one—I mean anyone in a long, long time. I don't know how good I'll be fer ya, but…"

Reggie pulled Calvin close and wrapped his arms back around him. "Oh, you beautiful man," he whispered in his ear, while brushing his lips against it. "I've gone for long periods, too, but don't worry, it's like riding a bicycle."

"Maybe I'll need a new set of training wheels t' keep me up 'n straight."

Reggie chuckled. He reached down to Calvin's groin and began to rub his hand against his erection, then smiled impishly when he felt the firmness of his cock, straining against the zipper. "You're already up and straight. Maybe you just need someone to stay by your side."

"You'll stay by my side?" Calvin asked.

"Always, Calvin … always."

"Your place or mine?" Calvin whispered with a chuckle and a glint in his eye.

"It doesn't matter, as long as we're together." Reggie took Calvin's right hand and moved it to his groin, rubbing it against the firmness of his own cock.

Calvin's head dropped back, and then he groaned. "Damn, Reggie," he exclaimed as he lifted his head back up. "You's a packin'!"

Reggie chortled.

"Yours," Calvin answered.

"Mine," Reggie said at the same time.

****

When Miss Honey came into the dining room, she found the table undisturbed, the stew, again untouched in its bowls. "Not a bite taken," she said quietly to herself. She placed the bowls and tureen back onto the tray then headed for the kitchen. "It'll keep for one more day. I'll just put this away 'til tomorrow." Then she giggled. "But they're certainly going to need something to keep up their strength tonight."

Once in the kitchen, she looked around. "Cinders, my little man," she called as she placed one of the bowls on the floor, "I have a second dinner for you."

But Cinders, sensing Roscoe and Calvin had left the dining room, had sneaked out and followed close behind. He was nowhere to be found, so she scraped the stew from both bowls into a container and then ladled the contents of the nearly full tureen into a larger one, putting them away in the refrigerator when she finished.

Before retiring for the night, Miss Honey took the service elevator to the second floor and pushed a cart with covered platters of sliced fruit, tea sandwiches, and caviar and crackers, resting on trays of ice, along with glasses and a bottle of champagne in an ice bucket to Reggie's suite. Leaving it outside the door, she deftly placed a note card in the center, then made her way to her room.

This wasn't the first time she'd supported one of Reggie's amorous encounters, but she hoped beyond hope it would finally be the last.

Chapter Eighteen
Round One

Reggie's bedroom

Holding Calvin's hand, Reggie led him through his suite toward the bedroom, but then hesitated a moment and walked toward his desk. He pulled a piece of paper from the top left drawer. "You need to see this first. I get tested several times a year, and this is the most recent. I had Doctor Waters do it last week, just in case."

Calvin smiled. "Just in case, huh," he said as he began to read. He nodded. "Thanks fer showin' me, but I didn't have no worries. I know you wouldn't never do nothin' t' put me in danger."

"I though it only right that you know my status, Calvin, seeing that I know yours."

"I'd never suspect you was positive, Reggie, and it ain't no tit fer tat."

"Well, now you know for sure."

On their way to the bedroom, Calvin stopped in front of a bookcase, its contents displayed in several groupings. The one at eye level included over twenty covers, all of which had Reggie's name on the spines. "You done wrote all these?"

"Guilty as charged, but you're not here to admire my work."

"They's a part of you, Reggie. They's important."

"True." Reggie wrapped his arms around Calvin from behind. "But there's something else that's more important right now. Come on." He took Calvin's hand and gave it a tug.

Once they reached the bedroom door, Calvin turned to Roscoe and Cinders, close at their heels. "You two stay out here," he said as he pointed toward a stuffed chair.

Cinders wasn't having any part of it and bounded ahead as he began to explore the new surroundings. When Calvin snapped his fingers, Roscoe rounded him up, pulling him by his neck, protesting all the way, out into the suite's main room. He turned to Reggie. "Best if they don't see this. I don't know how they'll react, and I want my first time with you to be private."

Reggie nodded and smiled as he closed the door behind them and then led Calvin to the foot of his bed. Placing both of his hands behind Calvin's neck, he pulled him in and tenderly kissed his mouth. His hands slid down until he reached the top of Calvin's shirt. He drew the shirttails from his pants and began to unbutton it.

"You'll go slow, right?" Calvin asked as he pulled away, breaking the kiss.

"Whatever you want, Calvin. We don't have to push this. We can just talk if you like."

Calvin's eyes began to twinkle. "Hell no," he said, seductively. "The time fer talkin's over. I want the full treatment." Then his face turned impish. "If you please, sir."

Reggie laughed out loud. "Well you certainly don't have any difficulty making your wishes known."

"That ain't never been one of my problems. I said it, 'coz, well, you know, I ain't had it in a while."

"I'll be very gentle," Reggie assured him, "It's been a while for me as well, but you have had sex before, anal sex I mean, right?

"Oh, hell yeah, but it's been more 'n a couple o' years. Things likely t' have un-stretched if'n ya know what I means."

"I do, and I hope you'll not be the only one to be *re-stretched* tonight, if *you* know what *I* mean."

"I'll do my best." Calvin reached for Reggie's shirt, but Reggie stopped him when he cupped his chin with his right hand and drew him toward him by the shoulder with his left. Calvin's arms fell to his sides as a moan escaped his mouth when Reggie ran his tongue up his neck and ended behind his ear.

"God, you smell good," Reggie whispered. "You taste even better, but there's something I've wanted to taste even more for days now." Reggie dropped to his knees and frantically yanked at Calvin's belt. He undid the top button, and slid down the fly of his pants, then pulled them to the floor in one fell swoop. Immediately his mouth was upon the thick, seven-inch, hard shaft, drawing it into his mouth through the boxers' fabric.

As Calvin's legs began to tremble, he grasped Reggie's head, steadying himself. "You're gonna make me buckle over if'n you keep that up."

"Mmm," Reggie moaned.

When he slipped the mushroomed head through the boxers' fly and sucked down the liquid-gold pre-cum oozing from the tip, Calvin grunted. "Damn, boy, you know what to do with a mouth!"

Spurred on by Calvin's words, Reggie began to bob his head up and down, sucking extra hard as his lips passed over the head's flange. He drew the shaft in further until his face bounced off Calvin's belly when it reached the back of his throat.

Calvin could feel himself being brought closer and closer to the edge of orgasm as his prostate began to shudder. "No, Reggie! Wait! Please slow down." He began to pant. "I want the first ... first time I come ... come with you to be ... to be with you inside me."

"So good ... you taste so good," Reggie moaned between breaths, not slowing down in the least.

"Reggie!" Calvin cried out as he stumbled forward.

As he fell toward the floor, Reggie's grip was

broken as Calvin caught himself against the footboard of the bed. "Damn, boy, I nearly came. You got yourself one hell of an appetite there!"

"And then some," Reggie said, with a leer.

Calvin sat down on the floor and held his hands out in front of him. "Please, can we slow this down a smidge? We got all night."

"Yeah, we do," Reggie answered with lust in his voice. "And I'm planning to dine on you several times before morning."

"Then let's do this right." How 'bout a shower, or a bath first?"

"Even better. Then we'll be all slick and slippery."

"This here's a different side of you I ain't never seen, fer sure. I think I like it, Reggie, but it's gonna take some gettin' used t'."

"Sorry," Reggie said anxiously. "I'm just so worked up right now. I can't believe this is really happening, not to me, not now, and I don't want it to slip by."

Calvin caressed Reggie's face. "Me neither."

"I was so sure I wasn't going to let it happen. I was determined to not allow my desire for you to ruin the friendship that began to develop between us. And besides, you're my employee."

Calvin leaned forward and reached out to caress Reggie's face. "I ain't makin' light of it, but I sure am glad you decided otherwise, 'coz I'm gonna need help with this," he said as he gazed into Reggie's eyes and drew his hand to his pulsating shaft. Then he lowered his eyes to Reggie's groin. "And I think you're gonna need help, too."

Calvin pushed Reggie back up and rose to his knees as he began to unfasten Reggie's pants. As the belt came free, and Reggie helped to shimmy them and his briefs down, his eight inches of manhood sprang free. It was so thick, Calvin's fingertips barely met when he wrapped his hand around it. So engorged with blood, its purpled veins contorted and seethed, begging for release, as the shaft swelled and bounced with each heartbeat.

Reggie moaned as Calvin caressed its length with his fingertips. "There's only one thing that will relieve it, Calvin."

"I know." Calvin answered as he licked his lips and leaned forward. "And I'm gonna help you out with that right now, as best I can."

The moment he pressed his lips to the swollen, purpled head, Calvin began to suck greedily, drawing in the briny nectar that oozed through the slit at the tip. He licked his thumb and index finger and formed them into a ring, then wrapped them around the sensitive spot behind the ridge, extending the pressure his lips exerted and gently milked back and forth across the sensitive glans. As saliva slid down the shaft, it lubricated his grip even more, sending shivers up Reggie's spine.

"Oh, fuck!" Reggie cried out. "Oh, fuck, just like that. Yeah, baby, just like that!"

"So good … tastes so good," Calvin moaned in response. "Gawd, it's been so long … so damn long."

Reggie began to slowly thrust his hips forward, advancing his cock until it pushed through Calvin's stretched lips. He continued to thrust until it reached the back of Calvin's mouth, nearly dislocating his jaw with its girth. Calvin gagged and his eyes watered, but he pressed on and swallowed as the head passed his tonsils, drawing the tip down his throat. Reggie shuddered as pleasure waves spread from his loins and out through his body when the thickened saliva that formed at the back of Calvin's throat slicked the path his cock followed.

"Baby, you're bringing me close. You're going to make me come."

Calvin slid off his cock, choking as it left his throat. "Ain't that the idea?" he said after wiping his mouth with the back of his hand.

"Oh, it is … eventually. I'm just warning you."

"You wanna hold off a little?"

"Yes and no," Reggie said. "I want this, but I also want it to last as long as it can."

"Okay, Reggie," he said as he leaned back. "It's been a while, n' yer size is gonna take some gettin' used t', but I still remember how t' give pleasure to a man. You up for a little extended play?"

"Anything, anything you want, Calvin."

"Then let's head fer yer shower. I'll show ya some things that'll drive ya mad."

Reggie leaned down and kissed him. "Lead the way," he whispered as he pulled away.

****

After cleaning himself out with the extension on the bidet, warm water gently cascaded down Reggie's body from the showerheads above and around the two of them. Calvin ran an almond scented bar of soap through the trimmed, brown hair that covered Reggie's chest and abdomen, while he worked it into a lather.

Standing an inch less than Reggie's five foot eleven, Calvin barely had to glance up when he looked directly into his eyes. "Gawd, you're gorgeous," he murmured.

"The feeling's mutual," Reggie whispered back.

As Calvin slid the soap down and around his new lover's shaft and balls, causing him to suck in a breath and exclaim, "Oh, fuck, yes!", Calvin didn't stop there. He dropped to his knees and began to work the soap between his legs and around to the back, sliding it up his crack, causing his body to shudder and his hole to spasm.

"Baby," Reggie moaned as his hips thrust forward in an uncontrolled lunge. "You know just what I like."

Calvin chuckled. "You ain't alone. All men like this."

"Yes, but you do it so well."

"I aims to please, Reggie. I aims to please. Now, how 'bout we pick up where we done left off," he said as he lathered the soap into and around Reggie's hole.

As Calvin slid his lips around the head of Reggie's cock, his soap-slicked, middle finger begin to work its way inside him. He slowly advanced while he caressed the first sphincter.

Reggie's legs began to quiver as his head dropped back, and he closed his eyes. Calvin added a second as he slid the tips of both fingers around the sensitive membranes as if he was greasing a cake pan.

Then Calvin's mouth was on him, drawing his pre-cum-oozing glans along his tongue, as he relaxed his jaw until it passed his tonsils once again. At the same time, Calvin added a third finger and advanced until he breached the final barrier, entering the sacred regions of Reggie's interior. Reggie winced at the assault, then sucked in his breath as he lunged forward again, driving his cockhead beyond the back of Calvin's throat, causing him to gag, but Calvin swallowed greedily anyway.

Calvin pressed his free hand against Reggie's lower back to steady him and keep his cockhead centered in his gullet. He withdrew his fingers and scooped out a generous portion of gelatinous coconut oil from a jar he'd placed within reach on the shower's floor earlier.

"I'm on fire, Calvin," Reggie panted. "I'm on fire!"

"I know you are," Calvin whispered. "I know,

and I'm a gonna help you put it out, but afore that … that fire's gonna rage."

As he returned his fingers to Reggie's beckoning hole, Calvin smeared the liquifying oil around the entrance then advanced all three together up to his last knuckles in one smooth motion and swiped his fingertips along the quivering orb, buried deep inside.

Reggie screamed in delight as the muscles in his legs, abdomen, and back locked into shuddering spasms, making it difficult for him to draw breath, but Calvin didn't stop there. Advancing and withdrawing his fingers and caressing Reggie's contracting prostate, each time he reached it, Calvin slid his lover's cock in and out of his mouth, working him into a pre-orgasmic frenzy.

As Calvin quickened his pace, Reggie drew near to the moment of release as guttural, animalistic sounds rose from his chest. Calvin pressed his fingers firmly against the ridge of his lover's now rock-hard orb while he focused his mouth to suck against the swollen cockhead, finally sending Reggie to the frenzied point of eruption.

Calvin's cock ached for release. Unable to use his hands, he arched his back and began to thrust his shaft against the shower's tile floor, now slicked by the globs of coconut oil that had dripped out and fallen from Reggie's hole. As he thrust his pelvis back and forth, he focused the underside of the flange of his cock between the recess of grout between two tiles, focusing on the friction they were able to offer.

When Reggie's body locked in a tetanic spasm, he grabbed onto a vertical railing attached to the shower wall as the first wave of thick, milky cum burst from the depths of his loins, filling the back of Calvin's mouth until it began to spill from his lips.

Calvin swallowed and swallowed as he pressed

forward to seal his mouth against Reggie's pelvis and began to devour jet after jet of the musky essence now propelled past his tongue and down his throat.

****

Both men became consumed by the sensations that coursed through their bodies as time stood still. The world became lost to them as everything else faded away. They existed only in this moment, only in this place, only for each other.

****

A room in the estate staff quarters
Two-way telephone conversation

"Dudley speaking." Slender, at five-foot-eleven, Dudley, with his graying Boy Scout haircut and waxed and curving mustache was the epitome of what most people would picture as a chauffeur.

"Dudley! It's Miss Virginia. We'll be landing in thirty minutes. You need to meet us."

"Miss Virginia? You're arriving tonight?"

"Yes, there's been a change of plans."

"Is all well, Madam? I received no notice."

"Heavens no! Poor Peabody, he's had a terrible fright. I had to take him away from there, immediately!"

"I see, Madam. Are you calling from the plane?"

"Of course! Where else would I be?"

As Miss Virginia was speaking, Bernard, the butler, who was also Dudley's secret lover—though it was no secret at all; it simply wasn't mentioned—approached and listened in.

"Yes, Madam, quite right, where else."

"I hope the hour isn't inconvenient," she said, not meaning it.

"Yes, Madam, of course … of course it's convenient. I live to serve." Dudley rolled his eyes toward Bernard.

"Come right away. You know how my little boy becomes when he is forced to wait."

"Yes, Madam, I'll be there directly."

"Good."

"She's arriving tonight?" Bernard exclaimed. Dudley covered the mouthpiece and waved him off.

"At which gate will I find you?"

"The private terminal, of course. I've chartered a jet. My nephew will take care of it. Poor Peabody, he's still quaking. And bring the limousine, not that hideous, monstrosity he drives, so vulgar with those immense tires and ostentatious chrome. To have to climb, she emphasized the word "climb", *into a vehicle. Uncivilized!"*

"Yes, Madam, of course I'll bring the limousine."

"Directly, Dudley!"

"Yes, Madam, directly."

"Good! Don't keep us waiting."

"Yes, yes, Madam. I was advised you were to arrive in several days. Is the family expecting you?"

"No time to call ... there was no time at all. We fled ... barely escaped with our lives, Dudley, but what does it matter? Preparations should have been well underway by now for my arrival. They've known for two months, and the estate is still my home. It always will be."

"Yes, Madam, I see. I will let Miss Honey know to have your suite prepared."

"Good! Everything must be made right."

"Yes, of course, everything will be ready for you, just as it has always been."

"I look forward to seeing you again, Dudley. Ta-ta!"

"Yes, I look forward to seeing you—" The phone clicked to silence as he replied, "as well."

Dudley Portnoy, still the chauffeur at the Scottsdale family estate, and "Dear Old Dudley" to Reggie, lowered the handset into its cradle. "Oh, dear," he sighed as he looked toward Bernard, who had already begun to put on in his tuxedo.

"Oh dear is right," Bernard said as he buttoned his pants. "I'll get things started downstairs."

Dudley nodded then lifted the handset again and dialed Miss Honey's room.

Chapter Nineteen
Round Two

Reggie's bedroom

"Damn, boy!" Calvin exclaimed as he walked back into the shower, after using the attachment on the bidet. "Never felt so clean, inside and out."

Reggie smirked as he drew his lover into his arms. "It is convenient, isn't it?"

"Damn convenient if'n ya ask me."

"Now it's my turn," Reggie said after a kiss.

"Anythin' you want," Calvin winked, "just go slow. I ain't never taken one that big before."

"I promise, I'll go slow."

"N' just as so we wind up in that fine bed o' yers."

Reggie ran his hands through the hair across Calvin's chest and along the dark treasure trail down his abdomen. "I'll make sure of it." He lifted Calvin's sack in his soapy hand and raked it with his fingertips.

Calvin jumped. "That'll get them juices a flowin', fer sher," he said. Then he planted his mouth on Reggie's and drove his tongue into its depths as he stood on his left leg and wrapped the right around his hips, thrusting his hard-on against the ridges of his lover's six-pack.

Reggie continued soaping him up, front and back, then reached down to lift his lover's buttocks to his waist. As he lifted him up and down, his hardening cock glided between its slick, meaty globes. "Oh, fuck," he moaned. "I can't wait to slide inside you.

"Me neither," Calvin groaned. "'Now quit yer talkin' n' start yer fuckin'.'"

"That was certainly direct. You really want this, don't you?"

Calvin laughed. "Damn straight."

"With pleasure." Reggie carried him into the shower's spray to rinse the soap from his body, then lowered him to the floor and dried him off after he turned off the water. "This way," he said after drying himself.

He led Calvin into the bedroom and guided him onto his back down on the opened bed. "My God, you're a sight," he said as he lowered his mouth to Calvin's chest, sucking in his left nipple as he raked his teeth around the ring of darkened skin.

Calvin's head thrashed from side to side as Reggie nibbled his flesh while he traveled up and down his chest and belly. He paused to suck in the thread of pre-cum that clung between the tip of Calvin's throbbing cock and the well that had formed in his belly button, then slid his mouth down the length of the shaft until it was buried in the mound of pubic hair at the base. "So sweet." He groaned as he pulled away.

Calvin began to smack his lips and twist his nipples between his fingertips when Reggie sucked in his sack and toyed with his swollen balls, undulating his tongue between and around them.

"Can't take it," Calvin moaned. "Can't take it no more."

"You're going to take it and a whole lot more," Reggie snarled. "Now prepare yourself."

As Calvin lifted his legs, providing his lover with unbridled access to his most delicate regions, Reggie slid his tongue along the length of his crack then zeroed in on his puckered hole as he began to lap and nibble at it. Calvin wrapped his arms behind his knees and cried out when Reggie formed his tongue into a lance and drove it along the sensitive tissues, forcing him open, as he delved deeper and deeper towards his goal.

While devouring Calvin's recesses, Reggie pressed his thumbs, again and again, along the rigid base of his cock from where it began at his opening until he reached his sack, milking more and more blood up towards the swollen head until it could hold no more. The veins snaked along the shaft as they contorted to the point of rupturing, once the shaft turned crimson.

For fifteen minutes Reggie feasted, not stopping after the second barrier was breached, until Calvin's hole lay so slack, he could pass four fingers through it unencumbered, but he knew it still wouldn't be quite enough.

****

Calvin had passed into another world, one filled with a kaleidoscope of colored emotions and textured sensations he'd never experienced with another lover. In the first moments after Reggie mounted him, Calvin was barely aware of the change when the shaft slid into him, not until the head of his cock grazed the ridge of his sensitive, walnut-shaped orb.

Calvin came alive, stunned that the sensations he was experiencing could be heightened even further when he first felt the thickness of Reggie's shaft roughly slide out of him. Even with the degree that Reggie had opened him and the amount of lubricant he'd spread into him, it still burned like fire as he advanced and withdrew. But Reggie's lips on his and Reggie's words of love and encouragement whispered into his ear, helped to ease the blaze.

"You're taking me, Calvin. You're taking all of me!" Reggie said. "You're doing so well. Are you okay? Am I hurting you? Please tell me if I'm hurting you."

"Reggie," Calvin moaned. "It burns. It burns so much."

"I'll pull out. I'll pull out right now."

"No! Don't you dare. It's a good burn, a beautiful burn, and now it's gettin' less."

"Oh, baby, I love you. You feel so good." Reggie began to slow his thrusts.

"Don't you stop, Reggie. Don't you dare stop!"

"Oh Calvin!" Reggie slowed even more.

"Fuck me, Reggie! Damn you, fuck my brains out!"

"I don't want to hurt you."

"I said fuck me!" Calvin roared.

As Calvin wrapped his legs around Reggie's hips and pulled him in tight, he began to thrust his hips upward, crashing the globes of his buttocks against Reggie's hips.

Looking deeply into Reggie's eyes, Calvin smiled. "This is what I want, Reggie. This is what I need."

"Me too, Calvin! The sensations your prostate is creating in my cock are so intense, and they're spreading through my body."

"I'm getting close, Reggie," Calvin moaned. "I'm so close."

"Oh, God, Calvin!" Reggie cried out. "I'm gonna come! Oh fuck, I'm gonna come!"

Seconds later, Reggie's sack pulled up tight, his balls contracted, and his prostate began to spasm as his second load rushed along its path until it erupted, spewing rope after rope of thick cum into the depths of Calvin's colon.

"Now, Reggie!" Calvin shouted. "Oh, fuck! Now! I'm comin'! I'm comin'! Oh, my Gawd, I'm comin'!"

With each lunge of Reggie's hips, cum rushed from Calvin's cock in arc after arc, landing on his chest, on Reggie's chest, and on their faces until the two of them were coated in his musky spunk. When it was over, Reggie collapsed, falling to Calvin's left side. As his cock slid from Calvin's hole, cum oozed from the stretched opening and pooled on the sheet.

They lay there, panting. Calvin reflected on what had just happened. From the look in Reggie's eyes he could tell it must have meant just as much to him. They were now a couple. After a time, Calvin rolled to his side and pulled Reggie to him as he wrapped his body around him, then pulled the sheet over them until they drifted into a brief sleep.

****

Two-way telephone conversation from Virginia Abigail Scottsdale's suite

"Hello, Miss Honey. Her plane just landed. How's the suite coming along?"

"We're still getting it ready, Dudley. I have Perky, Geraldine, and Cynthia here with me now. How long?"

"Any moment now. The plane is taxiing up to the gate as we speak. Oh, It's loud. I'm moving inside."

"So another five, ten minutes there and forty-five minutes travel time, right?"

"Yes, that sounds about right. Oh, goodness, the door is opening and the plane hasn't even come to a stop yet."

"That doesn't sound good. How does she seem?"

"I don't see her yet. Oh, there she is. She's waving. Oh good, she's smiling."

"Can't have been too bad then."

"Who's to say, Miss Honey? You know how she is—mountain out of a molehill and all that."

"Call me back from the road once you have a better idea of her mood."

"I will. I'm stepping outside." Then his voice muffled. *"Yes, Miss Virginia ... coming. Coming right away."*

"Better go to her then."

"Right, Miss Honey," he shouted quickly into the phone over the declining whine of the jet's engine. *"I'll call you back from the road. Give me about ten minutes."*

****

Reggie stirred to the sound of his stomach growling. "I wonder," he said softly as he disengaged himself from Calvin's embrace.

"What is it?" Calvin asked as he rolled onto his back and pushed himself up against the headboard.

"I'm hungry. Just going to check on something," he said as he opened the bedroom door. "Uh oh," he called from the main room, "we're about to have company."

Seconds later, Cinders came bounding into the bedroom, then onto the bed, followed close behind by Roscoe.

"What are you two doing here?" Calvin asked as he pulled the comforter over his groin. He lifted Cinders to his face and rubbed the top of his head. A moment later, Roscoe was in his lap, exposing her belly for a rub. "Oh, you two," he said with amusement as he hugged then petted them both.

A minute later, Reggie appeared, pushing a cart. "What's that?" Calvin asked.

"Miss Honey, always looking out for me."

Calvin scratched his head. "Huh?"

"Whenever I've, *entertained*," Reggie made air quotes, "Miss Honey has put together some refreshment for me and my guest."

"Mighty nice of her."

"Yes," he said, reading the note. "Do you want to know what it says?"

"What what says?"

"The card. She wrote *I'm so happy for both of you. Enjoy!"*

"That was sweet of her."

"She comes by her name naturally."

"What did she pack fer us?"

Reggie lifted a lid and smiled. "We have tea sandwiches, champagne," he said, nodding toward the ice bucket, then lifted another lid, "sliced fruit," then the last lid, "Oh, and caviar."

"You mean fish eggs?"

"Yes, and she's served the best fish eggs in the world, Almas. It comes from an old, albino, Iranian beluga sturgeon in the southern Caspian Sea."

"It's all yours," Calvin said as he crinkled up his face.

Cinders sniffed the air and began to squirm, and then he began to mew as he tried to break free from Calvin's grasp.

"Not so fast there, little man," Calvin said, holding fast as he began to chuckle. "I think Cinders want some."

"You should try it, Calvin. It costs nearly a thousand dollars an ounce."

"Fer fish bait? You gotta be kiddin' me!"

"No, I'm not. It's white, not black like most other caviars."

"Fish n' crawfish bait. That's all we ever used fish eggs fer."

"Come on, live a little," Reggie said as he spooned caviar onto a cracker with a mother of pearl spoon and handed to him. "Just try it."

Calvin sniffed it. "Like I s'pected, smells fishy."

"Go on, taste it."

Calvin touched his tongue to the caviar, then nibbled at the corner of the cracker as Cinders began to swat at his hand.

"No," Reggie said chuckling, "you have to put

the whole thing in your mouth and crunch down through the eggs. They pop in your mouth, releasing the most delectable, briny goodness."

Reggie lifted a caviar-covered cracker to his mouth. "Like this." He popped it in, bit down, and chewed. "Mmm," he moaned with his mouth closed.

Calvin broke the cracker in half, spilling some of the caviar onto the comforter. Cinders pounced on it immediately. After popping the half cracker into his mouth and chewing, he chose his words carefully. "It's all right, tastes like anythin' else comes out the ocean, but it ain't nothin' special."

Reggie laughed. "It's an acquired taste. You'll learn to love it.

"One thing's fer sure," Calvin said, smiling as he held the other half of the cracker in his lap, "Cinders sure does like it!"

Cinders purred and purred as he ate egg after egg.

****

From the kitchen
Two-way telephone conversation

"Dudley, what took you so long? It's been forty-five minutes."

"Miss Honey, you won't believe how much luggage she's brought ... and packages. The trunk and three-quarters of the passenger compartment are stuffed to the brim. It took forever to get it all loaded. We've only just gotten onto the freeway."

"Phew, I thought you might be coming up the driveway by now."

"Sorry, Is everything ready?"

"Yes, we've finished with her suite, and I'm preparing some light refreshment as we speak."

"Good, that might help to lighten her mood."

"What happened? How does she seem?

"Who can say? The old girl is in a real snit, but I suspect it's one of her own making. She went on and on, and still I have no idea what actually happened."

"Well, I'm sure we'll all hear about it … in detail."

"Right, once she gets her story straight. Oh, have you told Master Reggie yet?"

"No, not yet, he's … *entertaining* this evening."

"Oh, I see."

"What? Why do you say that?"

"She's indicated she wants to see him once we arrive."

"Then let her know he has company for the night. She'll know what that means, so I don't think she'll push it."

"I'll do my best, but I can't promise anything."

"Why do you say it like that?"

"She's off. It's a gut feeling, but something tells me there's more to this story than just a peeved little Peabody."

"Oh, dear!"

Chapter Twenty
On a Broomstick

Reggie's bedroom

Miss Honey stood outside the door knocking. "Reggie? Reggie, it's Miss Honey." When there was no answer after a few moments, she turned the knob and called into the suite again through the open door, but there was no immediate response. After she noticed the bedroom door was ajar, she heard water running. Then Cinders came running toward her, followed immediately by Roscoe. While Cinders wove himself around her ankles in a continuous figure eight, Roscoe sat patiently on the floor, wagging her tail.

"Where's your master?" she asked the dog as she lifted the cat to her cheek. Roscoe made a single, subdued "Woof."

"Where is he, girl?" she asked, looking down.

Roscoe turned her head towards the bedroom, then looked back.

"Oh, I see. What to do? What to do?" A moment later, she headed for the bedroom door. She knocked again. "Reggie? Reggie, are you there? Calvin?"

But still there was no answer.

****

"Hell n' tarnation!" Calvin exclaimed as he suddenly stopped walking into the bedroom, naked, well ahead of Reggie. He turned back around and bolted for the bathroom, crashing into Reggie at the door, nearly knocking him to the floor.

"What is it? What's wrong?" Reggie asked, confusion on his face, once he'd regained his balance.

"Miss Honey! It's Miss Honey! She's a sittin' in yer bedroom?"

"What? Did she see you?"

"No! No! She done had her back t' me."

"Reggie!" They both heard with an upward lilt in Miss Honey's voice. "I'm so sorry, but this couldn't wait. I need to speak with you right away."

"Just a moment, Miss Honey," he called. "I need to put on a robe."

"I'll wait," she called back.

As they walked in together, their bodies covered, Miss Honey said, "Let me know when it's safe to turn around."

Reggie chuckled. "We're appropriately attired, Miss Honey."

"Reggie, I'm sorry." Miss Honey stood up and turned to face them. "Hello, Calvin." She nodded as she continued to approach. "There's been a development."

"What development? What's happened?" Reggie asked as concern creeped into his face.

"It's your aunt. Aunt Virginia will be arriving within the half hour."

"The Aunt Virginia you mentioned the other night at dinner?" Calvin asked. "So I finally get to meet her?"

"What?" Reggie exclaimed to Miss Honey, then to Calvin, "It's not that simple, Calvin."

"Yes, I'm sorry, but…"

"How long? Why didn't you…"

"You were … preoccupied, Reggie, engaged in, um, I didn't want to disturb you right away, but now…"

"No matter, Miss Honey. But 'now' what?"

"I would have left it 'til morning since her suite is on the other side of the mansion, but there's an indication she'll want to see you upon her arrival."

"Do you know why?"

"No, I don't. Dudley called on the way back from the airport. I told him to let her know you were entertaining for the evening. She knows what that means, but she was undeterred."

"Something must have happened. Do you have any idea what it could be?"

"Not really, other than something upset Peabody. You know how she exaggerates, but she told Dudley something to the effect of, 'they barely escaped with their lives.' I'm sure it's all blown out of proportion, but…"

"But it doesn't matter."

"No, Dudley seems to think there's more to the story than what she has let on."

"There always is," Reggie said. "If she'll be here in a half hour, give it another fifteen minutes for her to make her grand entrance, another fifteen for her get settled in her sitting room…"

"So you have a hour to prepare," Miss Honey said, wringing her hands together.

"This needs to happen on neutral territory," Reggie said, rubbing his chin. "Don't let her go up to her suite. Set her up in the dining room. Tell her earlier this evening I asked you to serve a light refreshment for my guest and myself at—what time is it now?"

Miss Honey looked at her watch. "It's 8:55."

"Perfect. Tell her 10:00. Tell her once I learned she was arriving, I invited her to join us. If she insists I come to her, tell her I won't be able to because I have important company."

"That's a good idea, Reggie. I had already begun to prepare a light refreshment to serve her in her suite. I'll simply add to it to include the two of you."

"Thank you. If she really wants to see me, she'll have to come to me. The delay will force her to wait, and that should put her off balance and pique her interest at the same time."

"You're a sly one, Reggie," Miss Honey said with a smile.

"Not really, I just know my aunt, and I know how to handle her. It's going to take more than a few minutes to explain Aunt Virginia to Calvin, and then we'll get dressed. Expect us to walk into the dining room at ten, sharp."

"Very good, Reggie. Just remember, she'll have Peabody with her."

"And we'll bring Roscoe and Cinders. It should make for an interesting encounter."

"Are you sure that's wise?"

"Wise or not, she's going to meet them eventually. Might as well get it over with right from the start because this is going to be my life from now on, and I'll not have her interfere with it any longer."

"I suggest you allow me to keep them in the kitchen at first. I'll keep an eye out, and you can give me a signal when to let them in."

"Thanks, Miss Honey. That makes more sense."

****

At ten o'clock, Miss Honey met Reggie and Calvin at the bottom of the grand staircase and took Roscoe and Cinders with her into the kitchen through the service entrance at the back of the mansion.

****

"I do not appreciate being kept waiting, Reginald!" Aunt Virginia said with a shrill, upward lilt as Reggie and Calvin entered the dining room. Dressed in a dusty-rose, flowing, silk-taffeta gown, with a brocade bodice and inlaid antique-Belgian lace, her statuesque form was seated with Peabody in her lap at Reggie's place, the head of the table at the far end. "I've had a most trying day!"

"I'm sorry to hear that, Aunt Virginia, and by the

151

way, you're in my seat," he said as he approached. "I see you're having one of your snits, but hopefully, it will pass soon, now that you've arrived, several days early, mind you, for your visit."

"Snit! How dare you, Reginald! What a terrible thing to say when I have only just arrived, and you've known for months I was coming. This is still my home. I will sit wherever I like!"

"It *was* your home." Reggie said, as he leaned down and kissed her on the cheek. Then he moved to the chair to her left. "It was passed on to me *by Father*, but no matter." He paused and reached down to gather the place setting in front of the chair, then walked around behind her and gathered the other place setting. He nodded from Calvin toward the table top. "Grab a couple platters, Calvin, will you?"

"What do you think you are doing?" Aunt Virginia exclaimed, as she primped her floral-embroidered head comb, dyed to match her dress. "Where do you think you are going?"

"Two can play your game, Aunt Virginia. There are two heads to this table. Since you refuse to relinquish my seat, if you really need to see me, you can move with us to the other end." Reggie walked along the table and pulled out the opposing chair. After he and Calvin had set new places and Calvin placed the platters on the table, they sat down.

Reggie continued, "Otherwise, I'll see you in the morning."

"You will see me now!" Virginia was so worked up she was shaking. Peabody yelped when she pounded her fists down on the chair's arms.

"Well yes, I do see you. I can see you. I'm sitting right here, but you've arrived early, without advance notice, and your arrival has interfered with my evening.

I've made concessions by inviting *you* to join *us*."

Reggie spread and tented the fingers of both hands in front of him, then rested his chin against them. "The ball's in your court."

Virginia's face turned beet red as her body shook with rage, but she seemed to realize she'd make no headway once her nephew had taken such a stand. Hugging Peabody to her bosom as she rose from the table, she moved to the chair to her left. As she sat down, her voice broke.

"Oh, Reginald," she cried out as she pulled an embroidered handkerchief from the cuff of her sleeve. "It was terrible!" Her body began to shake as she cried, real tears.

"Calm down, Aunt Virginia," Reggie said as he stood up and walked toward her. Calvin followed. When Reggie reached her, he rested his hands on her shoulders from behind while Calvin took the seat across from her. Reggie leaned down. "Tell me what happened."

"There was a snake, a real snake, a rattlesnake. It nearly killed Peabody."

"A snake? Where in the world were you when this happened?"

"Arizona of all places."

"What were you doing in Arizona?"

"It was a spur of the moment decision. I heard about a new artist colony, with real native artists, so I left San Francisco a few days early and changed my itinerary to include a stop in Arizona. They create the most gorgeous jewelry with turquoise and silver, and one artist in particular, a painter, creates the most breathtaking landscapes. I just had to have some of her work for my dining room. I'm redecorating you know. All natural and all native works."

"The snake?" Reggie redirected. "What about the

shake?"

"The snake, yes, I put Peabody down for just a moment, just a moment, mind you, while I was examining one of the paintings in the artist's studio. He had scurried off, and I didn't realize it. Suddenly I heard yelling and shouting. I didn't pay it any mind until a Native American child came running up to me and began to pull at my skirt. It was full length, made from the most beautiful Native American dyed material, stunning really."

"The snake?" Reggie repeated.

"No, the skirt, the skirt!"

"Yes, I realize it was the skirt, but what about the snake? You keep changing the subject."

"Oh! The child pointed to the door and pulled me by the hand until we were outside. She practically dragged me down the stairs toward a cactus garden. That's when I saw it.

"Peabody was barking at something in the corner of a rock wall. He was darting from side to side in the gravel walkway when I realized what it was. Its rattle was so loud. I screamed when it lunged for him, but an old brave, I think he was a brave—he had feathers and beads woven into his braids—he was already moving toward poor Peabody. I barely saw what happened.

"He pulled Peabody to his chest with one hand and struck out with a huge knife, like a machete, in the other as he flipped over in the air. It happened so fast. The snake sailed through the air, right past the brave brave … courageous brave … Oh, you know what I mean. When it fell on the ground, it was in two pieces. He sliced through it right behind its head.

"Reginald, it was the largest snake I've ever seen, even at the zoo. He kneeled down and said a prayer over it. A group gathered around him while he said it. Imagine that, a prayer for a beastly snake!

"Someone said it was a Western Diamondback. I don't know what that means, but it was six feet long. Did you know they are responsible for more deaths from snakebites than any other rattlesnake? Poor Peabody, they told me he would have been dead within minutes." Aunt Virginia continued to tremble.

Reggie moved to her side and kneeled down. "What happened then?"

"I hugged the man, the brave, and rewarded him right on the spot. I gave him $100.00 from my wallet. He didn't want to take it, but I insisted. I laughed when he told me the snake was reward enough. He said it tastes like chicken. I couldn't stop laughing. Then I began to cry, and I couldn't stop myself. I was hysterical, crying.

"They helped me to my car. I was so upset I forgot all about the painting. The driver returned me to the hotel only long enough for my luggage and parcels to be loaded into the limousine that would take me to the airport. I had the concierge book me a flight. I told her my nephew would take care of everything and to spare no expense, so she hired a private jet when that unaccommodating airline said they were unable to change my itinerary again. We flew here directly."

"A private jet, Aunt Virginia?"

"Yes, I'm sorry, but I was so panicked. I couldn't stay in that state one minute longer. I had to leave immediately."

"We'll talk about that later. The important thing is you're safe. You and Peabody are safe."

Aunt Virginia lifted her head and smiled at Reggie as she sniffled and dabbed at her eyes. "Thank you, Reginald. Now enough about that horrible ordeal. Please introduce me to your new friend."

Reggie's body recoiled at his aunt's sudden

change in the topic of conversation. As he walked around behind her chair, he collected himself. When he was out of her line of sight, he mouthed "Sorry" to Calvin.

When he reached Calvin's side, he rested his right hand on Calvin's left shoulder and cleared his throat. "Aunt Virginia, this is Mister Calvin Chadwick. He's the new administrator for my foundation. He's been working closely with me for a month now, and he's made tremendous strides in streamlining our distribution processes and expanding the operation."

"A worthy endeavor I am sure," she commented, then to Calvin, "A pleasure, Mister Chadwick," as she looked him up and down.

"Oh, the pleasure's all mine, Miss Virginny," Calvin said with a smile.

Virginia stiffened. Reggie began to pat Calvin on the shoulder. Misinterpreting his pats as confirmation, Calvin continued. "Ya know, Miss Virginny, yer voice reminds me of a character from a movie I watched when I was a kid—ain't seen it in years—Aunty Shrew from *The Secret of NIMH*. She had a good heart like I suspects you do. A sharp tongue, too..." Reggie's patting became desperate. "But a good heart, nonetheless."

Virginia huffed and puffed, raising herself up to nearly twice her size. "Well I never!" She shouted as she struck the table with both hands so sharply, the china and silverware rattled and the crystal fell over.

"Virginny you call me! Shrew you say! Reginald, who is this rogue, this heathen, you've brought into our home? We have our family to consider, our standing within the community. The scandal this could cause, the outrage among the foundation's benefactors.

"I imagine your *entertaining*," she emphasized the word, "means what it has always meant. Did you not consider how such an involvement, with such a *peasant*, could ruin our reputation? And now you have involved this *rube* with the foundation?"

****

No one noticed the doors from the kitchen begin to bulge outward. Hearing Calvin's voice and then the shrill voice of a human female, Roscoe launched from her bed where Miss Honey was keeping her and Cinders quiet in order to protect her master. Cinders followed on her heels.

****

As Virginia's onslaught of insults continued, Calvin froze in his chair. He looked up at Reggie, who also stood frozen in place. "Reggie?" Calvin said meekly. "What'd I do?"

Virginia was on a roll. "Who is this foulmouthed degenerate, this bumpkin, Reginald?"

Reggie's voice strained. "Aunt Virginia, please."

"Virginny indeed!" She pounded her fists against the table again. "The insult! This further proves your immaturity, you lack of discretion, particularly where the foundation is concerned. Such behavior has no place at its head. I will call a special meeting. I will have you removed..."

****

The kitchen doors pressed open. When Roscoe squeezed through, Cinders leapt over her head, and together they raced toward the commotion, barking, hissing, and caterwauling all the way. As Cinders flew to the tabletop, Roscoe jumped to Reggie's chair, then onto the table to meet up with her adopted son, but their momentum kept them going, and they slid along the tablecloth crashing through place settings and platters, right past the screaming human.

"Saints preserve us!" Virginia screamed.

As Roscoe and Cinders turned around, the

tablecloth slid beneath their paws, as they tried to get traction. Silverware flew and dishes crashed to the floor until both were perched at the table's edge in front of the hysterical human female, barking and hissing up a storm.

While Calvin launched over the table to grab them, Peabody climbed up Virginia's chest, peeing all the way as she tried to push him down to her lap. Unfortunately, once she got ahold of him, she instinctively used him as a shield in front of her face, but Peabody hadn't quite finished. His golden stream sprayed into each and every orifice and crevice in its path.

By the time Miss Honey reached the dining room it was nearly over, but she bore witness to the conclusion.

As Calvin reached his charges, Virginia sprang up from her seat and ran from the dining room, screaming and flailing her arms in the air like one of those inflatable figures that whips back and forth at a roadside establishment.

Peabody followed close behind, yipping all the way.

Chapter Twenty-One
Caught in a Lie

Reggie's office, the following morning

Miss Honey sat in a chair facing Reggie's desk while Calvin sat beside her in another. Their faces were drawn tight, their expressions dour. Reggie drummed his fingers on his desk. No one spoke.

A knock on the door brought Dudley into the mix. Reggie waved him to a third chair. "Thank you for coming, Dudley."

"Certainly, Master Reggie, I'm always at your disposal."

"I'm sorry to involve you in all of this, because I know you really aren't involved at all, and I know this will sound strange, but I need to know whether you know anything about my aunt's encounter with a rattlesnake yesterday. It's very important. The future of the foundation depends on this."

"I see," Dudley answered solemnly.

"What can you tell me?"

"Certainly, sir. On the way from the airport last evening, your aunt related an incident where she spied a snake while she was shopping for artwork."

"That's it? She saw a snake?"

"That was her accounting to me, sir."

"What about Peabody, the brave who saved him, the machete, the child?"

"They seemed to be insignificant, sir, and there was no mention of a machete, as I recall."

"I apologize, Dudley. Can you please tell me what she said … exactly?"

"I believe so sir. She was in Arizona, shopping for artwork, I believe, but she wasn't able to get the artist to come down to her price. As she was leaving the artist's studio, she encountered a young Native American girl. The child tried to sell her a beaded necklace, but your aunt wasn't interested. Apparently, the child's pleading was quite incessant, and she began to tug on Miss Virginia's skirt. To get the child to stop, she relented and purchased the necklace."

"What about Peabody? What happened to Peabody?"

"Oh, yes, she mentioned she had to put him down to reach into her pocketbook for twenty dollars. When she did, he ran out of the studio. She said she called after him, but he didn't come back.

"When she reached the doorway, an elderly gentleman was holding the dog. She told him the dog was hers and asked him to return Peabody to her. Then she handed the gentleman a five-dollar bill for his trouble."

"So she was holding Peabody the whole time except for when he first ran out of the studio?"

"She did mention that she had to put him on the ground a second time to get the money for the gentleman, and as she did, she heard a sound coming from a rock garden.

"When Peabody began to bark at the sound, she turned toward it and realized it was coming from a snake. As she picked Peabody up, she asked the gentleman what it was. He told her … now what was it called? It had diamond in the name … a diamond, diamond. A Western Diamondback, that's it.

"The man told her to keep a hold of Peabody, because a bite from that kind of snake could kill him in minutes. She said she found that to be disconcerting, so she decided to end her shopping trip and return to her hotel.

"From her recounting of the incident, I was

perplexed by her … shall we say, unsettled mood."

"That's it? That's everything?

"To the best of my knowledge, sir."

"Did she say whether Peabody encountered the snake directly?"

"No, sir, it's as I told you."

"Did she happen to mention anything about arriving here early?"

"Yes, sir, briefly. She told me seeing the snake and then learning it was poisonous caused her some trepidation, so much so, she decided she didn't want to stay in a state where such creatures were permitted. It upset her greatly when the hotel concierge was unable to change her flight to an earlier one."

"So that's why she chartered a private jet? Because she was upset she saw a snake?"

"Sir, the more she spoke of the incident, the more agitated she became. I did my best to steer the conversation elsewhere, but it was to no avail. She eventually became so worked up, she raised the window between us and rode the remainder of the time in silence."

Reggie looked between Calvin and Miss Honey, then back to Dudley. "I see. Thank you, Dudley, you've been very helpful."

"As always, my pleasure, sir."

****

"I told you, Miss Honey," Reggie said, after Dudley left. "I told you something wasn't right about her story."

Miss Honey nodded. "And you were right, Reggie. I'm sorry you had to go through that. I'm sorry for the both of you," she said turning to Calvin.

Calvin shrugged. "It don't … sorry, doesn't change the facts of what happened with Roscoe and

Cinders."

"No, it doesn't," Reggie said, supportively, "but none of that would have happened if she hadn't become so agitated ... and lied ... if she hadn't arrived early ... if she hadn't booked a private jet!"

Calvin shook his head. "Facts are facts, Reggie. Can't change what happened. And there I went, soundin' like a yokel from Appalachia. It's as much my fault as it is hers."

Reggie looked kindly at his lover. "You were nervous, Calvin. You were overwhelmed and intimidated by her. Many people are. She can be a real—"

"Reggie," Miss Honey warned, cutting him off.

"Witch!" he exclaimed.

"Reggie," Miss Honey continued, "that kind of attitude will not resolve anything. The question is, what do we do about it? How do we fix this?"

"Well the first thing I'm going to do is confront her about her lie. It's her fault, all of it. Who does she think she is, threatening the foundation, my position? It's my foundation, damn it! Her seat on the board is only honorary."

"Yes, Reggie," Miss Honey warned, "but she still has friends, powerful friends on the board."

"I don't believe she still wields that kind of power. Not anymore."

"Perhaps not," Miss Honey said softly, "but given the right circumstances, she can influence donors, give the foundation a bad name, you and Calvin bad names. It only takes one sympathetic ear to start sour gossip. You don't want to allow that to happen."

"What's in it for her?" Calvin asked. "What does she want? Everybody wants somethin'. What would make her happy?"

"Being the center of attention," Reggie scoffed.

"That's always made her happy."

"So how do we make her the center of attention without it costin' anything important?"

Reggie's eyes widened. A look of astonishment spread across his face. He jumped up from behind his desk. "Calvin! You're a genius!"

"I am?"

"Yes! We'll throw a charity event!"

"That sounds wonderful," Miss Honey said.

"Yes, we'll have a dinner, a charity dinner for the foundation.'"'

"Better yet, Reggie," Miss Honey offered, "a ball, what about throwing a charity ball?"

Reggie sat back down. "That could be pricy, Miss Honey."

"Not if it's done right, Reggie." Miss Honey smiled, slowly. "Have it here. Open up the estate. The grand ballroom hasn't been used properly in years. Make it by invitation only, with a pricey, two-tiered donation initiative to accompany acceptance. You know the greater the cost, the more exclusive it must be..."

Reggie stood up and began to pace behind his desk. "And the more exclusive it is, the greater the prestige of attendance."

Miss Honey stood. "And the greater the prestige, the more the wealthy will clamor for an invitation!"

Calvin stood up. "Hell's bells, you got your answer, Reggie!"

The three of them began to jump up and down and high-five each other.

Once they calmed down, Calvin raised a finger. "So how do we make Aunt Virginia the center of attention?"

"Trust me," Reggie said, "she'll make herself the center of attention.

Miss Honey leaned forward. "Yes, Reggie, she'll draw attention to herself, but how do we ensure she remains the center of attention?"

Everyone became quiet, and then Calvin smiled. "I know." He paused.

Reggie grew impatient. "Out with it, Calvin!"

"You really don't know, do you?" he answered. Calvin smiled like the Cheshire cat, extending the pause until the others began to fidget. "We hold it in her honor, fer her years of service to the foundation."

"Calvin!" Reggie exclaimed, "You're a genius, twice over!"

Miss Honey clapped her hands. "Calvin, that's a wonderful idea! She'll be beside herself. Oh, you are brilliant! You are so brilliant!"

"The names of the upper tier donors could appear in high relief immediately below a bronze bust of her that will be commissioned. The names of lower tier donors would appear in bas-relief, further down."

Reggie walked around his desk and placed his hands on Miss Honey's shoulders. "Yes, a bust, and it will be displayed in the lobby of the foundation headquarters." He kissed her forehead.

"Okay." Reggie pressed his hands down through the air, indicating for everyone to sit down. "First things first. Before we can begin any preparations, I must confront her about her lie … and how she treated Calvin."

"Careful, Reggie," Miss Honey cautioned. "She must be treated delicately. Perhaps you should drop it."

"No, Miss Honey, it must be done immediately and directly. I need to inform her that I know the truth, that she was wrong, and I must convince her to make amends."

"That's a tall order," Miss Honey said.

"It's okay, Reggie," Calvin added. "Don't go 'n do nothin' on my account. It was my fault after all. I wasn't at my best. Neither were Roscoe and Cinders."

"She's the one who was wrong, Miss Honey, and no, Calvin, she started this whole thing. You're important to the foundation, but more importantly, you're important to me. She's going to have to accept that."

"Warts n' all?" Calvin asked.

"Yes, Calvin, warts and all."

"It will be her word against Dudley's, Reggie." Miss Honey said. "You mustn't put him in such a position."

"Don't worry, Miss Honey, Dudley will be safe. I'll put Mister Tasker on it, and I won't make a move until he confirms what Dudley told us."

****

Virginia Scottsdale's suite, the same afternoon

Tapping a foot on the floor, telephone to her ear, Virginia sat in her chair with Peabody in her lap, looking out an immense window with diamond-cut, leaded panes. Mumbling to herself, she dialed the number.

"Who does he think he is, bringing that bushwhacker into our home? Me, always me, but who is left to be tasked with saving this family? Well, I'll do it, I tell you, Peabody, I'll save him from himself, just as I always…"

"Rutledge Investigations. How may I direct your call?"

"Bartholomew, please. Tell him Virginia Scottsdale is on the line."

"Right away, Miss Scottsdale."

After a moment a voice came on. *"Virginia, my dear! Wonderful to hear from you! How can I help?"*

"Bartholomew, I'd like you to look into something for me, actually a someone."

"Hasn't the family been using Wallace Tasker?"

"The family? Yes, I presume, however, I cannot be certain Reginald would not learn of my query from him. This is personal—for my ears only. Understand?"

"Yes, certainly, my dear. Now who is this person you'd like me to investigate?"

"One Calvin Chadwick."

"I'm not familiar with the family. Who is he?"

"I doubt anyone we know would be familiar with the name. He is a lowlife, ill-bred scoundrel, and Reginald has gotten himself entwined with him!"

"Entwined as in…"

"Yes, entwined!

"I see. For how long?"

"I cannot be certain, but Reginald now has him working for the foundation. Reginald has put him in charge!"

"When did this happen?"

"Sometime before I returned from my travels, but I have heard the staff talking. Several weeks at least."

"Good. Then it shouldn't be too difficult to identify him. All his particulars will be on file."

"With discretion, Bartholomew, it must be with the utmost discretion."

"Always. How deep do you want me to dig?"

"To China if you must! I want everything you can learn about him—his history, his family—everything. My family's reputation is at stake."

"Consider it done, Virginia. I will provide you with a thorough accounting of his entire life's story. You know you can always count on me."

"Yes, I do. We go back a long way, Bartholomew. Our families have known each other for generations. That is why I am calling you."

"I should have something for you in a few days."

"Thank you, my old friend. I'll wait to hear from you, Ta-ta!"

Chapter Twenty-Two
Extending an Olive Branch

Reggie's office, two days later

"Aunt Virginia?" Reggie said into the phone. "We need to talk."

"I have nothing to say to you, Reginald."

"You've threatened the foundation, and you've threatened me. That warrants a conversation."

"Nothing! Absolutely Nothing!"

"I know your story about the snake, about Peabody, about everything is untrue, Aunt Virginia, and I have the proof to back it up."

"Reginald Montgomery Scottsdale, how dare you accuse me of such a thing!"

"Look, I don't want a fight with you, Aunt Virginia, but I'll give you one if the foundation, my life's work is at stake. I promised Mother I'd carry on her mission, and I mean to keep that promise!"

The other end of the line went quiet.

"Aunt Virginia? Are you still there?"

There was no reply.

"Aunt Virginia?"

"Yes ... Yes, your mother, my dear, dear friend, my Penny. I forgot. I forgot that it was she who started it all."

"Will you talk then?"

"Yes, for the sake of your mother's memory, I will speak with you, Reginald, but I warn you…"

"Thank you, Aunt Virginia. I'll be there in five minutes. Goodbye."

Reggie hung up the phone.

"Reginald? Reginald, I am not finished. Reginald? Reginald! Oh, damn that boy!"

****

Perky, a short, portly, middle-aged woman with graying strawberry blonde hair, woven into a bun, knocked on the door to the sitting room. She was the primary household staff member whose duty it was to serve as Miss Virginia's lady's maid whenever she visited. "Miss Virginia, Master Reginald is here."

Virginia lifted Peabody from her lap and placed him on a plushily stuffed-stool beside her, then smoothed her gown as she rose from her chair beside the leaded, diamond-paned window. "You may show him in, Perky."

"Yes, ma'am. Right away."

When Reggie entered, his aunt was standing askance to him in front of the window, overlooking the snow-covered flower garden. "Your mother planted that garden, Reginald." She nodded below, as she saw him approach from the corner of her eye.

"Yes, Aunt Virginia, I know. I helped her many times when she worked in it."

"I know you did. You were always a good boy, Reginald. What happened to you?"

"Really, Aunt Virginia, is that how you want to begin … with a deprecatory comment?"

"I have no other option. You have as much as called me a liar. And now you say you have proof, as if you have had me investigated, like a criminal."

"Before you paint yourself into a corner any further, Aunt Virginia, I'm going to show you the courtesy of offering you the opportunity to retract your prior statement."

"Retract you say! Retract? I am owed an apology!"

Reggie's ears began to burn as blood rushed into them. He realized he would need to extend the first olive branch. "Very well, I'm sorry you were frightened by your encounter with Calvin, Roscoe, and Cinders, but that doesn't excuse…"

"*That* is a beginning. What kind of names are Roscoe and Cinders? They're the names given to mongrels … mongrels I say, and in this house! And who is this Calvin person? Dudley informed me you were *entertaining* for the evening. Does that mean what I think it means? Satisfying your carnal needs … and with such a cretin?"

The veins in Reggie's neck stood out. "Don't you dare call him that!"

Peabody began to growl.

"He is unrefined … a foul-mouthed, ignorant, commoner. Shrew! Shrew indeed!"

"He was intimidated by you. He meant no disrespect."

"Intimidated? By me? Indeed! Is it not enough you donate vast sums to the downtrodden? Is it not enough you mingle with them at the … what are they called … shelters? Obviously not! Now you bring them here, into our home?"

Reggie splayed his fingers as he waved his arms outward, like an umpire declaring a runner safe. "Enough!" he shouted. "Sit down, Aunt Virginia, or I'll cut your visit short."

Peabody's growling intensified.

"You? You would throw me out … like the help? You would not dare!"

"I swear to you." There was steel in Reggie's voice. Then to Peabody, "Shut up, Peabody, or I swear I'll…" Peabody cowered.

"Don't you dare speak to Peabody in that tone!" Virginia began to tremble as she reached for the chair's back.

Reggie raised his right hand and pointed his index finger. "I'll have you packed up and on your way so fast it will make your head spin."

Virginia recoiled at Reggie's rage, as if she'd been struck.

Reggie's fury grew. "This is my home! *My* home now! Don't forget, that! I control the family accounts. I administer your trust fund."

Virginia drew the back of her hand to her mouth.

Reggie continued his barrage. "I'll not have you insult who and what I hold dear, not in my home. Not now. Not ever! Now sit down!"

Virginia faltered as she landed in her chair with a thump.

Reggie's breathing became ragged. He pounded his fist onto the back of the high-backed stuffed chair that was facing his aunt. "Damn you! Damn you for angering me so. I came here to make amends. Now look at what you've done to me!"

"Reginald, I…"

"Save it! Don't speak! Just listen!" Reggie grabbed hold of the back of the chair to steady himself as he tried to regulate his breathing. Once he'd calmed down enough, he sat down in it, across a small table from her.

"After an extensive and costly investigation, I have received an accounting, with sworn statements, of what was witnessed during your shopping trip."

With steel in her eyes, Virginia collected herself as she stared across the table at her nephew, but there was also fear there. "You actually had me investigated? Me?" She thought about her conversation with Bartholomew just that morning. *Damn you, Bartholomew. Why must you be so thorough? If only you had found something scathing, some treachery committed to counter with.* Unsatisfied with the dossier he had assembled on Calvin, she had instructed him to dig deeper.

"Do you care to comment?"

Virginia looked down. She was a skilled swordswoman who realized she would need to be cautious until she learned what her nephew had discovered. "No," she said calmly as she motioned Peabody to her lap. She closed her eyes and envisioned the conversation going in a different direction. *Not yet, my boy,* she thought, *but soon, very, very soon—just as soon as Bartholomew uncovers something.*

Reggie continued. "Peabody never encountered a snake. There was no rescue of him. No snake was ever killed. There was never a threat to Peabody's or to your life. And there was no machete."

"Yes, there was!" she answered with a quiver in her voice, "The man who held Peabody had one. It hung from his belt. It extended to below his knee!"

"That may be, but the rest … the rest, Aunt Virginia?"

She hesitated as she began to frantically pet Peabody. Peabody yelped. She'd been caught. She knew it, and so did Reggie. He'd discovered the truth. She reviewed her options and realized she was backed into a corner and had nothing to counter with. After a long pause, she spoke.

"Manufactured." She looked down and to her left, avoiding eye contact with him. "I'm sorry, Reginald. I don't know what came over me."

Reggie exhaled as the tension began to drain out of him. "Why? Can you at least tell me why?"

"I became frightened. I panicked. My imagination ran away with me. Then, after I was in the air, after the concierge had chartered the private jet, I felt foolish. I knew you would be angry about the expense, but everything I told you, everything I said were things I saw happening. I must have conjured them in my mind."

"Good grief, Aunt Virginia!"

"I know, Reginald, I know. I'm sorry."

"Do you understand what you've done? How your actions and words have affected Calvin?"

"How could I? I didn't know ... don't know him."

"I realize he's of a different class, from a different background than you, from both of us, but he's a good man..."

Reggie had presented an opportunity for Virginia to riposte, and she saw took it. "Good or not, Reginald, our family's reputation is at stake. I think sometimes you forget that."

"I don't care about our family's reputation!"

"Obviously," she said in a measured tone. "But I do and thank goodness for that. Someone must. Otherwise this family's world would devolve into anarchy."

"Why are you so worried about our reputation? Only two generations back, my grandfather was a homeless man. If it wasn't for a chance encounter with great-grandmother..."

"That is *your* family's history, Reginald, on your mother's side. It is not mine."

"How dare you! How many times have you referred to my mother as your 'dear friend'? Was that ever true?"

"Yes, of course she was, but that is not the point. By birth, you carry the Scottsdale name. That means something."

"Don't be a hypocrite! If Mother was good enough to marry into this family, why isn't Calvin?"

"Marry? Marry you say? You wish to marry this man?"

"No, I was not implying that. I was trying to make a point. Mother did not come from an aristocratic background, yet she was your dearest friend. You're talking out of both sides of your mouth."

"Do not be vulgar, Reginald. Your mother came to boarding school from another state. Nothing was known of her background for some time, and by the time I had grown to love her, it was already too late, so none of it mattered anymore."

"Yet you still introduced her to Father."

"Of course I did. By then we had been school chums for two years. She had transcended her circumstances. She was quite extraordinary.

"When I brought her here, to this home, to spend the summer, I knew everything there was to know about her. Her family had done quite well, but even more so, Penny was a unique and remarkable girl in her own right. Regardless of any of that, it was all a moot point, because your father fell head over heels in love with her."

"That may be, Aunt Virginia, but if you hadn't brought her, they never would have met. If you had learned of her history, before you became friends, would it have ever happened?"

"Who is to say?"

"It's the same where Calvin is concerned. You just don't know him. He is a good man, a kind man, who has sacrificed for his dog and cat. He's served and sacrificed for his country, in the military, overseas, and his country dismissed him as if he was rubbish, for something he cannot help."

"Oh, I see."

"He's made great strides in redirecting the foundation onto a path that will accomplish so much more than I was ever able to accomplish when I was running things. I've practically turned the reins over to him."

"So you have implied. What is it about him? What has attracted you to him?"

"It's a long story, Aunt Virginia."

****

Virginia couldn't have cared one way or the other about whether her nephew was having carnal relations with another man. That was not an issue. It had been a pattern followed by some members of the family, for generations, both male and female, and it rarely skipped one.

Though Reginald didn't know it, his father, Montgomery, was a perfect example. Despite his indiscretions, at least Montgomery had the good sense to honor his family obligations and marry so he could produce an heir and carry on the family name and in truth, he really did love Penny.

Eventually, Penny discovered her husband was bisexual when she found him in bed with another man, but she never pushed Virginia to learn how long she had known. Though she had accepted who he was, from that day forward, Penny took a separate bedroom, never bedding Montgomery again.

Montgomery knew better than to protest. He remained faithful to her in that he never lay with another woman, but he also took solace in her rejection because it allowed him to engage freely with men, his preference, once again.

In public, and in the presence of their son, they lived out the remainder of their lives as a happily married couple, but privately, though they inhabited the same home, they lived separate lives. Until her death, and though she offered an easy smile, there was always sorrow behind Penny's eyes.

Regardless of the pain Montgomery had caused

his wife, Virginia still loved her brother dearly, for he had been her protector and her champion her entire life. It never became more evident than when he shielded his younger sister from the wrath of their father, Everett, once it was realized she would never acquire a husband and by doing so, expand the reach of the family dynasty.

Early on, while courting, her first few suitors left her high and dry, once she revealed her inability to bear children, but only their mother and father knew the true reason. While away at school, Virginia had been raped and became pregnant. The ensuing botched abortion she'd secretly undertaken at the insistence of Everett—in order to save the family the disgrace of a child conceived in such a way and out of wedlock—destroyed her womb, preventing her from ever conceiving, let alone carrying a pregnancy to term. Once word got around, her prospects dried up, and she accepted her fate to become a spinster.

Everett refused to take responsibility for her barren womb, even though it was he who had forced her into the abortion. He chastised her for revealing the truth about her inability to conceive, but Virginia could not enter into marriage with such a lie hanging over her head. In those days, little was known about reproductive difficulties, and Everett had said as much, insisting her inability to conceive might have been accepted as fate and nothing more.

As a consequence for her betrayal to the family, as he saw it, Everett nearly disowned her, changing his will to ensure she would be left with practically nothing, but Montgomery had protected her. He'd secretly taken her under his wing until their father's death, and he continued to provide for her after his own death by creating a trust fund in her name.

****

With Reginald, there were two issues to consider,

the most important, but not presently urgent was an heir. The other was immediate, this Calvin person, his breeding, his background, what social status he held and how it would affect her nephew because what affected Reginald reflected on the family. She'd already sacrificed too much for the family name. She would not allow it to be destroyed, not for love, not for money, not for anything.

There was nothing in the dossier Bartholomew had assembled on Calvin that revealed any promise for a viable future between him and her nephew. He simply didn't have the necessary breeding. Reginald's love interest might be of service to the foundation, and that was important to him. It and his writing gave him purpose, but compared to the future of the family, they were insignificant.

How to get her nephew to focus on producing an heir would take some doing, but with the right leverage and the right incentives, she believed she could manipulate him to not only achieve that, but also be done with Calvin.

Thanks to Bartholomew's reputation for thoroughness, she believed she might yet still have cards to play, if necessary, and she'd hold them close until the time was right to play them. There were many games she'd mastered over the years. For the time being, she'd go along with Reginald's game, and as unlikely as it might be, the family could still gain something from it.

More might yet be learned about this man from Reginald himself. She would give her nephew every opportunity to provide her with the ammunition she could bring to bear against Calvin in some future battle.

****

"I have the entire afternoon, Reginald. If this man is so important to you, I think I should know everything there is to know about him."

"Then settle in, Aunt Virginia. There's much to tell."

"One moment." Virginia lifted a finger, and then she rang a small bell on the table.

Geraldine appeared a moment later. "Yes, Miss Virginia?"

"Where is Perky? Oh, never mind. Please tell Miss Honey we'll be taking tea … high tea, with all the trimmings."

"Yes, Miss Virginia, right away."

Virginia looked across at her nephew. "Proceed, Reginald."

Chapter Twenty-Three
Amends

Calvin's suite

"Guess who's coming to dinner?" Reggie announced after knocking and entering Calvin's suite. At Reggie's voice, Roscoe began to bark and Cinders bounded ahead as the two ran to meet him.

"Huh?" Calvin said, rising from the sofa with a confused look on his face. "Who?"

"Aunt Virginia, that's who."

Calvin stood up from the sofa. "How? Why? What happened?"

Reggie walked to Calvin and pulled him into his arms. "Do you want the long or short version?"

"It don't matter. Whichever one works best."

Reggie leaned in for a kiss, then pulled away. "It got ugly at first, but eventually I confronted her. When she realized I knew everything, she capitulated, admitted it was all fabricated."

"But why? Why would she do that?"

"She became scared, and then her imagination ran away with her. She made it all up. It's happened before. Everything she told us was a lie, based on hysterical delusions."

"And how was she after all that?"

"We had tea."

"Tea?"

"Yes, a formal, high tea with finger sandwiches and scones and tarts, baked brie with preserves, in other words, the works."

"Like them British do?"

"Exactly."

"From where? How? I seen them on TV. There's a lot of stuff to 'em."

"Miss Honey, of course. She serves an abbreviated version of high tea to her every afternoon. I imagine she just went the extra mile."

"No wonder you been gone so long."

"And now she's joining us for dinner."

"Oh, Reggie, I don't know about *us*. I'm likely t' put my foot in it again. You know what happened the first time. You go by yourself. You don't want a repeat."

"It's all good, Calvin. I've told her all about you, how we met, about Roscoe and Cinders, and an abbreviated version of your story, only enough for her to get a general idea of what you've faced, and I've told her what you're doing now with the foundation."

"And she still wants to meet me, proper like?"

"Of course! There were actually tears in her eyes when I related how you found Roscoe and how Roscoe rescued Cinders."

"Well, I'll be."

"I'm so happy right now, Calvin, and I'm so horny for you. I want you to make love to me."

"Damn, boy, you sure do change gears mighty fast!"

"Sorry, I can't help it. I'm so hard right now I feel like my cock will break if you don't."

Calvin reached down and ran his open palm up and down along the bulge in Reggie's pants. "I see what you mean. You poor man. You got yerself a problem."

"And you're the only one who can take care of it," Reggie said as he thrust his hips forward."

Calvin narrowed his eyes and bared his teeth, smiling wickedly. "Then I'll do my best." He dropped to his knees and pulled down Reggie's fly. As he reached in and slid down the elastic of the boxers, Reggie's cock pushed its way out.

Calvin leaned in and ran his tongue around the

head, then flicked it upward across the spread lips of the slit, drawing the bead of pre-cum that was forming there to his tongue.

"Mmm," he moaned as he savored its salty, muskiness across his taste buds. "Like the nectar of the gods, Reggie, boy. Like the nectar of the gods."

Calvin slid forward, past the ridge of the head, just to the shaft and back again, concentrating pressure on the sensitive region, over and over again. Reggie's head fell back as guttural noises emanated from his throat. "Fuck," he moaned as he began to lick his lips.

When Calvin looked up, Reggie was unbuckling his belt, and then his pants dropped to the floor when he undid the top button. He moved his hands beneath his shirt and began to tweak his nipples between his fingertips. "Just like that, Calvin," Reggie groaned. "Yeah, suck me just like that."

As Calvin slid his mouth along the shaft, taking the head to the back of his throat, he reached behind with both hands and began to knead the firm globes of Reggie's buttocks. Reggie's knees began to buckle when Calvin's fingertips pulled his cheeks apart and began to graze up and down, along the cleft, but he righted himself at the last moment. When Calvin's fingertips circled his twitching hole the first time, he stumbled forward, but Calvin caught him and steadied him.

"'Bout time we get you into the bedroom, buddy-boy," Calvin said as he pulled his mouth away, "before you go and hurt yourself."

"As much as I want you to ravage me, let me take a quick shower," Reggie said as he looked down into Calvin's eyes. "Then you can fuck me proper."

Calvin leered up at him. "Oh, baby, I'm a gonna fuck ya more 'n proper! And I ain't lettin' you outta my sight. I'm gonna soap you up and tease ya int' a frenzy afore I take ya t' bed. Then I'ma gonna make such sweet love t' ya, I'm gonna make ya cry!"

"Then what are we waiting for?" Reggie answered as he reached down and took Calvin's hand, pulling him up, before leading him into the bedroom.

****

Calvin adjusted the spray of water in the shower and opened a jar of lube as he waited for Reggie to finish using the bidet attachment. Once they were together, he focused his attention on Reggie's semi-erection, bringing it back to life in seconds as warm water cascaded down around them. Reggie spread his legs wide apart, allowing unrestricted access to the recesses of his body, and Calvin took advantage of it.

He reached for a bar of scented soap, then slicked his lover's hole and began to open him up with his lubed fingers. Reggie moaned as Calvin worked the first of several fingers through the outer, then inner circular muscles. Reggie grunted and curled his toes the moment he passed through the opening. Calvin advanced immediately to reach his sensitive spot and began to stroke the firm orb, making it grow harder and harder.

At first contact, Reggie cried out in ecstasy as his hips thrust forward. When Calvin drew one ball, followed by the other into his mouth, Reggie reached down and began to stroke his shaft, bringing himself up to the precipice of release in less than a minute.

Suddenly, Calvin stopped, causing Reggie to shout out in dismay. "Why'd you stop? Fuck! I'm so close, so fucking close. Please!" he pleaded, "Please take me over the edge."

"On yer knees, boy!" Calvin ordered. "On yer knees right now!"

Reggie staggered forward, grabbing onto a support bar before lowering himself to the floor, then onto all fours. He was immediately rewarded when Calvin dove in with his mouth and began to devour his ass, lapping and sucking at the still open hole, as he inhaled and tasted the muskiness there.

As Calvin continued to feast on the sensitive tissues that led to Reggie's treasure trove, he reached around and grabbed his lover's shaft and began to gently caress across the turgid veins that snaked along its length, barely making contact.

"Fuck!" Reggie shouted. "Fuck! You fucking bastard! You're driving me insane! Make me come, damn you! Make me come!"

Calvin leered, then laughed. "But you said you wanted me to fuck you proper."

"Fuck what I said!" Reggie growled. "Then fuck me now! Take me now!"

"Ya don't hav'ta ask me twice!"

Calvin reached into the jar of lube, taking a handful, then began slathering it around and into Reggie's gaping hole. He finished up coating the length of his shaft with what remained and then positioned himself to enter. Slowly he teased with the head of his cock, pressing it just within the beckoning hole, then drawing it back, only to slide up and down the cleft and beneath, along the base of his lover's throbbing cock.

Reggie reached back and grabbed at the cock's shaft as he guided it to his opening. When it was in position, he thrust his hips back, forcing it deep inside him. "Now," he demanded. "Fuck my brains out, Calvin. No more of this teasing, I need to come! I need to come now!"

Without a word, Calvin grasped Reggie's shoulders and withdrew, then thrust forward in one smooth, continuous lunge, driving the length of his shaft inward until his thighs slapped against his ass, sending water droplets flying in every direction. He withdrew again, just as smoothly, until the head of his cock sat cradled within the sensitive opening, then thrust forward, repeating his assault over and over.

As he picked up speed, Calvin leaned forward and wrapped his arms around Reggie's torso, shifting the path of his cockhead to drive glancing blows along the cleft between the globes of his prostate. Then he lowered his right hand and grabbed his lover's cock tightly, drawing the stream of pre-cum that oozed from the tip along the shaft to slick the path of his hand as he began to pound his fist against Reggie's groin.

Reggie's chest dropped to the shower floor as his mind, overwhelmed by the sensations coursing through his body, began to reel. Flashes of colors passed before his eyes. Smells and tastes that weren't really there rushed past his nose and tongue, and waves of pleasure overwhelmed his brain's ability to distinguish between what he felt inside and what bombarded it from every other part of his body.

As Reggie's moans grew louder and louder, Calvin began to thrust his hips in a frenzied assault, as he pushed himself closer and closer to the edge of release. When Reggie's shaft began to spasm within his grasp, Calvin began to roll his palm around the sensitive glans, overwhelming the nerve endings there, then alternately drawing it back and forth along the shaft, pushing Reggie toward the point of no return.

****

A warmth began to spread from deep within Calvin's core as he felt fluids begin to shift deep inside himself. When his sack pulled up tight, squeezing his swollen balls against the floor of his abdomen, he began to grunt and groan as the first orgasm he'd experienced while fucking another man in years began to seethe through his entire body. His cock began to spasm as its veins snaked tightly along the shaft and the head turned purple, swelling by half its size as more blood rushed in until it could hold no more.

****

Reggie's chest lifted from the floor. His back crashed into Calvin's chest, as he rose to his knees, but Calvin held on tight as he continued to thrust his hips, finally pushing them both beyond the threshold. Then Reggie's head tilted back as the veins in his neck bulged outward and his mouth opened, but his throat clamped shut at the last moment. Silently he screamed towards the ceiling as tears streamed from his eyes.

****

A warmth began to spread through Calvin's body, then turned to a burning so hot he became drenched in sweat as he made his final lunge, driving his cock deep within Reggie's core. His shaft quivered as an orgasmic spasm overtook it when the first jet of cum seethed along its path, spraying against Reggie's turgid prostate, as it traveled its course, into his depths.

As Calvin came inside him, Reggie released the first rush of his thick, milky essence. As stream after stream of musky cum flew from both of them, Calvin cupped his palm over the end of Reggie's cock and scooped up his nectar, then drew it to his mouth. He lapped hungrily, swallowing his lover's seed greedily, then returned his hand for more. As he drew his hand up again, Reggie grabbed hold of it and pulled it to his mouth to swallow his own spunk, then turned his head and pulled Calvin's mouth to his, driving his tongue inward.

Together they sucked and slurped, consuming each other, savoring Reggie's seed as their orgasms raged. Guttural, animalistic sounds rose from deep within their chests as they moaned in ecstasy while their bodies shuddered with the passion only new lovers could experience.

****

When it was over, Reggie fell forward, catching himself at the last moment, as Calvin fell with him, but Calvin's cock refused to relent. Still turgid, it continued to spasm against Reggie's prostate, sending wave after wave of pleasure coursing through his body, causing Reggie's cock to remain just as firm as it thrust against the shower's tile floor. Overwhelmed and unable to speak, he grunted in protest at the overwhelming, painful waves of bliss until finally, Calvin's shaft began to soften and slide from him, leaving a gaping hole through which cum began to ooze.

Several minutes passed before they were able to stand. Wearily, Reggie steadied himself against the shower wall while Calvin sat on his knees as he tried to rise several times before he was able to pull himself to an upright position. Reggie drew him to himself as he wrapped his arms around his back and began to murmur words of love and gratitude.

Seeming unable to speak, Calvin smiled meekly as he looked deeply into Reggie's eyes, but his look said enough. Reggie knew what he felt because he felt the same.

****

After a time, as their strength returned, they showered again together then walked into Calvin's bedroom. Slowly and cautiously, Calvin began to dress for dinner. Once finished, they went to Reggie's suite where he dressed. For over a half hour, he coached Calvin on how he should act, move, and speak for when he met Aunt Virginia again.

Calvin was overwhelmed but determined to make

a better impression this time. As they made their way from Reggie's suite, down to the dining room, a glow radiated from both of them, the glow of post-coital bliss.

Chapter Twenty-Four
Second Impressions

The dining room

At 8:00 PM sharp, Reggie and Calvin, dressed to the nines, stood waiting by the doors that led into the dining room.

"Well," they heard, coming from the center landing, "don't you two gentlemen look handsome."

As Virginia, with Peabody in her arms, descended the staircase with her semi-precious-stone-encrusted cane hanging from her forearm, her cream-colored gown with its lace bodice, flowed behind her.

"And aren't you captivating, Aunt Virginia," Reggie said as he advanced to meet her at the bottom of the stairs. "I haven't seen you wear feathers in your hair in years."

"It's a special occasion, Reginald. I'm meeting your gentleman, and this time it will be done properly."

As Reggie escorted her to where Calvin stood at the dining room's entrance, he began to make introductions. "Aunt Virginia, this is…"

"Reginald, don't be foolish, we've already been introduced." Virginia stepped forward and extended her hand. "Calvin," she said, drawing out both syllables.

Calvin nearly swallowed his tongue as he took her hand and began to stammer. "Miss … Miss…"

Virginia went on. "It's lovely to meet you properly. Please allow me to apologize for my abhorrent poor manners and hasty retreat the other evening. I hope you can forgive me."

"Yes, ma'am," Calvin answered. "Certainly. It's … lovely, um, to meet you as well."

Reggie smiled brightly.

Calvin waved his arm through the doors. "Shall

we go in?" He lifted his arm and waited for Miss Virginia to take it. A moment later, he led her to her chair with Reggie, beaming, following close behind.

After seating her to the left of the head of the table, Calvin walked to the other side and waited for Reggie to move into position at the head, and then together, they sat down.

Virginia moved Peabody to one leg. "Where are Roscoe and Cinders this evening?" She unfolded her napkin and placed it in her lap.

"I believe they're keepin', um, keeping Miss Honey company in the kitchen, Miss Virginny, um, Virginia."

The moment the word left his mouth, Calvin turned a deep shade of red. "My apologies, ma'am," he said as he averted his eyes. He began to fiddle with his napkin, lifting it to tuck into his collar. Then recognizing his error, he abruptly lowered it to his lap.

Virginia's eyes sparkled as a look of amusement crossed her face. "Well, I must meet them soon. What trials they must have faced, that is, until they met you, Calvin. You are to be commended for how you have cared for them."

"Thank you, Miss Virginia."

She cleared her throat. "Now, about *Virginny...*"

If Reggie's chair had been without arms, he would have fallen off of it.

"I have grown, Calvin, to not be comfortable with such familiarity. Sadly, it's been lost to me for years, but I know you didn't mean any harm. There is only one person who ever called me Ginny, and that was Willie, or William to be proper, our cook's boy, when I was a child. Willie was my closest friend before I was sent away to boarding school. We did everything together.

"I never saw him again after that day. When I

returned home the first summer, I was told his family had moved on. After hearing the staff talk, I came to believe Father had sent them away in my absence. In those days, you can imagine, I'm sure, it was looked down upon for a white girl to befriend a black boy, even at our young age, and even though it was completely innocent, and we were quite young, I'm certain Father wanted to end it to avoid the possibility of any future scandal.

"I used to think of him often, but not for years now. I thank you for returning his memory to me."

"Yes, ma'am."

"Calvin?" Virginia smiled invitingly. "If you like, I will allow you to call me Virginny in private, but never in public and never in front of the staff, understand?"

"Yes, ma'am. Thank you, ma'am, but I can't see as hows I ever could again."

"Calvin, I am giving you permission."

"Yes, ma'am."

"Good. Each time you do, you'll remind me of my old, dear friend, Willie."

Through dinner, Virginia listened attentively as Calvin related his life's journey, asking pertinent questions whenever she needed clarification of a military term or any words of dialect when Calvin let them slip through. Similarly, she shared many superficial aspects of her life as she directed the conversation to ensure it never became stale until the meal was consumed. For the most part, Reggie sat back and observed, adding to the conversation only when needed.

Virginia laid down her fork. "Now, when may I meet Roscoe and Cinders?"

Reggie smiled. "When would you like to?"

"As soon as possible, of course."

"I'll go see about them," Calvin said as he began to get up.

"I'll get them, Calvin," Reggie said. "You keep Aunt Virginia company." With that, Reggie headed for the kitchen. A few minutes later he returned carrying Cinders as Roscoe walked by his side, barely taking her eyes off of the no longer kitten in his arms.

"Down, Peabody," Aunt Virginia ordered. When Peabody balked, she lifted him to the ground to her left and reached out for the cat. "You are the most handsome little fella I've ever seen," she said into Cinders's face, as she held him in front of her. "I had a gray cat when I was a girl, Calvin." She pulled the cat to her chest and began to stroke his head and neck. "Though she wasn't nearly as handsome as this fine, young man. She didn't have the lovely pattern in his coat or his dazzling golden eyes."

"Woof!"

Aunt Virginia looked down to find Roscoe sitting on the floor to her right while Peabody walked in circles, humphing, on the other side of the chair. "And look at you," she said. "Your coat has the pattern of an orca." She handed Cinders to Reggie and leaned over the chair's arm to reach down and pet Roscoe. "A lovely animal, Calvin, and so well behaved. Peabody could take lessons from her."

At the mention of his name, Peabody came running around the back of the chair and growled, then nudged Roscoe out of the way. "I'm sorry, Roscoe," she said, "Peabody has a terrible jealous streak." Roscoe disappeared beneath the table only to appear a moment later in Calvin's lap.

"In truth, Calvin, I'm glad you've brought them here. They will provide Peabody with some playmates. He bores easily, and then becomes extremely demanding. He requires all of my attention. Perhaps he will learn some patience from them."

"If you like, ma'am, I can spend some time with

'im, do some behavior trainin' with 'im," Calvin said.

"That would be wonderful, Calvin. Thank you."

"Certainly, ma'am."

"Please, call me Miss Virginia … or Virginny," she said, with a glint in her eyes.

"Yes, Miss Virginia."

Virginia lifted her napkin from her lap, folded it, then set it on the table. "I should return to my rooms. It has been years since I have had this much conversation, and I require sleep. Thank you both for a lovely, informative evening."

Reggie moved to pull out her chair. "I'll walk you up."

"That will not be necessary, Reginald. I know the way. Though I am getting old, I am not so old as to require an escort." She stood up to take her leave. "Good night." Her words carried an upward lilt.

After Reggie and Calvin stood, she made her way from the room, using her cane as more of an ornament and disappeared through the door. Reggie took a deep breath and exhaled, loudly.

"You did it, Calvin," he said, taking his lover's hand. "You've won her over!"

Calvin shook his head, doubtfully. "You sure, Reggie? I slipped up more 'n a few times."

"No, you did wonderfully. I know how to read her, and unless she was faking it, which I seriously doubt, she was impressed."

"Not likely."

"Yes, she was. You even amused her a few times, and that doesn't happen often. I could see it on her face."

"Then I'm glad. I was afeared I'd mess up somethin' fierce, 'n I didn't want t' do that on your account."

"Not at all, you held up your end of the

conversation splendidly."

****

Two days later

"You must be so pleased, Miss Virginia," Perky said as she buttoned up the back of her dinner dress.

"Pleased? Whatever do you mean?"

"Yes, about the ball."

"The ball?" *What ball?* she thought. "To which ball do you refer, my dear?"

"The ball the foundation is holding in the spring, the one in your honor. I overheard Ryan, Mister Calvin's new assistant, talking about it. It sounds like it's going to be quite extravagant. I've been here nearly fifteen years, and I've never seen the grand ballroom used."

Virginia's stomach did a somersault, and her heart nearly leapt from her throat. "Yes … quite." *A ball? In my honor?* she thought. "Though I don't believe it will be all that grand," she said, not wanting to let on she had no idea what Perky was talking about.

"Are you kidding? Ryan mentioned some of the names on the provisional invitation list—only top drawer. It's going to be quite a night. A night to remember for years!"

The silver, the crystal, the china! Virginia began to mentally take inventory. *The invitations need to be designed. The seating charts must be arranged! The photographer must be hired! The guest list, oh I must review the guest list! The wine and music! The waitstaff! There are so many things—so, so many! Reginald doesn't know the first thing about etiquette for a ball— and in my honor?*

****

After dinner was cleared from the table and dessert, a multi-layered chocolate almond torte with an orange cream filling, was served, Reggie cleared his

throat. "Aunt Virginia, there's something I'd like …
sorry," he took Calvin's hand, "we'd like to discuss with
you."

Virginia had barely made it through dinner, so
anxious she was to be told about her ball. *Here it comes*,
she thought. Her face was completely neutral, but her
heart began pounding so hard she was sure they could
see it. "Discuss?" she said as she took her first forkful of
torte. After swallowing, she replied "What would you
like to discuss, Reginald?"

"I was thinking about the foundation, about all
the good works we've done, and I thought about how you
stepped in after Mother passed away and about your
guidance over the years."

"It was the least I could do for her, my boy. She
was my dearest friend, all through school. Then when she
became my sister-in-law, well, that was simply icing on
the cake."

"Yes, I know. We've begun to consider the
hosting of a ball, an annual ball in Mother's memory, the
Penelope Turner Scottsdale Foundation, Memorial Ball,
and we'd like you to be the first inductee of honorees."

"Me? Oh, Reginald, I'm deeply touched." Tears
began to flow from her eyes. As she dabbed at them with
a handkerchief, pulled from her sleeve, she lowered her
head. "My dear Penny. My dear, dear Penny. What a
wonderful tribute to her memory. Thank you, Reginald. I
would be honored."

"Though I must give credit where credit's due,"
he said, squeezing Calvin's hand. "We were
brainstorming the other day, trying to come up with
charity events that would help to elevate the foundation
in the minds of contributors, old and new. Miss Honey
came up with the idea of a ball, and it was Calvin who
insisted you be the first honoree."

"I don't know what to say." She sniffled into her hanky as she looked at Calvin. "I'm speechless."

"We'll need your help…" Calvin hesitated. "Virginny."

Virginia's eyes twinkled as she nodded. "Yes, go on."

"If you think you're up to it. We don't know the first thing 'bout throwin' no ball, and with you being so refined 'n all, well, it seems only natural."

Though it was subtle, Reggie noticed the way his aunt's posture changed and the slightest of smiles that crept into her face. His eyes scrunched up in the corners, smiling.

"What?" Calvin asked. Then he realized what had amused Reggie. He laughed. "See, there I go again. I get all excited, and the hick slips out!"

"No, Calvin," Virginia said, smiling. "You were quite eloquent, quite eloquent indeed, and yes, I would love to help."

Though this doesn't change a thing, she thought. *There can still be no future between you and my nephew, for his sake and for the family's.*

Chapter Twenty-Five
Preparing for a Ball

Reggie's office, one week later

Ryan, a youthful looking, twenty-two-year-old and Calvin's administrative assistant, at a fit, one-hundred eighty-five-pounds, with light brown hair and dark brown eyes, stood a tanned and muscular, five-foot ten. Wearing a gray-tweed, three-piece suit that day, he knocked on the door and hurried in, minus the jacket.

"Good morning, Mister Scottsdale, sir, I'm sorry to bother you, but I have that updated list of names you asked for. Mister Chadwick said to get it to you right away."

Reggie looked up from behind his desk. As he finished typing a sentence for his current work in progress on his laptop, he smiled from his chair, as he watched the young buck hurry in. *I envy the man who gets to wrap his legs around that piece of prime meat,* he thought. *If he swings that way.* Then aloud, "Now, Ryan, we've been through this dozens of times. I know you're new here, but please call me Reggie."

Ryan blushed. "Yes, sir, Mister Reggie, sir. Those names you've been waiting for, sir, Mister Chadwick just finished putting them together."

"Here," Reggie held out his hand, "let me see them."

Ryan handed him a bound folder with several pages containing a list of names divided into three groupings. It revealed some known well to Reggie, some he was familiar with, and others of whom he had no knowledge. He rubbed his chin. "Pretty impressive list, wouldn't you say, Ryan?"

"Yes, sir. Mister Chadwick has been refining it for the past two days."

"I think Calvin must have had some help with this. I find it unlikely he knows any of the names here."

Ryan blushed. "Yes, sir."

"Did you help Calvin with this, Ryan?" Reggie asked, amused.

"Yes, sir, a little. After assembling the names of known contributors I acquired from your files, I tapped several databases, then followed up with web searches of press releases from multiple charities and offered him suggestions of new names for the list, based on their known philanthropic donations, business associations, personal income, and corporate profit statements. Mister Chadwick made the final selections himself."

"How many names did you initially provide him with?"

"Well over five hundred, sir."

"And he boiled them down to one hundred sixty-five all by himself, with no additional help?"

"Yes, sir, sort of, sir."

"Sort of?"

"Yes, sir. When he had questions, I explained who the people were, and what the numbers meant, based on what I surmised about their potential disposable income and the charitable donations they'd likely made for tax deductions, and my knowledge of the philanthropic or," Ryan made air quotes, "'good-will' charitable donations their spouses made."

"Whatever we're paying you, Ryan, it's obviously not enough."

"Yes, sir. Thank you, sir."

"I see there are three on the list who are circled. Two of them include two names and then there's a third."

"Yes, sir. One of the individuals, Jason Ackerman, is a military veteran who's also a billionaire. Mister Ackerman is the CEO of Jaron Enterprises, and

Aaron Jaeger is the president of Jaron Rehabilitative Services. They're a married couple.

"Toby Jacobson owns Jacobson Construction, and Cliff Turnbull is his husband. Jacobson Construction was the builder for Nathan's Promise, a rehab center in Idaho, operated by Jaron Rehabilitative Services.

"The last name is Doctor Conrad Tolbert. I found your name associated with all three on the list during my research. Based on what I told Mister Chadwick, he thought they might be more than interested in supporting the foundation."

"He was right. I've had dealings with both couples, and I've met the doctor. I visited them a while back when I flew out to offer my support for the rehab center. Its mission is to serve injured and disabled LGBTQ law enforcement and military veterans and professional and amateur athletes, but it also accepts straight members from those groups. All care and services were provided free of charge. Doctor Tolbert was the medical director for the center.

"As I understood it at the time," Reggie continued, "they planned to branch out nationwide, but I don't know how far they've progressed."

"Sir, from what I've been able to ascertain, they have, and recently they've surveyed dozens more sites, several of which are here on the East Coast."

Reggie leaned back in his chair. "Then they've moved forward quite nicely."

"Yes, sir."

"I'll talk to Calvin about the list myself, and I'd like another copy for Aunt Virginia. She'll be much better at enticing the names in the first group to attend. We should try to narrow the total down to one-hundred invitations. The ballroom can accommodate just over two-hundred guests, as can the dining room. I'd prefer to hold it here, and that number will be perfect.

"If we go too far over, we'll need to rent a venue somewhere else, and that would significantly cut into any profit generated by the event."

"Yes, sir, from what I've seen of the rooms, that number sounds about right. Here is the extra copy." Ryan placed a second bound copy on Reggie's desk. "Miss Virginia," he made air quotes again, "*stopped in* several times to offer suggestions of several dozen names, some of which I had not found myself. I thought she might want her own copy."

"There's one thing you'll learn about Aunt Virginia, she knows all the ins and outs of high-society. We'd do well to give her free rein where they're concerned."

"Agreed, sir. She's … I don't mean to seem indelicate, sir."

"Speak your mind, Ryan. You've earned it."

"Well, sir, she's a force to be reckoned with. A good force, but a force nonetheless."

Reggie laughed out loud. "Your powers of observation are dead on, Ryan, dead on."

"Yes, sir. Thank you, sir."

"I'll give the additional copy to my aunt at dinner this evening. Good work on the invitation list, Ryan. Now, if you'll excuse me, I have some of my own work to finish." Reggie returned his attention to his laptop and began to read the last paragraph he'd written in his manuscript.

"Certainly, sir. Thank you. Oh, there was one other thing."

Reggie stopped reading and looked up. "What's that?"

"A Mister Wallace Tasker left a message asking you to return his call at your convenience."

"Thank you, Ryan. I'll take care of it." Reggie turned his chair toward the phone on his desk.

"Very good, sir."

After Ryan had left, Reggie placed the call.

"Wallace Tasker, at your service."

"Wallace? Reggie Scottsdale returning your call."

"Thanks for getting back to me, Reggie. I have some bad news."

"Bad? What's happened?"

Perhaps disturbing would be more accurate. I've lost contact with Calvin's sister, Eloise."

"Lost? In what way?"

"I haven't been able to reach her. The service for her number has been terminated. I checked, and it turns out it was a disposable cell phone so I had no way to trace its origin. I'm so sorry."

"On no, Calvin will be so upset."

"I'll keep working on it, Reggie. It may take some time for me to pick up the trail again, but please know I will find her, eventually."

"Thank you, Wallace. I don't know how I'm going to break this to Calvin."

"I'm sorry, Reggie."

"I know it's not your fault. It's just a damn shame, that's all."

"Yes. People who don't want to be found have all the advantage. I just don't understand it. She seemed to be so excited at the idea of a reunion. Something must have happened, but what, I have no idea."

"You're probably right. I just hope we can get this all straightened out."

"I'm sure we will, sooner or later."

"I hope you're right. Thanks, Wallace."

"I'd usually say, 'my pleasure,' but in this case..."

"I know. We'll wait to hear from you, Wallace. Again, thank you."

"Right. Well, bye for now."

"Good bye, Wallace."

After Reggie hung up the phone, he called Calvin, asking him to come to his office, and then he moved to take a seat at the coffee table. A moment later, Calvin came in and walked toward him.

"What's wrong, Reggie? Are you okay? You look like your world's come to an end."

How am I going to tell him? Reggie thought. He looked into his lover's eyes and saw only concern. "Sit down, Calvin. I'm afraid I have something to tell you, and it's not good."

****

Virginia Scottsdale's suite, later that morning

Virginia reached for the ringing telephone. "Hello?"

"Hello, Virginia. Have you had time yet to review my latest correspondence? I sent it by courier early yesterday afternoon."

"Yes, Bartholomew, I received the updated dossier, though unless I missed something, I could find nothing incriminating."

"You are correct. There is nothing there, but I thought it best to send it along anyway, seeing as it was everything I found."

"You did your best I'm sure. Pity it turns out the lower class is just that, lower in class. One would think there would be much more in the way of unsavory elements."

"Yes, though I have learned poor does not mean bad, directly, and welfare does not mean criminal by itself. Is there anything else you require by way of my assistance?"

"No, and thank you for trying, Bartholomew. You were the first person I thought of."

"As always, it was my pleasure, Virginia. If there's nothing else…"

"Actually, there is, but it is unrelated to this matter, for the most part."

"What do you mean, 'for the most part'?"

"Believe it or not, they are throwing a ball for me."

"A ball? Who? What is the occasion?"

"In memory of Penny … for the foundation of all things, Reginald and his companion."

"Well isn't that lovely? You must be tickled pink."

"You will be receiving an invitation in the near future, once I've finished designing it. Be sure to keep the weekend of May fourth open."

"I will and thank you for the heads up."

"My pleasure, Bartholomew. Ta-ta for now."

"Good bye, Virginia."

****

In the ensuing weeks, preparations for the big event took form. Replies to Virginia's ornately designed invitations to the ball came flooding in, and as word spread, those not included in the initial mailing of one-hundred clamored for an opportunity to attend. As a result, an additional fifty invitations were sent out and the ensuing upper tier donations were so numerous, the base for Virginia's bust had to be redesigned to accommodate them all. Because the guest list had grown beyond the ability of the estate to host the event, the hunt began for an alternate location.

Initially, Virginia's visit was to last six weeks, and though she had planned an extended trip to Italy months earlier, she believed it would not interfere, for she would be able to return with plenty of time to attend the ball. However, as the day grew closer, Reggie, Calvin, and Miss Honey realized how important she had become to the preparations for the event, for none of them possessed knowledge adequate enough to hold the fort down in her absence.

When the subject was brought up at dinner one evening, Virginia voluntarily cancelled her trip and extended her stay at the mansion, which relieved Reggie to no end, quite a turnaround from his feelings only a few weeks earlier. Her life's experience as a member of high-society and her knowledge of etiquette were invaluable in ensuring the preparations for the ball met all the requirements society demanded.

When Calvin brought up the subject of security, Virginia balked, claiming a security force, no matter how discreet, would sully the event. She also emphasized several of the elected officials attending would have their own security and that would be more than enough. When Calvin countered with his concerns, Virginia put the matter to rest, stating she simply would not have it, and the matter was dropped.

Between becoming immersed in the ball's preparations and the camaraderie and love she witnessed between her nephew and Calvin, Virginia became less and less resolved to break up their relationship. Even Roscoe and Cinders, the mongrels, as she once referred to them, had become permanent, welcome fixtures to her.

In addition, Peabody's behavior improved dramatically, thanks to Calvin's obedience training. He grew to not only tolerate the additional animals' presence, he became quite enamored with Roscoe, and he adopted Cinders as his little brother.

Nary a day went by when Virginia didn't find herself leaving her suite to search for him in some other part of the mansion. Often, she found him bedding with Roscoe and Cinders in Reginald and Calvin's suite—for they were now living together, in their office—they now shared just one, or at Miss Honey's feet in the kitchen, where she fussed over the three of them while she cooked, but there was more afoot than the animals simply getting along.

****

The only person to notice the change in Roscoe was Miss Honey. When she placed her hand against Roscoe's belly one morning, she felt the swelling that had begun to take place, swelling that could not be explained by an improvement in her diet alone.

Miss Honey smiled. "Oh, you little dear," she said softly. "You're going to be a mother, aren't you? Your daddy is going to be so excited. And you little man," she said to Peabody. "It could only be you. You're going to be a father, though I'm not so sure how your mother is going to feel about it.

"We'll tell Calvin and Reggie, but we'll have to keep this a secret from Miss Virginia for the time being. With just two weeks to go before the ball, everything is coming together according to plan, but there's simply too much going on right now, and this kind of news will distract her."

The following day, Doctor Littleton confirmed Miss Honey's suspicion, which helped to alleviate some of the stress Calvin and Reggie had been feeling as they dealt with Aunt Virginia's eccentricities over etiquette.

"She's right," Doctor Littleton said, nodding to Miss Honey, as she lifted the ultrasound probe from Roscoe's abdomen. "She's between three and four weeks along. I counted six, but there could be more. I think you can expect her puppies in a little over a month but definitely within six weeks. Just be prepared, they're going to be little hellions. Terrier and Pomeranian, what a combination!"

Then a call arrived from Wallace Tasker, Reggie's private detective. It changed the future for everyone.

****

Reggie and Calvin's office

It had been a hectic morning taking and making phone calls as preparations were coming to a head when Ryan, who had since become the executive assistant to both Reggie and Calvin, answered the phone.

"The Penelope Turner Scottsdale Foundation. How may I direct your call?"

"Good morning. Wallace Tasker calling for Mister Scottsdale."

"I'm sorry, sir. Mister Scottsdale is in a meeting at present. May I take a message?"

"I think he'll want to take my call ... and right now. Would you please put me through to him?"

"I'm sorry, sir, but you're not on the list. Again, may I inquire as to the reason for your call?"

"It's a private matter."

"I'm afraid I'll need more than that if I am to interrupt him, sir.

"Certainly, if you must. Tell him it's about Calvin's family."

Ryan sat up straight in his chair. "I see. One moment, sir, while I check whether he can be interrupted. Please hold."

Ryan stood from his desk and hurried to the group surrounding the coffee table. He leaned down by Reggie's side, and whispered in his ear. Immediately Reggie signaled for Calvin to accompany him to his desk, and a moment later, he answered the phone, putting it on speaker.

"Wallace," he announced, "I'm here with Calvin. You're on speaker. What's up?"

"Hello to the both of you, I have new news about Calvin's family. May I speak openly?"

"Yes, certainly," Calvin said, anxiously. "I'd nearly given up hope after your last call when you told us you'd lost contact with Eloise."

Virginia was holding Peabody in her lap while she reviewed the seating chart. She perked up when she overheard the mention of Calvin's family. "Who is Eloise?" she asked Miss Honey, without lowering her voice.

Reggie waved his hand to try to shush her.

"Reginald!" she exclaimed. "You do not wave your hand at me as if I were a child!"

Shhh, Miss Virginia," Miss Honey whispered, "this is important. She's Calvin's sister."

"Calvin," Wallace continued. "Eloise called just a few minutes ago. She had news about your mother. She's had a mild heart attack. She's asked to see you."

"Mama!" Calvin cried out.

"There's more," Wallace said. "Your brother, Caleb, has also been located. He made contact with them before they left the homestead a few years ago. They moved close by, but now he's living with them, has been for the past couple months. They're in a single room above a tavern where Eloise found a job as a cook. Eloise got him a job as the bartender. Right now, they're taking turns holding vigil at your mother's bedside at the hospital."

"Ryan," Reggie exclaimed, "Get me Doctor Waters on the phone immediately. Ask him to contact the hospital to learn whether Mrs. Chadwick is stable enough to be transferred to a local hospital. I'll have the number for you in a moment. If so, I'll need you to arrange for a medical flight. Tell them wheels up within two hours. Then get someone to pack a bag for both Calvin and myself, enough for say, three days."

"I'll take care of that," Miss Honey said as she stood up.

"Thank you, Miss Honey." Again to Ryan, "Call Dudley, have him get the Escalade ready. We'll be leaving as soon as preparations are completed. Oh, and we'll likely need ambulance transportation for Mrs. Chadwick between the hospital and airport and then again after we return, if she does in fact return with us."

"Right away," Ryan answered as he hurried to his desk. Miss Honey passed him on her way out of the office.

"Mister Tasker," Calvin said into the phone, "how'd you ever find them?"

"Eloise called from the hospital. She wasn't allowed to use the phone at the bar, as otherwise she would have called much sooner. It seems someone had stolen her cell phone while she was at work. That's why I wasn't able to reach her. She said she had planned to reestablish contact once she'd saved up enough money to buy a new one. Fortunately, the hospital allowed her the use of a phone so she could get word to you about your mother."

Reggie interrupted. "Wallace, send me everything you have on Mrs. Chadwick."

"I've already emailed it all to you, Reggie. Check your cell phone."

"Great!" Reggie said as he lifted it from his desk and opened his email. "I've got it. Thanks so much, Wallace. We'll be in touch."

"You're welcome, both of you. I'll wait to hear back from you. Bye."

Reggie scanned the email. "Ryan, here's the

hospital's phone number for Doctor Waters."

Chapter Twenty-Six
Family

The bedroom of the third guesthouse, two days later, in the afternoon

After reviewing her case with the attending physician in West Virginia, Doctor Waters learned Calvin's mother would be ready for discharge to home within a day or two.

Gathered in the same bedroom Calvin occupied his first night at the estate were Jean, Doctor Water's nurse; Eloise, and Caleb; Calvin, Reggie, and Virginia.

"Mama," Calvin said softly to the frail woman lying in the bed, "this is Reggie's aunt, Miss Virginia Scottsdale." He turned toward Virginia. "Miss Virginia, Mrs. Freda Chadwick, my mother."

"How do you do, Mrs. Chadwick?" Virginia said, as she leaned down next to the bed, extending her hand. She was drawn to the woman's pale blue eyes. "It is a pleasure to meet you."

There was something familiar about the woman's face. Though aged with years and pale with sickness, the color of her eyes caused Virginia to spin back through time.

Miss Honey entered after having just finished setting the dining room table with an assortment of light refreshments and whispered to Reggie. "I've shown Doctor Waters out. Finger sandwiches and a variety of fruit and various sweet cakes along with coffee and tea are ready for when you're all finished visiting in here."

"Thank you, Miss Honey. I'm sure we won't be long."

Slowly, Mrs. Chadwick's eyes came into focus as Reggie's aunt's name began to trigger her memory. The frail, bed-bound woman looked up at Virginia as a sense

of recognition slowly spread across her face. She took
Virginia's hand. "Virginia Scottsdale!" she suddenly
exclaimed, though her weakened state diminished her
speech. "Miss Virginia? Miss Virginia, from The
Brookside School? Could that really be you?"

"You know me?" Virginia was stunned as images
from years past began to take form. It couldn't be. It just
couldn't be her.

"Oh, Miss Virginia, you's safe, you's alive!"

"No! It can't be!" Virginia cried out.

"It's me, Alma Mae, Alma Mae Primrose! Oh,
you's safe, you's safe!"

Virginia faltered, then plopped down on the edge
of the bed.

"Alma Mae Primrose?" Calvin, Eloise, and Caleb
all said at the same time.

"Your name is Freda, Freda Chadwick," Calvin
said, confused.

Calvin's mother continued. "I thought about you
so many times over the years. We both did, wonderin'
whether you was alive … didn't know if Johnny Blue
had done ya in n' some others found ya n' took yer body
away. But now I knows, now I knows you's alive and
well."

"Alma Mae? My Alma Mae? My savior, Alma
Mae?" Virginia cried out as tears began to spill down her
cheeks.

"What the hell is going on?" Reggie exclaimed in
shock as he looked at Calvin. Calvin shook his head just
as confused, speechless. Everyone in the room stood still,
stunned in silence.

"Oh, Miss Virginia, me n' Rosie was so plumb
scared fer ya. We done ran after we scared 'im off. Only
way we was able t' pull him off ya was 'cause he was a
burnin' with the manly fever. Then he got his wits about

'im, n' he come after us.

"Rosie got aways, but he caught up t' me at the edge of the woods n' knocked me t' the ground. Got his hands about my neck and pert near done squeezed the life out'o me, that is 'til Rosie bashed him upside the head with a rock. Last thing I 'member was him atop me with his neck veins a bulgin', n' his face, crimson with rage. Then I passed out."

"We never knew what happened to you, Alma Mae." Virginia's voice shook as she spoke. "The two of you simply vanished. And they never found Johnny Blue. They said he must have run away, never to be heard from again."

"It wasn't like that a'tall. When I come to, he was lying on the ground with a pair of kitchen shears stuck in his heart, his chest a bubblin' n' gaspin' fer air. Then he just plumb stopped breathin'. Rosie said he turned on her after she hit him off me, got her by the neck, too, and started to squeeze. She pulled out them shears from her apron n' stabbed n' stabbed him real good, 'til he fell t' the ground.

"We dragged his body deep int' the woods, n' then we ran t' the barn t' fetch ya, but you was gone. We hoped you done come to and made yer way back t' safety, but we really didn't know what happened t' ya fer sure.

"We was so scared, Miss Virginia. We was so plumb scared so we got us some shovels out the shed n' dug a real deep hole n' buried him, then covered it all up with leaves n' sticks.

"We was afeared fer our lives, Rosie fur killin' him, 'n me for helpin' t' bury him. What chance did two fifteen-year-old girls, one white trash n' the other colored, have with the law, 'specially after killing a Reverend's son, so we snuck int' our rooms n' grabbed our things n' then we ran away.

"We ran and hid fer weeks, jumpin' trains a couple times 'til we made it out west. Rosie found us work scrubbin' pots and cleanin' rooms fer our room n' board at a roadside cafe n' motel in Nevader. After five years passed, we figgered the heat cooled down enough so we come back east n' settled in Gopher's Holler, West Virginie.

"Lived next door t' each other all them years, too, keepin' an eye out fer each other."

Calvin, Eloise, and Caleb looked at each other. "Does she mean Miss Sarah?" Eloise whispered. The other two shrugged while tilting their heads.

Alma Mae continued to relate what happened. "Had t' change our names t' keep the law from findin' us, after … after it was all over.

"I felt real bad leavin' poor Rosie behind a few years back, but I had t' go, 'cause I couldn't afford t' stay in my home no more, not after my husband up n' died. Poor Rosie was heartbroken 'coz she couldn't put us up, seein' as she didn't have no room, but we still keep in touch, now n' again."

"Yes," Virginia said, "I remember. The last thing I remembered was you and Rosie screaming, just before I lost consciousness. When I woke, I was alone. Johnny Blue was gone, and so were you. I made my way back from the barn, but I collapsed outside the front doors. They found me the following morning."

"Oh, Miss Virginia," Alma Mae said. "You's alive and you's well. I'm so relieved."

Virginia leaned down and hugged Alma Mae to her, then kissed her forehead. "You're home now, Alma Mae," she said, smiling. "This will be your home, from now on, and I will take care of you."

The room broke out in chaos as shouting erupted

and questions flew through the air. Neither Virginia nor Alma Mae heard any of it. They simply sat together, holding hands, looking into each other's eyes, smiling, in silence.

****

After things settled down and after Virginia, Reggie, and Calvin returned to the mansion, Virginia called them to her suite.

Having discerned what had happened to his aunt so many years ago, Reggie began to understand why she was the way she was. He leaned down where she sat in her chair and kissed her cheek. "What was so urgent, Aunt Virginia?"

"Please have a seat, Reginald. You too, Calvin. I have something I must say to you both."

After they were seated on the sofa she continued. "Please allow me to say what I must say before you speak." Reggie and Calvin nodded.

"I owe the two of you a sincere apology. I have acted hideously toward you. I have attempted to drive you apart at every turn. I have done my absolute best to destroy what you have tried so hard to build, but your love for each other has been stronger than my most flagrant efforts, and I thank God I failed.

"Calvin, I did not trust you, I believed you, like others in Reginald's past, were trying to take advantage of him. I could not have been more wrong. Your love and support of him, your kind and gentle ways, and your genuine good will are all reflections of the spirit that dwells within you. You are a good and decent man. I hope you can forgive me."

As she spoke, tears had welled up in Calvin's eyes. "Yes, Virginny," he said as his voice broke and the tears spilled. "Of course."

"Thank you." Virginia took a breath and

continued.

"Reginald, I have always had your best interests at heart, but I have failed you terribly because in my attempt to protect you, I believe I have crushed your spirit. I have erected roadblocks wherever and whenever I could with the hope you would be guided toward a course I believed you needed to travel, but I was fooling myself.

"What do I know? I'm an old spinster who never knew love because I wouldn't allow myself to know it, and I put you on the same path.

"Not until Calvin came into your life have I seen the spark of the boy and young man you once were return. I am so grateful you persevered with this relationship and proved me wrong, and I am happy beyond measure that you have found your soulmate. Can you ever forgive me?"

Reggie rushed to her side and knelt down, resting his head in her lap as he wept. As sobs escaped his chest, his aunt gently caressed his cheek until they passed. He lifted his head and was met with the first, genuine smile he had received from her in years. "Yes, of course, dear aunt. Thank you."

After they left, Virginia spoke to Peabody. "Well, my boy, I didn't think I had it in me, but I pressed on. Let us hope this will open a new chapter in our lives."

Peabody barked and sat up in a begging posture. "Oh, you silly dog. You have no idea about what I said, do you?"

Peabody barked again and panted with his tongue lolling from the side of his mouth.

"No," she said, "I didn't think so."

****

Later that afternoon, Virginia made a call from her suite. "Bartholomew? This is Virginia. I need you to do something for me, urgently. It is of the utmost importance."

"Certainly, Virginia, anything."

"Have you ever heard of Gopher's Hollow, West Virginia?"

"Can't say that I have. What about it?"

"You must go there to find someone and bring her to me."

"Did I hear you say, 'Bring her to you?'"

"There is nothing wrong with your hearing, Bartholomew."

"I see. I guess I know better than to ask."

"Quite."

"Her name?"

"One Miss Rosie Freeman, though she goes by the name of Sarah Trumbull."

"Um ... okay ... can you give me any additional details? It might help me to begin my search."

"That will not be necessary. Someone will be accompanying you, a Miss Eloise Chadwick, Calvin—Reginald's friend, his sister. She will take you directly to Miss Rosie. You will need her with you in order to bring Rosie back. Rosie knows and trusts her."

"Again, something tells me I shouldn't ask you to elaborate."

"That would be wise. You know me well, and the less you know, the better for all involved."

"As you wish, Virginia. When do I leave?"

"As soon as possible, Eloise is packed and ready to go. The sooner you pick her up, the sooner you can leave for West Virginia."

"Do you know how old this Miss Rosie is?"

"Why is that important?"

"I'm thinking about logistics and how a sudden change of scenery might affect her. Does she even know

someone's coming for her? Has anyone telephoned her to advise her I'm coming? Is it just her or will she need to pack? Will she need to bring belongings back with her?"

"Darn you, Bartholomew. Why must you make things so complicated? No, of course she has no idea anyone is coming for her, she has no telephone, and she is of my generation. About belongings, I have no idea."

"May I offer a suggestion then?"

"If you must, go on."

"Then she is old ... er, um, sorry, let us say, of a mature age. Allow us to leave first thing in the morning. I can arrange for a private jet, though at the moment I can't find a Gopher's Hollow anywhere in West Virginia, but a flight to any part of that state shouldn't take more than two hours. We can get in and out the same day, and depending on how far she is from the airport, I can have her to you by evening at the latest. If necessary, I'll hire movers to take care of her belongings and have them delivered after we return. If we leave now, we'll likely be flying back late, in the middle of the night. Without knowing the particulars, would such a flight create any difficulties for Miss Rosie?"

"It might. I failed to consider that."

"That's why you pay me so well, Virginia. It's my job to think of such things."

"Very well, Bartholomew. Have it your way. Call back to the house and ask for Eloise. She will be able to tell you where Gopher's Hollow is located."

"I'll do that, Virginia. Just leave the particulars to me. I'll take care of everything."

"I know you will, Bartholomew, and thank you."

"Of course, Virginia, as always. Um, if I may?"

"What is it, Bartholomew?"

"This turn of events. Has something changed?"

"Only that I have come to the realization I have been acting like a conniving witch. I have been so wrong, on so many fronts, about so many things, it will require the remainder of my life to make amends."

"I see. You shouldn't be so hard on yourself, Virginia. You were only looking out for your family."

"Well, that may be, but my blindness certainly made me put my foot in it. That will be all, Bartholomew. Good day to you."

Chapter Twenty-Seven
Silk and Satin

The kitchen, the big day

Dressed in a flowing, salmon-colored house-gown, her hair tied up in a matching-silk scarf, Virginia entered, cane in hand, through the grand dining room into the mansion's kitchen just after one-o'clock where food preparations were well underway. They extended through the outside kitchen doors into a connected mobile kitchen, nearly twice its size.

With the Chef de cuisine (executive chef)—one Charity Hopewell, care of Jaron Enterprises–along with her three Sous-chef de cuisine, her two daughters, Fiona and Evelyn, and her son, Eugene; two Pâtisseries (pastry chefs), four Chefs de partied (line chefs), a Saucier (sauce), Poissonier (seafood), Entremetier (soups), and a Rotisseur (meat), all with their own staff of Commis (line-cooks), as well as the Chef garde manger (pantry/cold items), the Expediter (go-between kitchen and waitstaff), Maître d' (whose job it was to attend to the comfort of the guests), Head waiter (supervisor of waitstaff), and the Sommelier (wine)–who was busy opening bottles and tasting the wines and champagne to ensure they met with her approval, both kitchens were jam-packed and in a near state of turmoil. Acting like a symphony conductor, Miss Honey knew her domain and kept everything flowing.

With all one-hundred and fifty invitations accepted, three-hundred guests would be arriving. Miss Honey knew there were always a few, last-minute, surprise guests who showed up, so with herself, Reggie, and Calvin; and Miss Alma Mae, Eloise, Caleb, and Miss Rosie she rounded it up to three-hundred and twenty dinners to be prepared.

The dining room's rear doors opened into a throughway for the staff. It was connected to an immense, donated, heated tent, where the guests would be seated, complete with hardwood flooring, sheer drapery, hanging and pedestal-mounted, grand floral arrangements, crystal chandeliers, a bar, and a small bandstand for a chamber ensemble.

Once Virginia had it in her head the ball would be held at the estate, there was no convincing her to move it elsewhere when the guest list grew to three hundred. To accommodate her wishes, it was decided the additional tent—the rental fee waived by one of the foundation's board members—would serve as a temporary dining room. An additional throughway on the far side of the tent, connected into the grand ballroom, located on the other side of the mansion's grand foyer, where an orchestra would provide music for dancing after dinner.

Because it could not accommodate that number of guests, the dining room had been converted into a staging area for serving. In a corner, the maître d' and head waiter were busy orienting the waitstaff to the facility, place settings, and the evening's menu.

Virginia scanned through the scene of controlled chaos until she found who she was looking for and approached them. "Miss Rosie, Eloise, and Caleb," she projected, softly clapping her hands together. "You've done quite enough now. It is time to begin your preparations for the evening."

Rosie looked up from where she was chopping vegetables while Caleb stopped in place with a thirty-pound crate of romaine lettuce on his shoulder, and Eloise ceased peeling carrots. "Miss Virginia," Rosie answered, "we's not nearly done helpin' as of yet."

"I'm sure everyone appreciates all of your assistance, as do I, but that is what the additional staff are for." Virginia flicked her left wrist toward the kitchen staff. "Now come along, the three of you. There is much to accomplish before the guests begin to arrive."

"But, Miss Virginia," Caleb said as he lowered the crate to a stock table, "I don't feel right, not 'til I done earned my keep."

"You, my dear boy," Virginia said with a kindly smile, "*you* are a guest of honor, one of *my* guests of honor this evening," she waved her right hand to include all three of them, "and your attendance is not only desired, it is required. Let us not keep your mother waiting any longer. She is quite eager to witness your transformations.

"Tonight will be an evening like none you have ever experienced before, and proper preparations are de rigueur. I'll hear no more of this. Now please, stop what you are doing and come with me. The dressers, beauticians, barber, and all the rest are waiting."

"What's de rigueur mean?" Caleb half-whispered to his sister and Miss Rose. Eloise shook her head.

Rosie elbowed him. "Don't know, but sounds like a highfalutin' way of sayin' proper."

"Precisely," Virginia replied, "Now come along."

Then she turned and led the way up to Reggie's mother's former suite, which was located down the hall from his and Calvin's suite of rooms. Because it already contained a beauty salon, Virginia had it transformed into a dressing area that would rival those found at any of the top fashion shows.

****

At six o'clock, Reggie and Calvin entered the guest suite to see how everyone's final preparations for the evening were progressing. Calvin barely recognized his mother as the beautician put the final touches on her hair. Dressed in a shimmering, midnight-blue, silk gown with a matching headpiece and satin slippers, she beamed. Even with the oxygen tubing beneath her nose, its tank effectively concealed within the workings of her wheelchair, she radiated sophistication and elegance.

"Mama," he said, leaning down beside her on her right as she admired herself in the full-length mirror "You are glowing." He squeezed her shoulder and touched his lips to her right cheek.

"I'da nev'a believed it ma'self," she said, eyes glinting, as she turned her cheek up to receive him. "And jus' look at yer brotha n' sista," she said, pointing towards them. "They's a glowin', too." Eloise twirled in her pink chiffon gown, and Caleb, in his black tuxedo, bowed slightly.

"N' so is Rosie," Alma Mae continued. "Jus' look at what they done fer Rosie!"

Rosie, in her shimmering-peach, silk gown with a similarly matching headpiece and dyed satin shoes, lifted the back of the fingers of her right hand to beneath her chin, tilted her head, lowered her eyes, and curtsied. "I ain't nev'a had nothin' so fine," she said as she looked up. "Nev'a imagined such finery in all my life."

Alma Mae reached up to her left and took Virginia's hand. "N' I have you t' thank fer it all, Miss Virginia. We all do. I'll 'member this night fer as long as I live."

Virginia, dressed in a shimmering-scarlet, silk gown, fashioned similarly to Alma Mae's and Rosie's, but with more enhancements, and a necklace of diamonds, sapphires, and rubies around her neck, with earrings to match, took in all of them as she squeezed Alma Mae's hand in return. "You are an image of beauty, Alma Mae. You are all the epitome of elegance and refinement. Now," she said with a twinkle in her eye as she struck one hand with the other, then leaned on her cane and lifted her left leg as if she was about to dance a jig, "what say we get this shindig underway!"

Caleb let out a guffaw and slapped his leg while the rest of them laughed and giggled aloud.

"Aunt Virginia," Reggie said through stilted laughter, once he'd regained his composure, "you never cease to amaze me."

"There is much you do not know about me, Reginald. I have been known to cut a rug or two in my day. Alma Mae's arrival has reminded me of much of my past. I have long forgotten too, too much, and I am going to remedy that. Shall we?" she said, lifting her arm to him.

"My pleasure," Reggie answered, taking it. "We'll meet you at the elevator doors downstairs," he said, looking briefly at the nurse, but focusing on Alma Mae. Then, as they turned toward the doorway, he whispered, "Your gown will create quite the scandal this evening, Aunt Virginia. Scarlet! Who'd have thought."

"One can only hope, Reginald," she said, batting her eyes, as she withdrew a fan of the same color from a concealed pocket and dramatically snapped it open, then energetically fanned herself. "One can only hope."

Arm in arm, they led the group to the top of the stairs and down to the grand foyer where music from a chamber ensemble drifted in. After picking up Alma Mae, they made their way to the guest entrance leading into the tent and awaited their announcement to enter.

****

After an hour of wine, champagne, and hors d'oeuvre-served socializing and mingling, Reggie positioned himself at the podium's microphone and asked the guests to take their seats. After everyone found their places, he began to speak.

"Good evening, ladies and gentlemen. My aunt,

Virginia Scottsdale; Calvin Chadwick, the foundation's new administrator; and myself thank you all for coming tonight. We are honored by your presence, and we are grateful to you one and all for your generous support of The Penelope Turner Scottsdale Foundation." He paused briefly for applause. "Your compassionate contributions have exceeded our wildest expectations, and because of your benevolence we will now be able to expand our support into areas well beyond those of which we had ever dared to dream.

"You are members of a very special ensemble in that tonight marks the first annual charity ball in my mother's honor. Founded a decade ago, the foundation continues the work she began out of the trunk of her car where she distributed food and clothing to anyone in need, and she continued that work until her death.

"Today the foundation supports the less fortunate members of society across a broad spectrum of charities and outreach programs year-round. Through the efforts of Calvin Chadwick, the foundation is now associated with many new partners from the clothing, food, and healthcare industries, and this has allowed us to extend its reach and services well beyond anything my mother could have ever imagined.

"In addition, with the assistance and guidance of Mister Jason Ackerman and Mister Aaron Jaeger, two new board members from Jaron Enterprises, we have begun to not only coordinate housing assistance for homeless military veterans, we are now able to direct them to organizations that provide healthcare, mental health services, and assistance in finding gainful employment, often within the foundation or our affiliated organizations.

"Now I know you are all as anxious as I am to indulge in the gastronomical marvels created by our special guest, the world-renowned, three-star-endorsed chef, Miss Charity Hopewell, but before we begin, I ask you to indulge me for a moment in another way. There is a very special lady who is receiving specific recognition this evening as the first inductee into The Penelope Turner Scottsdale Foundation's Legion of Honor, a charter member of the foundation, my mother's best friend, and my aunt, Virginia Scottsdale." Reggie paused for a roaring round of applause.

"Through her perseverance, guidance, and goodwill over the past ten years, the foundation has grown and flourished. Her insight into all levels of society has been invaluable in helping us to focus our efforts where they have been needed most, and we look forward to her continued participation on the board." Again, Reggie had to pause for applause.

"Ladies and gentlemen, I give you, Miss Virginia Scottsdale!"

As Virginia rose from her seat, the applause from the guests roared. When she reached the podium and stood beside Reggie, he surprised her with a golden medallion suspended on a blue, satin ribbon, which he then draped around her neck.

She leaned forward and whispered into his ear. "None of those words were true, Reginald."

"Perhaps in the past, Aunt Virginia," he whispered back, "but now I'm certain they will be."

After the applause died down, he turned toward his left and pulled a drape revealing the bust of his aunt. "This bust will become a prominent and permanent fixture in the foundation's lobby." Again, applause broke out. As it died down, he spoke again. "Without further ado, I give you my aunt, Virginia Scottsdale."

Virginia waited for the room to quiet again then cleared her throat and leaned in to the microphone.

"Thank you, Reginald," she said, looking toward him at her left. "Your words are much appreciated, though in truth, I feel I have much to live up to in receiving them." Then she turned towards the seated guests.

"Ladies and gentlemen, for many years, and I am ashamed to admit this, I did not endorse my nephew's work with the foundation wholeheartedly. In truth, I barely tolerated it.

"I found his passion to continue Penny's one-woman, direct-contact mission as a somewhat foolish endeavor because I was under the belief that people from our level of society should not involve ourselves with the needy. I believed it was enough to write a check. I could have not been more mistaken.

"Very recently, I became reacquainted with two people from my past, two people I had not thought about in years. When they reentered my life, I realized how great a disservice I had done to them, for without them, I would not be standing in front of you here today. You see, ladies and gentlemen, they saved my life, and I forgot them." For a moment, Virginia looked across to where Alma Mae and Rosie sat at the dais. She smiled as tears threatened to spill from her eyes.

Virginia cleared her throat. "Not only did I forget them, I failed them because by saving me they sacrificed their futures, and as a result, led very different lives than those they had envisioned for themselves. They became members of the neediest socioeconomic class in our country while I continued on with where you and I find ourselves today, the wealthy, privileged, upper class. It is something I will have to live with, but I do not need to accept my failure as the end result, because there is something I have done … and will continue to do about it.

"I hope you will use my example as an

opportunity to look back upon your own lives and recognize the sacrifices many others have made on your behalf and where necessary, make amends where appropriate and to a degree that is warranted. I am grateful to you all for this honor," she said, lifting the medallion. "I only hope that by continuing Penny's work I will someday become worthy of it."

As the applause rose, Virginia turned towards her nephew and received his kiss on her cheek and his embrace. As the applause settled down, Reggie motioned to the maître d' to begin serving, then led his aunt to her seat at the dais.

Chapter Twenty-Eight
Fatigue and Felons

The dais, the dessert course

After Virginia waved him to her, the waiter leaned down beside her. "Yes, Madam?"

"I shall have tea with my dessert," she said, not making eye contact with him, "English Breakfast, if you please, and I wish to splurge. I would like a small sample of each of the desserts. Small ones, mind you, just enough for a taste."

"Gladly, madam," he said. "Right away."

****

The staging area, the dessert table

The waiter signaled to another, who quickly approached. As he sliced portions from the six different desserts and placed them together on a dessert plate, he nodded to the second waiter.

"It's perfect, Ralphie," he whispered. "She wants a dessert sampler." Then he spooned tea leaves into a silver pot and filled it with hot water from the tall dispenser.

"Great, Mikey, I've got the stuff right here," he said as he pulled a small plastic bottle that had once held eyedrops from his pocket. He turned his back to conceal his hands above the plate, shook the bottle, and then squeezed several drops of liquid onto each of the six pieces of dessert. Once he finished, he handed the bottle to Mikey. "Make sure you slip four or five drops into her cup before you pour the tea. Remember to do it before and only that much, got it? That way it'll get good and mixed."

"Will do."

"Remember, only four or five drops, Mikey. We want to knock the old dame out. We don't want to kill her, now do we?"

"Right," Mikey said as he took the bottle and slipped it into his pocket. "Four or five drops." As he placed the plate, cup and saucer, and silver teapot onto a silver platter, he whispered. "You see those rocks around her neck? Oh, buddy boy, we're gonna be rich." Then he turned, and headed for the dais.

Ralphie smiled, barely able to conceal his glee, as his body trembled. Then he settled himself and lifted a large tray filled with dessert plates and followed the other waitstaff into the tent.

****

A half hour later, the grand ballroom

While a band played music, dancing ensued. Virginia made her way through the crowd, leaning heavily on her cane. "Reginald, it seems we will need to postpone our dance. I have come to the conclusion that I no longer possess the vim and vigor of my youth, for my stamina appears to have left me."

"You look a little peaked, Aunt Virginia," Reggie said with concern on his face. "Do you feel okay?"

"I'll be fine, my boy, just fine. It has been quite a long day, that is all, but I will take my leave of you now." Virginia stumbled forward, ever so slightly.

Calvin braced her forearm. "Miss Virginia, me n' Reggie 'll take you up to your suite."

Virginia shook her head. "I will not hear of it, Calvin. You have guests to entertain. Think of the foundation."

Calvin signaled to his sister. "Yes, ma'am. Why don't you let Eloise go upstairs with you?"

"I am fine, Calvin, thank you," she said as Eloise arrived, but then she wavered. "Oh!" she exclaimed as she wavered again. Then she pitched forward.

Calvin waved frantically to Caleb. "Miss

Virginia, are you sure you're okay?"

"Yes, I will be fine. I need to lie down, that is all." She clutched Calvin's arm as she began to teeter. "I am very tired all of a sudden."

Reggie grabbed a chair from one of the small tables around the dance floor and placed it behind his aunt. Then he set her down.

"Don't you dare make a scene, Reginald," she said in a strong whisper. "Think of your guests."

"I'm not making a scene, Aunt Virginia. I'm simply preventing you from landing on the floor."

"What's going on?" Doctor Waters said as he appeared suddenly from the crowd. Caleb arrived right behind him. Doctor Waters immediately lifted Virginia's wrist and felt for her pulse. People began to turn and stare.

"My aunt seems to have taken ill," Reggie said as he stepped out of the way.

"Her pulse is slower than I'd expect for a woman of her health and age," Dr Waters announced. "Miss Scottsdale, do you take any heart or blood pressure medications, eyedrops for glaucoma, beta blockers perhaps?

"I take no medications of any kind, Doctor. I'm as healthy as a horse."

"That's very strange. I need her supine, Reggie, so that I can perform a proper examination on her."

"Not here, Doctor," Virginia said calmly, as she chuckled and patted the back of his hand.

Doctor Waters tightened his lips, and then frowned. "I need two strong men. We'll carry her in this chair. Is there somewhere close by I can have her lie down?"

"Don't you dare, Doctor!" Virginia said vehemently.

"Aunt Virginia, please!" Reggie pleaded. "You're not well."

Virginia shook her head and then called on all her reserves. She grasped her cane and with a determined look on her face, rose from the chair. "I will allow you to escort me from the ballroom to my suite, Doctor. We can take the elevator, if you like. There and only there will I permit you to conduct your examination."

The doctor smiled tightly. "Very well, Miss Scottsdale, if you insist."

"I do indeed."

Virginia turned and nodded to Eloise, then took her arm. "If you will, my dear, I would be most appreciative."

"Yes, Miss Virginia, of course."

Virginia looked over her shoulder. "You may follow, Doctor."

As they began to make their way from the ballroom, Calvin whispered to his brother. "Go with them, Caleb, just in case."

"Course, Calvin."

Just then, four men approached Calvin and Reggie as they watched Virginia exit the ballroom.

"Reggie!" a dark-bearded, muscular and tanned, handsome man in his forties said as he reached them and extended his hand. "And you must be Calvin. It's good to finally meet you in person."

"Howdy," Calvin said with a smile as he shook his hand. "And from the pictures I've seen, you must be Jason."

Jason smiled warmly. "Guilty as charged."

"Hello, Jason," Reggie said. "Aaron," he nodded toward the tall, blond Adonis, a former professional quarterback, who stood at Jason's side. "Thank you both for coming."

"Our pleasure, Reggie," Jason said. "Is everything okay?"

"I don't really know. My aunt said she was tired, but she nearly just fainted. The family doctor is accompanying her to her suite."

"Do they need any help? I'm still a medic."

"Yes, I know, Jason, but no, I don't think they do. Thank you just the same though."

"Okay. I'd like you to meet my friends, Toby Jacobson and Cliff Turnbull."

"Gentlemen," Reggie said, shaking their hands, noting how similarly built Cliff was to Aaron. "How do you do? This is my partner and the administrator of the foundation, Calvin Chadwick."

As they all shook hands, a shout came from the direction of the grand foyer. Caleb came back, walking very quickly. "Reggie, Calvin, Miss Virginia just went down like a sack of taters. She's okay, but I don't know as to how she's gonna make it upstairs. She says she's okay, and she says she'll skin you alive, Reggie, if you leave your guests."

"Skin me alive? My aunt said that?"

"You know what I means, Reggie. The doctor's sayin' he thinks it might be somethin' t' do with her ear, messin' with her balance. He don't think it's food poisonin' on account of nobody else is sick. I started to pick 'er up t' carry her up t' her room, but she started pitchin' a fit."

"Why don't you let Aaron and Cliff go to her?" Jason offered as he nodded towards the two men. They're the same height so they can carry her upstairs using a two man lift. "No offense, sir," he said to Caleb, who was a good head shorter than either of the two men.

Caleb nodded. "None taken."

"Thanks. I'm sure she won't like it, but yes."

Reggie turned to Caleb. "Caleb, tell her if she doesn't, allow it, I'll rip down a drape from the dining room and roll her up in it and have her hauled up that way."

The three men didn't wait. Aaron and Cliff followed Caleb out as he led the way.

****

Thirty minutes later

As Doctor Waters approached, he was smiling. Aaron, Cliff, and Caleb had returned as soon as they'd taken Virginia to her suite. "She's resting comfortably, Reggie," the doctor said as he reached him. "Eloise is sitting with her at present. I really don't know what it is, but she just seems to be very tired. I performed an EKG with the app on my phone. Her heart rate is a little slow, sixty-two, but it looks fine. I also drew blood for analysis, and I've already sent it off via courier. I'll have most of the results, including a drug screen in a few hours.

"Everything would have gone much quicker if she had allowed me to call an ambulance to take her to the hospital, but she forbade it."

Reggie nodded as he spoke. "I'm not surprised. In her mind it would have been scandalous, and if you know anything about my aunt…"

Doctor Waters smirked. "I do. The toxicology will take longer, perhaps a day or two."

"Toxicology? Drug screen? What are you thinking, Doctor?" Reggie asked.

"It's purely precautionary, my boy, purely precautionary, but if there's anything to find, we'll find it."

"Okay, if you think it's for the best."

"I do, and it is."

Reggie shook his hand. "Thanks. We'll go up and visit her in a little while."

****

After several more hours, and all the guests had left, Caleb, with the help of the nurse, took his mother back to the cottage. While the hired waitstaff were cleaning up and packing up all the rented tables, chairs, and place setting items, and the kitchen staff were packing up their equipment, Reggie and Calvin retired to their office, accompanied by Jason, Aaron, Toby, and Cliff to discuss the possibility of them stepping up their involvement with the foundation. As Reggie and Calvin explained the new direction they wanted to take the foundation, the four other men listened carefully, gave their input, and offered suggestions based on their perspectives and their areas of expertise.

The meeting was abruptly disrupted by a scream that came from the hallway outside the office.

"Reggie!" Miss Honey shrieked as she opened the door and came rushing in. She was carrying a small form in her apron. Crimson spots began to bleed through. "It's Peabody! He's bleeding all over. I found him at the bottom of the grand staircase. He's having a seizure!"

"What?" Reggie shouted as he ran to her. "He should be with Aunt Virginia! He was when we left her."

Jason followed him and immediately felt Peabody's groin. "There's a pulse. He's still alive."

"I was carrying a tray with hot cocoa for Eloise to the elevator when I saw him out of the corner of my eye."

"Where's Roscoe n' Cinders?" Calvin yelled. "They was with her, too! They wouldn't let Peabody go nowheres alone."

"Eloise put them in your suite," Miss Honey cried. "Cinders wanted to play, and she thought the commotion would disturb Miss Virginia."

As Reggie ran to the door, he yelled over his

shoulder, "Call Doctor Littleton!"

The rest of the group followed. In less than ten seconds, Miss Honey stood alone in the office.

Having already been to Virginia's suite, Aaron and Cliff knew the way. They reached the top landing and were heading down the second-floor hallway, with Reggie, adrenaline pumping, close on their heels, when the others had cleared the first set of stairs.

"Football players, ya gotta love 'em," Toby said to Jason and Calvin as they watched them disappear from sight.

****

As the men ran from the office, Miss Honey followed. Not thinking clearly, she hurried to the telephone on a table in the grand foyer and dialed Doctor Littleton about Peabody's condition, rather than calling from the office. Her call lasted less than a minute. Doctor Littleton was on her way.

****

With Reggie right behind them, Cliff and Aaron rushed through the bedroom door when a gunshot rang out, immediately followed by shouting and screaming. As Calvin, Toby, and Jason reached the suite's outer door, the shouting and then a second gunshot erupted from the bedroom. In mid-stride, Calvin and Jason's military training kicked in. Jason turned to look for cover. Because he knew the layout of the suite, Calvin grabbed Jason and Toby by their shirt collars and turned them 180 degrees towards the library.

****

While on the phone with the veterinarian, Miss Honey jumped when she heard what sounded like a gunshot. Then there was distant shouting. After hanging up, she immediately picked the phone back up and dialed 911.

Chapter Twenty-Nine
Pint-Sized Cavalry

Virginia's suite, the bedroom

Ralphie yelled at the three men as he waved the gun in their direction. "I said, everyone down on the floor!"

"Ralphie!" Mikey yelled back at him, "Where'd the gun come from? You said no guns!"

"Shut up, Mikey, it's insurance. Good thing, too. Look at those two." He waved the gun towards Aaron and Cliff. "You think you could take 'em? You think you could take even one of 'em?"

"No," Mikey answered, sullenly.

Reggie seethed. "What do you want?" He looked at his aunt and Calvin's sister, both gagged and tied up on the bed.

With adrenaline pumping through her system after the assault by the two burglars, Virginia was wide awake. Reggie saw terror reflected through both his aunt's and Eloise's eyes, but with Virginia, rage also burned.

"You've already shot one man!" Reggie turned toward the other two. "Cliff, are you okay?"

"No talking!" Ralphie screamed.

Cliff was breathing hard and fast. He was gripping his lower left abdomen. Aaron was holding pressure over Cliff's hands. While Cliff smiled weakly and nodded, Aaron looked towards Reggie, shook his head, and mouthed *No*.

"You've shot a man in the abdomen. He could die!" Reggie shouted, ignoring the burglar's order for silence. "You've gagged and tied up two women. What kind of men are you?"

"I said shut up!" Ralphie pulled the trigger again.

The bullet struck the dresser, just above Reggie's head. "That missed on purpose. The next one'll be between your eyes."

****

Immediately after Miss Honey hung up from the 911 operator, the phone rang back. She picked it up.

"Hello?"

"Hello? Hello? Is this the Scottsdale residence?"

"Yes, who is this? It's not a good time."

"Miss Honey?"

"Yes, who is this?" she insisted.

"It's Doctor Waters. Is something wrong? You answered the phone strangely."

"Oh, Doctor! There was a gunshot. Peabody's been injured. He's covered in blood. He had a seizure."

"A gunshot? Let me speak to Reggie."

"He's gone up to investigate. All the men have."

"Miss Honey, get out of there immediately! I'll call the police."

"I already have, Doctor. They're on their way."

"Miss Honey. When you see Reggie, tell him his aunt has benzodiazepines and narcotics in her bloodstream."

"What does that mean, Doctor?"

"It means she's been drugged. She must be taken to a hospital immediately."

"I will, I mean we will, but right now I must attend to Peabody. Good bye, Doctor."

Miss Honey hung up and turned to carry Peabody to the kitchen where she kept first aid supplies in the cabinet next to the sink. So focused on getting him to where she could bandage his wounds, she was completely unaware of the heads that turned and followed her progress as she hurried through the grand dining room. Most of the waitstaff were still packing up.

Most of them saw the blood. Some of them saw the small dog suspended in her bloodied apron. Then one of them screamed.

Miss Honey looked up. It took a moment for her to realize who all the people were. "I heard a gunshot!" she yelled. "He's been injured," she said more calmly, looking down at the limp body, suspended in her apron.

What had once been a scene of organization and purpose turned into one of bedlam. People began to shout and run in all directions.

Hearing the commotion going on beyond the kitchen doors, Miss Charity Hopewell, the visiting, three-star chef came hurrying out. "What's happened?" she asked, noting the blood as Miss Honey approached.

"He's been injured. I heard a gunshot from the second floor. He was with Miss Virginia."

"Where's Mister Jason? Where's Mister Aaron?"

"They went up to investigate. All the men did."

"Come with me." Miss Charity put her arm around Miss Honey and guided her through the kitchen doors. "Mister Jason knows what to do. Now we gotta get ourselves out of here and help this wee one in the process. You just stick with me, Missus. Miss Charity's gonna take care of you, too."

****

"Are there any guns in the house?" Jason whispered to Calvin as he held his hand over Toby's mouth. Both he and Calvin were holding Toby down. The three were crouched down behind a bookcase in Virginia's library on the other side of the living room, two rooms away from the bedroom.

All three men had a vested interest in the goings on inside the bedroom. All three had someone to lose. All three were scared to death.

"Only huntin' rifles as I knows of," Calvin

whispered back, "down in the study."

"Shit." Jason looked into Toby's eyes. "Toby, stop struggling," he whispered. "You can't do anything for him right now. We know he's still alive. You go in there now and you'll get yourself killed and maybe everyone else, too."

Toby was scared to death for his husband. Based on what he'd heard Reggie say, he believed Cliff was the one who'd been shot, but he didn't know how bad. He didn't know for sure. He could hear Reggie's voice coming from the bedroom. Why was he antagonizing the gunman? Then he'd heard a second shot, and he heard what the gunman said, but he didn't know who he was talking to. All he wanted was get to his husband.

Toby nodded and tapped his hand over Jason's.

"If I let go," Jason whispered, "you promise you won't call out to him?"

Toby nodded again so Jason released his hand from his mouth. "Sorry, Jason, it was a reflex," Toby whispered. "I understand."

"I know," Jason whispered back to him, "but it doesn't make it any easier, does it?"

"No." Toby began to shake.

****

As they passed Cynthia's room in the staff quarters, Bernard rapped on the door. When she opened it, he whispered, "Did you hear it?"

Cynthia shook her head as she twisted and folded her blond, waist-length hair into a headscarf. "No. What?"

"Two muffled gunshots. I'm afraid there's trouble afoot. Lock your door, then call the police."

"Where are the two of you going?" she asked as she looked from him to Dudley.

"To investigate. I'm bringing Betsy." He patted

the shotgun he was holding. Then, as he tilted his head backward toward Dudley. "And help if necessary."

"You old fool, you'll get yourself killed, the both of you killed," she whispered as she furrowed her brow, then gave Dudley a quizzical look when she noticed him lift up a second shotgun, "if there's any real trouble."

"And I have Bertha," Dudley said meekly, as he patted the barrel of the second shotgun.

"Just call the police, Cynthia," Bernard said. Then they moved on.

****

From her bed in her master's suite, Roscoe cocked her head and listened to the sounds coming from the other side of the mansion. Cinders had already left their bed and was frantically scratching at the closed door. When the first shot rang out, Roscoe jumped into motion and raced to join her adopted son. Together they scratched and chewed at the wooden door, but it didn't budge.

****

Armed with "Betsy", his double barrel shotgun, the first barrel loaded with a double aught cartridge and the other with a slug, Bernard stealthily approached the suite. Carrying the second double barrel, loaded the same, and a .32 caliber Walther PPK with an extra magazine, and hugging Bernard's heels, Dudley trembled with fear.

"I don't think I can do this, Bernard," Dudley said, shivering, when they reached the open door. "I can't shoot another human being."

Bernard turned back to Dudley. "It will be all right, my love," he whispered as he patted Dudley's forearm. "All will be well. I promise. You don't need to do anything. Just hand me what I ask for as quickly as you can."

Quaking in his slippers, Dudley nodded.

****

"Central to Unit One," the 911 dispatcher said into her headset.

"Unit One, go," the watch commander answered.

"Unit One, be advised a second call has come in from the residence confirming a gunshot at the location you're responding to. We also received another call confirming it from a third party."

"Unit One received. Will proceed as planned."

"Do you want additional units, Unit One?"

"Not at this time, Central."

"Unit One," the dispatcher answered. "Call in to Central via landline."

A moment later the shift supervisor, Alfie, at Central Dispatch answered the back line.

"Hey, Alfie," the watch commander said. "What's up? Wanda said to call in."

"Wanda wants to talk to you. Putting you through to her now."

Wanda, the dispatcher, answered the line. "Hey, Jackson, you know who lives there, right? The residence you're responding to?"

"No," Jackson said, "Who?"

"That's the Scottsdale estate, you know the one where that big shindig was going on tonight. The one that the governor and mayor were attending. Where they still might be right now."

"Oh shit!" Jackson exclaimed. "Dispatch SWAT to that location and a half dozen more units."

"Thought you might say that," Wanda said as she smiled to herself. "Don't worry, Jackson. We've got you covered."

"Thanks, Wanda. You just saved my ass."

"Yeah, I know, and what a lovely, um derrière it

is."

****

No sooner had Cynthia hung up the phone with the 911 operator than she left her room to investigate. She took the old servants' staircase at the far end of the mansion up to the second floor. As she made her way down the hallway, she passed Master Reggie's suite where she heard scratching and whimpering coming from the other side of the door. She opened it to investigate.

Roscoe and Cinders were gone in a flash. Like a pint-sized cavalry, down the hallway they raced towards trouble.

****

"Now hurry up," Ralphie yelled. "Get it all! Here," he said as he yanked a pillowcase from a pillow. "Stuff it in this."

Mikey lifted the carved, wooden jewelry box and shook the contents into the pillowcase while Ralphie held it open. "And don't get any funny ideas," he said as he waved the gun towards the three men, now tied up at the foot of the bed. He gripped the pistol in his right hand while also holding the one side of the pillowcase. "I can still take out all three of you."

"That's all of it, Ralphie," Mikey said.

"Good, then let's get out of here. Down the back staircase right into the dining room, and then we blend in with everybody else and make our escape, real leisurely like."

Chapter Thirty
Shotguns and Helicopters

Roscoe knew from Calvin's training not to bark when trouble was afoot. As she crossed the landing above the grand foyer, she started to pant and began to slow down. Having put on extra pounds the last several weeks, she wasn't as fast, and she couldn't keep up with Cinders. As she looked ahead, Cinders had already crossed above the foyer and was headed down the far hallway. Roscoe called on all her reserves and stepped up her pace.

****

Unaware of the two armed men just beyond the suite's outer door, or the three men lying in wait on the other side of the living room, and keeping their eyes on the three men they'd tied up, Ralphie and Mikey began to back out of the bedroom.

Like a whisper, Cinders blew into the suite, right past Dudley and Bernard. He passed them before Bernard even noticed him and headed for his favorite observation spot in Miss Virginia's living room, atop the illuminated display cabinet, beside the bedroom doorframe.

Watching from the shadows, outside the suite, Bernard saw his chance. He inched through the open door and planted his feet shoulder length apart, the left forward of the right. While raising Betsy to his right shoulder, he aimed her at the back of the burglar holding the gun. As he began to speak, the sound of heavy, grunted breathing reached the ears of the two burglars.

As Ralphie began to turn around, Bernard called out, "Hold it right there, you two."

When Roscoe blasted past Dudley and Bernard, she saw the gun in the burglar's hand. While she ran toward both humans, at the far end of the room, she assaulted them with a barrage of shrill barking.

Momentarily disoriented, Ralphie froze as he looked down both of Betsy's barrels, pointed at his chest.

Hearing his adopted mother's call, Cinder's leapt from his perch and landed on Ralphie's head.

Seeing the shotgun's barrel aimed at his partner and brother, Mikey dropped the pillowcase and dove toward the pajama-clad man holding it.

As Cinders began to shred the face of the human with his claws, Roscoe jumped up and clamped her jaw down on the man's crotch. Ralphie cried out in pain.

Seeing the second burglar leap toward him, Bernard shifted Betsy's aim and pulled the trigger of the first chamber, sending the double aught shot toward its new target. A moment later the burglar's left shoulder shattered in a spray of blood, bone, and muscle, but his forward momentum kept him coming. After Bernard pulled the second trigger, a section of the burglar's chest, where his heart once sat, vanished in a spray of liquids and tissue.

****

As the watch commander, Jackson's car, and the police cruiser behind it pulled to a stop, dozens of people, dressed in waiters' and cooks' uniforms came flooding out of the mansion, heading in all directions.

Jackson immediately radioed into Central dispatch and called for more backup and multiple ambulances. As he opened his door, two muffled, but thunderous shots rang out from the second floor of the mansion right above him. "Shots fired," he called into the microphone of his portable radio. "I repeat, advise all units, shots fired at this location."

****

Bernard dropped Betsy and reached his arm back to Dudley. Dudley came through the door and slapped the barrel of Bertha into his hand and then crouched down on the floor, holding the Walther pistol at the ready, while Bernard brought the sights of the second shotgun to bear on the burglar holding the gun.

At the same time, Calvin and Jason, with Toby behind them, came rushing out of the library. "To me," Calvin called to Dudley when he saw the pistol. "Throw the gun to me."

Unable to see, and pulling at the creature shredding his face with his left hand, Ralphie aimed the gun in the direction of the shouting. Toby ducked, and Jason dropped to the floor. At the same time, Calvin leaped towards the pistol that had left Dudley's hand and was flying across the room. He caught it in mid-air and tucked and rolled across the oriental carpet, then came up onto one knee.

As Ralphie pulled the animal from his face with his left hand, he squeezed the trigger of the gun in his right. As the shot rang out, a porcelain vase above Calvin's head shattered, and then the left column of the doorframe of the library exploded as the bullet found its destination.

Cinders twisted his body as he flew through the air and landed stealthily on Virginia's favorite stuffed chair. Spitting out the chunk of nose still in his mouth, he turned around and headed back to join his adoptive mother's fight.

Ralphie reached down toward the pain in his groin. He staggered back through the doorway into the bedroom and struck downward with his fist, landing a blow against Roscoe's spine. As she opened her mouth to yelp, Ralphie struck again, driving her to the ground.

When Ralphie pointed his gun toward the dog on the floor, Calvin raised his weapon and squeezed the trigger, while Cinders, in the same moment, leapt and landed on the head of the human once again. At the same time, Jason and Toby rushed forward to take him down. Thrown off kilter by the return attack of the cat, now ripping at his flesh, Ralphie's body was driven back and to the right just enough so that Calvin's bullet missed its mark of dead center and lodged in the burglar's left shoulder.

Ralphie stumbled backwards into the bedroom, then staggered to the left, then stumbled again to stand in front of a window with diamond-cut, leaded panes.

While Bernard, Dudley, and Calvin followed, and Jason and Toby rushed toward the bedroom, Virginia and Eloise, along with Reggie, Aaron, and Cliff watched in horror. Once inside the room, Bernard lifted the shotgun and aimed the barrel again. Then he saw a figure come from behind him and to the right as it rushed toward the burglar. He removed his finger from the trigger and lowered the barrel just in time as Toby dove over Jason into the belly of the man with the gun. As Toby made contact, Roscoe launched again and sank her teeth into the burglar's crotch while Cinders continued to shred his face.

Together, the two humans and two animals crashed into the window, shattering it. They teetered for a moment and then fell towards open air, out the window. Jason jumped up and reached for Toby's body, grasping his left calf at the last moment. Calvin also leaped, but he was too late to reach his beloved animals. He cried out their names and then collapsed into a heap on the floor as they disappeared from sight.

****

At the sound of shattering glass, Jackson, the watch commander, the other officers, and more than a dozen of the temporary staff who had fled the mansion looked up to see a mass of forms hover, momentarily suspended in the air at the window above them. Then the forms began to fall as they followed the shards of glass to the ground. A small form seemed to shoot away as it sailed down to disappear into a tall, narrow ornamental evergreen tree at the front of the mansion.

The largest form continued to fall while a second, hung, dangling from the broken window by one leg. The larger one continued down, as it released a bloodcurdling scream, until it was silenced as the sound of crushing bone echoed across the front lawns. At the last moment, as the scream ended, those witnessing the horror could have sworn hey heard a yelp. Then all was momentarily silent.

A moment later, shouting could be heard coming from the window above. As hands reached out, the dangling form disappeared as it was pulled back into the mansion. Jackson along with several others rushed through a dormant flowerbed toward the twisted form, now lying still on the ground. It was the body of a man … and a dog.

From the base of the tall, narrow, ornamental tree a shadow appeared and shook itself off. Jackson directed the beam of his flashlight toward it. It was a cat, a striped, gray cat, and it made its way, limping, toward the jumbled bodies in front of the crowd that had gathered. The cat began to nuzzle the body of the stilled dog. Then it began to paw at it, but the body refused to move.

The cat began to mew, mournfully, as it continued to paw at the dog and nudge it with its nose. Finally, it lifted its head and cried out the most soul-shattering cry ever heard coming from an animal by any of the humans who watched. The cat then curled its body against the dog, lowered its head and began to purr. Several humans reached for the cat, but it lifted its head and hissed, baring its teeth, only to curl up again against the dog's body and continue to purr.

****

Recognizing it was all over, once she heard all the shouting, Cynthia came rushing into the suite. After seeing the dead body of the burglar and blood spatters everywhere, she froze in place and began to scream.

"Reginald!" Virginia yelled as Bernard pulled the gag, made from a head scarf, from her mouth. She strained against the torn-sheet-bindings around her wrists. "Reginald! Are you injured? Bernard, damn you!" she shouted as the butler struggled with the knot between her hands, "Untie me at once! And you!" She jutted her hands toward Jason. "Attend to this young girl!" She motioned to Eloise. "They began to assault her, were *attempting* to assault her when you all came rushing in! It was the one with the gun!"

"Aunt Virginia! Oh, Aunt Virginia, this is all my fault!" Reggie cried out. "I thought you were right. I thought the governor and mayor's security would have been enough! There should have been more security, our own security!"

"It was me! It was my fault!" Virginia cried out. "I was the one who forbade it!"

Calvin began to untie Reggie. "No, Reggie, it ain't! It ain't yur fault a'tall!" he said sobbing. "'N it ain't your fault, Virginny. It ain't none of y'alls fault. Oh, Roscoe! Oh, Cinders! My babies. My babies is gone!"

"He's right, Reggie," Jason said as he lifted Aaron and Cliff's hands from Cliff's lower abdomen to examine it. "All the guests have gone. Any security you would have hired would have been gone as well."

"I'm so sorry. I should have hired security!" Reggie moaned. "This would have never happened…"

Calvin continued to sob at the loss of his family

as he pulled Reggie to him and hugged him. "Like Jason done said, Reggie, no, that wouldn't've done it. They would've been long gone. Wouldn't've made a lick of difference."

"Where are the doctors?" Virginia shrieked. "Where are the paramedics? This child requires immediate attention! No! Do not waste time on me," she shouted at Dudley as he tried to comfort her. "Eloise! Eloise requires care!"

"Calvin!" Jason yelled. "Start ripping up sheets, pillowcases, I don't care what, and tie pressure bandages around Toby's legs. He's losing a lot of blood. I'll be there in a minute."

Seeing Cynthia in the other room, through the doorway, Virginia called to her. "Cynthia, put that body of yours in motion and get in here and help. There are people injured! Help Calvin rip up sheets, anything you can find! Hurry!"

"Who let Roscoe and Cinders out?" Eloise screamed the moment Dudley removed her gag. "I had them safe. They was safe in Calvin's room. I put 'em in there. Oh, my God, Calvin! I'm so sorry. I'm so, so sorry. I had 'em safe. They was safe!"

"Peabody!" Virginia shrieked. "Where is Peabody? The mirror shattered when that bastard threw him into it. Where is my Peabody?"

****

As news helicopters circled above, shining their spotlights onto the scene below, and rooftop lights from the police cruisers and ambulances bathed the mansion and its grounds in red and blue, Cliff was loaded into the medevac chopper while Toby, Virginia, and Eloise were put into ambulances.

Shortly after the ambulances pulled out, the chopper took off, and Jason and Aaron headed to the

Scottsdale estate's private limousine. Jason turned to Reggie while Aaron continued on. "You need to get yourself checked out, too. There's nothing more you can do here."

"I can't leave Calvin. Not after what happened to Roscoe. He just sits there holding her. He won't leave. Doctor Littleton is attending to the other two right now."

"I understand, Reggie, really I do, but you're going to need those wounds looked at, sooner than later."

At the mention of them, Reggie rubbed his hands around the abrasion burns on his wrists. "Doctor Waters called a few minutes ago. He said he'll be here in a little while to look after Calvin. I'll have him check me over once he's finished."

"Of course, of course." Jason nodded.

"What about Aaron?"

"I'm worried about him." Jason turned and nodded and smiled at Aaron, who was now in the limo. "I'm sure he won't even consider getting checked out until we get an update on Cliff. They're close, have been since they were kids."

"Oh, I didn't know. I'm sure Toby is beside himself with worry right now. How bad do you think Cliff's gunshot wound is?"

"It wasn't bleeding as much as it could have, but regardless, it's going to have to be explored to ensure no underlying structures were damaged. How's your aunt doing?

"As well as can be expected. Doctor Waters said her blood work showed benzodiazepines and narcotics. Looks like she was drugged. I'm guessing the burglars did it because as far as I know, no one here is on those medications. She certainly doesn't take them. He told Miss Honey over the phone while we were in the middle of it all, but obviously, she couldn't tell us."

"Make sure the police are made aware of that. It could have been anybody. They could have had an accomplice."

"Doctor Waters already did. He called them after he hung up with Miss Honey."

"Good, and thanks, Reggie. Thanks for the use of your limo. Thanks for everything." Jason rested his hand on Reggie's shoulder. "I'll call you from the hospital as soon as I know something about Cliff."

Reggie hugged him then leaned back. "Please do, but I'm the one who owes you. We all do. Let me know if Cliff and Toby need anything. I don't want them to want for a thing. Whatever they need or want, I'll provide."

Jason nodded, keeping a hand on Reggie's shoulder. "I will, I will. Oh, our chief of security got back to me a few minutes ago. Expect a division of officers to arrive first thing in the morning. They'll work with you to develop a plan around your needs. They're very good at that. They'll be as visible or invisible as you want them to be."

"Great. I'll wait to hear from them. Now get going. Aaron needs to get checked out, and he needs to check on his friend."

"Thanks, Reggie. Bye for now."

Jason let go and ducked into the waiting limo. "I'll have you at the hospital in less than thirty minutes, gentlemen," Dudley said from the driver's seat as he pulled out. Then he closed the dividing window to give the men behind him their privacy.

Epilogue

After an extensive investigation of all the evidence collected, the police determined the small bottle, found in the pocket of the burglar who'd had his chest blown out, contained a combination of lorazepam and codeine in their liquid forms, a lethal combination if given in the right amount. Fortunately, sensing they tasted off, Virginia didn't eat much of her six-dessert assortment or drink much of her tea.

Floor plans for the estate were found in the apartment shared by the two burglar-brothers, along with jewelry and other high-priced items from other recent burglaries committed in the region. The police were unable to discover evidence of the involvement of any other individuals in the crime. The case was closed.

After exploratory surgery, Cliff recovered from his gunshot wound. He was lucky. The bullet had entered just above his groin, but missed the major arteries and exited his side above his hip bone. His blood loss was minimal. Later, a plastic surgeon repaired the scars, leaving only a trace of evidence that there had ever been an injury, but that didn't stop Toby from paying special attention to the area for years and years, whenever they made love.

Toby wasn't as fortunate. He initially required three units of blood to replace what he had lost, and he needed additional units of fresh frozen plasma and several more units of blood over the course of several weeks while multiple, extensive surgeries were required to repair the long, deep, multiple leg lacerations created by the jagged, leaded glass from the window. Initially, the wounds were left open to prevent compartment syndrome from occurring.

His last surgery to finally close his wounds was

performed by the same plastic surgeon who treated his husband. Not to be outdone, Cliff lavished just as much attention to Toby's scars as Toby did to his.

Eloise found gainful employment with the foundation, and she continued to receive counseling after the attempted sexual assault committed by the burglar with the gun. Though her physical wounds had healed, and the psychological trauma she'd suffered would diminish, it would remain with her for the rest of her life. Her greatest supporter of course was Virginia, for she more than anyone else understood what she had gone through.

Virginia, Reggie, Calvin, Jason, and Aaron also recovered from their various minor lacerations, abrasions, and bruises, and life began to return to a new normal for all of them.

The division of officers from Steinecker Security Systems, a subsidiary of Jaron Enterprises, moved seamlessly into the estate. Though their presence was all but evident to the staff, one buff, young officer in particular caught the eye of Ryan, Reggie and Calvin's assistant, clarifying Reggie's long held curiosity as to Ryan's preference.

In a private conversation, Miss Rosie apologized to Calvin for not telling him she was still in contact with his mother when he came looking for his family all those years ago. She admitted to having been shocked by his return and didn't know whether revealing he'd come looking for them would add to her dear friend, Alma Mae's misery after having been forced to leave her home. Of course, Calvin forgave her.

Like his sister, Caleb joined the foundation's team of employees, and Alma Mae and Rosie settled into their new home in the cottage briefly occupied by Calvin. Though weakened from her heart attack, Alma Mae traveled to the mansion every day where she assisted preparations in the kitchen. She particularly enjoyed observing her lifelong friend, Rosie, share her secret family recipes and cooking methods with Miss Honey while the three of them spent each afternoon preparing dinner for what soon became a new, multi-generational, blended, family.

****

The Scottsdale Estate, mid-spring, Miss Virginia's suite

"Are you excited, Miss Virginia?" Perky asked as she set down the breakfast tray.

"Excited. Excited about what? I'm too old to become excited."

"No, you're not, Miss Virginia. As I understand it, we're expecting a delivery today."

"A delivery? What kind of delivery?"

"The babies of course," Geraldine chimed in as she entered carrying fresh bed linens. Her striking chestnut hair served to highlight the twinkle in her eyes, and her dazzling, effervescent smile.

"What babies? What on earth are you girls talking about?"

"Puppies! The puppies are coming!" Cynthia added with glee as she came in carrying the mail.

"Oh, good lord, what has my nephew gone and done now? What are we going to do with more puppies running around the estate?"

Cynthia began to bounce up and down. "No, not Mister Reggie, Roscoe and Peabody! Their puppies! They're arriving today."

"Roscoe? Peabody? How is that possible?"

"Miss Virginia, you do know how babies are made, don't you?" Geraldine asked.

"Of course I know, Geraldine!"

"Well, Roscoe's been pregnant for eight weeks now." Geraldine put her hands on her hips. "And Peabody's the father."

"What? But no one told me! Oh, my lord, I'm going to be a grandmother!" Virginia jumped up from her chair. "I'm going to become a grandmother!"

"Yes, ma'am, sort of," Perky answered.

"Sort of, nothing!" With a wave of her hands, Virginia moved away from her chair. "Take me to her, right away! Geraldine, Call Dudley and have him bring the car around. I must get to Doctor Littleton's office immediately. Cynthia, call the office. Get me an update. I must be there to support her.

"Oh, that dear little girl! She saved my life, you know. She's going to have so much on her hands, I mean paws, but I'll be there to help her every step of the way. Perky, help me to get dressed. I must look my best for her."

"Miss Virginia, she's not at Doctor Littleton's hospital any more. She's here, has been for a week," Geraldine said.

"She's in Mister Reggie's suite," Cynthia added.

"They're setting up for the delivery as we speak." Perky began to dance around. "It's going to be so wonderful!"

"Puppies!" the three maids chimed together.

"What?" Virginia exclaimed. "Oh, that nephew of mine. I'll have his head!"

****

Thirty minutes later, Virginia, stomped her cane along the hallway as she made her way from the north wing to the south wing. Announcing her arrival at Reggie's suite, she nearly drove it into the floor.

"Reginald! Explain!" she projected into the room while she stood there in a flowing, myrtle-green gown and waited, but no one noticed her.

"Here comes the first one," Doctor Littleton whispered. "Oh, it's a boy, and he has his father's markings."

"Where?" Virginia shouted as she lifted her dress and hurried toward the group clustered in a semicircle on the floor. "Let me see my grandson."

As Doctor Littleton pulled the sack away and moved the puppy to his mother's head, she watched as Roscoe began to clean it. A moment later the first squeak came from the new arrival. Immediately, Cinders leapt down from his perch on the bookcase and entered the birthing bed to sniff his new little brother while Peabody panted and turned in circles nearby, and Doctor Littleton dried it off with a towel.

Satisfied that everything was well with the puppy, Cinders jumped from the birthing bed and sauntered over to Virginia. As he pranced and rubbed up against her ankles, he looked up at her and began to purr, loudly.

"Reginald," Virginia said softly. "Calvin, why was I not told she was expecting when I visited her in the hospital?"

"We didn't want to get your hopes up, Aunt Virginia," Reggie whispered. "It was touch and go for a while. We weren't sure she would be able to carry the pregnancy to term. We weren't even sure she was going to make it, with her extensive soft tissue injuries and bruised lungs."

"But you told me her recovery was miraculous. You told me…"

"Yes, I know what we told you, and I'm sorry. We wanted to stay positive, and we didn't want to upset you even more than you already were after the attack.

"Doctor Littleton said had it not been for Cinders, keeping her warm after she landed on the ground, she would have never regained consciousness. She would have just slipped away. Everyone else thought she was dead, but she was in shock. Cinders knew. He knew to keep her warm."

"May I hold the puppy?"

"I don't know whether Roscoe will allow it just yet," Doctor Littleton said. "Let's wait for the next one to appear. She'll be preoccupied while she's pushing it out and then cleaning it. While I examine number two, we can try then, but I may have to put it right back. It all depends on what Roscoe wants."

"Of course. Of course," Virginia said as she kneeled down, extending the end of the semicircle.

"Aunt Virginia!" Reggie exclaimed, "You're on the floor!"

"Oh, hush, Reginald," she said with a flourish of her hands. "If this is where the puppies are then this is where I will be."

As soon as Virginia knelt down, Cinders put his front paws on her lap. Then he jumped up to her shoulder and began to nuzzle her cheek. "There, there, Cinders," Virginia murmured as she rubbed his neck. "I know, I know, it's all so exciting, isn't it?"

While watching his aunt, Reggie's jaw dropped open. "Someone, wake me!" he exclaimed. "For I must be dreaming."

"Don't be dramatic, Reginald. He saved my life. We must make allowances for these things, and dear, sweet Roscoe has helped me to realize we are a family, a different kind of family, but a family nonetheless. You, me, Calvin, Miss Honey, Bernard, Dudley, Perky, Geraldine, Cynthia, Roscoe, Cinders, Peabody, Rosie, Alma Mae, Eloise, Caleb, and all the babies. We are now one, big, happy family."

"Here it comes," Doctor Littleton announced.

"Here comes number two." She lifted the first puppy and gave it a quick once over then handed it to Miss Virginia. "It's a girl. Number two is a girl, and she looks just like her mother! Veronica, make a note."

"Oh, you dear little boy," Virginia cooed as she brought the puppy to her face. "You dear, sweet little boy." Cinders leaned forward and licked the pup along its cheek. "What are you going to name him?" she asked, looking toward Calvin.

Calvin smiled back. "Why don't you name him, Miss Virginia?"

"May I?"

"Of course."

Virginia thought for a moment, and then her eyes misted over. "William, I'd like to name him William, after my dear old friend, Willie."

Calvin nodded. "Then William or Willie it is."

"Oh, thank you, Calvin." She handed the puppy back to Doctor Littleton then cleared her throat. "Now you know, Reginald, Peabody has done his duty to carry on the Scottsdale name. It is about time you consider alternatives."

"We already have, Aunt Virginia. Calvin and I are investigating the possibility of hiring a surrogate through our attorney, and we're evaluating possible egg donors. It wouldn't surprise me if we don't have two or more new additions to the family by this time next year."

"Reginald!" she exclaimed. "What wonderful news. You have made me so happy!"

"We were going to tell you after the puppies were born, once we knew everything was all right with them … and Roscoe."

"You will get married of course." She lifted Peabody to her lap. "But don't worry, I'll plan the entire wedding. You won't need to do a thing."

A broad smile spread across Reggie's face. "I had a feeling you were going to say something like that, but it won't be for a while yet."

"Of course, of course, Reginald. We have time for all of that, but these two lovebirds," she hugged Peabody and nodded toward Roscoe. "These two need to be properly married. We must have a ceremony at once."

"You're kidding of course," Reggie said. "Please tell me you're kidding."

"Kidding? Why Reginald, think of the scandal. A Scottsdale? Fathering children? Out of wedlock? I could never show my face in public again! Peabody will never be able to enter another show."

"Aunt Virginia! There's no way! No way in hell I'm even going to even consider entertaining this harebrained idea of yours."

Virginia nearly fell sideways onto the floor she began to laugh so hard. After she regained her composure, she looked lovingly across at her nephew.

"Gotcha!" she said with a twinkle in her eye.

The End

EVERNIGHT PUBLISHING ®

www.evernightpublishing.com